# Buck Naked

Also by Joyce Burditt

*The Cracker Factory*
*Triplets*

# Buck Naked

## Joyce Burditt

Ballantine Books • New York

Library of Congress Cataloging-in-Publication Data
Rebeta-Burditt, Joyce.
Buck naked / by Joyce Rebeta-Burditt.
p.  cm.
ISBN 0-345-40136-0
1. Television actors and actresses—United States—Fiction.
2. Private investigators—United States—Fiction. 3. Women
detectives—United States—Fiction.  I. Title.
PS3568.E27B83  1996
813'.54—dc20  95-45699
CIP

Text design by Debbie Glasserman

Manufactured in the United States of America
First Edition: May 1996
10  9  8  7  6  5  4  3  2  1

# Buck Naked

# Prologue

Dear Gus,

I don't mean to worry you. Honest I don't.

I've heard every message you've left on my machine. The times you've come over and banged on my door, I've been sitting here in the dark with my hands over my ears.

I know this is no way to treat an old friend. Please, please, forgive me. If I could do better, I would. If I could take you to dinner and convince you that the past three months were just a bad time I'm over, I'd do it. But I can't.

You'd know. You'd see what I see in the mirror. Three months of uppers and downers washed down with Kahlúa. A one-night stand with coke. Muscle relaxants. Vicadin, Percodan, fast, fast relief. Only none of it worked, not for a second. I've dropped twenty pounds, spent days in bed, had to look at the newspaper to see what day it was, and then didn't care. But I didn't forget.

The escape I was chasing down a blind alley turned around, reared up, and bit me. Took a chunk out of me, Gus. Bone, blood, and muscle. Mind. Nerves. My alleged edge. Fast, fast relief is the lie I lied to myself. Damn. You know how much I hate liars.

So now that I no longer resemble the twenty-one-year-old

*girl you hired ten years ago or the woman you like to call your semitough cookie, I give up. I even know where to go to surrender.*

*You've been right about me all along, Gus. I'm only tough on the outside. Inside I'm the kind of woman I've always pretended not to understand, a woman with her soul on fire for the one man who fills up her heart. You knew and I didn't. You told me. I wouldn't listen.*

*I don't know why he left me. I don't know.*

*I only know that three months ago I was whole and happy and knew myself.*

*Do you know that a heart really breaks? It shatters inside into twisted, sharp pieces. They cut and I bleed. And I hurt. I can't believe how I hurt.*

*I wish I'd never met him. If I hadn't, I wouldn't have known how a love like this feels. I wouldn't have had it and lost myself in it, then lost it and lost myself with it.*

*I'd be in the office with you, watching you chew on your stogie and bitching because you're handing me my fourth cheating-husband case in a month when you know how much I hate those all-night stakeouts. Another hubby banging the girlfriend in a nice, warm apartment while I'm in the car with a telephoto lens and cold thermos of coffee, listening to the best of L.A.'s sincerely whacked-out on all-night, all-talk radio.*

*But I'm not. I'm everything I don't want to be. I'm disgusted with myself, Gus. With my weakness, with my grief, with the longing that overtakes me. That's why I can't see you. You'd be gentle and kind. Your pity added to mine for myself would destroy me. What I need is a kick in the ass. You'd try, but I'd see the concern in your eyes and I couldn't bear it.*

*I'll be gone for a few weeks. I'd call—but I'll be busy*

*shaking, sweating, and swearing. We've both seen junkies. We know the drill. When it's over I'll either be pure or dead.*

*Not the vacation I wanted, but the one I deserve. The ass-kicking I need, I have to do myself. There's no other way.*

*There's something else, Gus. Don't hate me for this. Beyond my "vacation," I need a time-out. A change that will spin me around in a different direction, just for a while.*

*I've been offered a job and decided to take it. It's a weird job, Gus, as a technical consultant on a television show—but it'll keep me busy and that's what I need.*

*That's it. When I'm me again, I'll call you. I promise. Be well.*

*Your not so tough cookie,*
*D.*

*Chapter 1*

Buck Stevens delivered his final speech straight into the camera. He smiled, a slight upturn of his lips that stopped at a point midway between dumb yahoo and foxy grandpa. Above the folksy smile, his benign blue eyes twinkled with wisdom and humor. He delivered the final line, emphasizing his words with a mellow shake of his leonine head, crowned with the thick, wiry white hair God gives to symphony conductors and winos.

From behind us, the director yelled, "Cut!"

Buck grinned, then farted, his own version of *cut*. On cue, the crew laughed, in expected homage to his down-home humor. He glowed in their laughter. He was their star. They were his guys. This was his set. The world according to Buck.

He looked around. Someone was missing.

"Where's Amy?" he asked.

The director, Cleve Morton, an old buddy of Buck's, answered reluctantly. "She said she had to go."

Buck cocked his head to one side, like a spaniel who's just heard a whistle. "Go? I didn't tell her she could go."

Morton moved closer to Buck. "I . . . uh . . . think she had an appointment, Buck, but she left you a note." Morton jammed the note in Buck's hand, pivoted on one heel, and fled.

Still smiling, Buck unfolded the note while everyone looked away except me.

In my experience, getting a note from a woman you've been sleeping with is not a good sign. Especially when the woman is supposedly dependent on you.

I hadn't needed to hear the rumors to know that Amy Westin, the young actress who plays Buck's daughter in the series, was sleeping with him. The minute I walked on the set and saw them together, I knew that if I dusted Amy for prints, I'd find Buck's in all the wrong places.

Buck read the note.

His smile vanished. His skin mottled. His eyes narrowed to angry slits. His eyes darted around, looking for a target, and found one.

He lowered his head and strode across the set to Bess Hollander, the sixtyish script girl, who cowered reflexively.

"You fucking old cunt," Buck bellowed. "Shake your head at me one more time when I'm in the middle of a scene and you can get the hell out of here."

White-faced, Bess whispered, "But I didn't . . ."

Buck leaned over her menacingly. "You calling me a liar?"

Bess shook her head slowly. "No, Buck. Of course not."

"Good." Buck nodded, straightened, and saw that the whole crew was watching him. "What the hell you looking at?" He grunted and moved toward the stage door. "I'll be in my trailer. Don't nobody bother me."

As Buck slammed the stage door behind him the crew exhaled a sigh of relief. Compared with most days, Buck was in a great mood.

Personally, I find Buck's antics more entertaining than his

television show, a lumpy blend of down-home hokum and mysteries that often don't make any sense. Before being hired on the show, I'd never watched it—and I'd said so when the producers offered me the job. They didn't seem offended or even surprised, maybe because they thought private investigators never watch television or more likely because they watched it themselves only when they had to. But ten minutes after I accepted the job, a messenger arrived with twenty-two tapes and a note "suggesting" that familiarizing myself with the series might be "helpful."

I watched all twenty-two and discovered that *Stone, Private Eye* concerned a private investigator who works out of his home in Sassafras, Arkansas, and that most of his clients are his Sassafras neighbors or folks passing through Sassafras just long enough to be murdered—or occasionally an outsider, when a big enough star could be coaxed by money or sweet-talked by Buck into playing the part. Each episode begins with a murder that Sam Stone investigates by ambling all over town—dropping in at the barbershop, filling station, and the Koffee Kup Diner—where he asks foxy questions and dispenses folksy advice. Somewhere along the way he solves a friend's personal problem, such as a buddy whose hens aren't laying until Buck changes the radio station in the henhouse and gives those Rhode Island Reds the Dolly Parton they've been craving instead of that "big city rock 'n' roll crap." Then along toward the end of each episode Buck gets a hot idea, usually while sitting alone in his kitchen. He jumps up and yells "I got it!" then runs off, solves the murder, and nabs the killer. Cut to commercial, tune in next week.

Watching twenty-two episodes has taught me three things. All the shows are the same. Under no circumstances, unless I have a burning desire to be murdered or jailed, will I ever set foot in Sassafras, Arkansas. *Stone, Private Eye* is the cure for insomnia.

On nights when my nerves scream like a cheap car alarm and I toss, haunted by Michael, I slip a tape into the machine, watch Buck amble for ten or twelve minutes, and am dulled into a drift that's almost sleep. Sometimes, dull is comforting, even necessary. Dull soothes the soul. Dull quiets the mind. Dull heals the body. Late at night I know I've made the right choice. I've picked the right job. Because nowhere else will I find a world as predictably, resolutely, unrelentingly dull as *Stone, Private Eye*. I know I've lucked out and keep watching.

Of course, that's an opinion I keep to myself. Though most people who work on the show would agree, no one dares even to think it, for fear Buck will read something less than worship in their eyes. Buck demands worship. Buck demands groveling. Buck demands stuff Buck hasn't thought of yet. Buck may not know what he wants, but he does know that if he doesn't get it, he'll fire every last son of a bitch and good riddance. The show might be turgid but the set is a circus where, at any given moment and for no reason at all, the ringmaster can get pissed and set the tigers on the crowd. Diverting.

It's been three months since I checked into an upscale loony bin that promised "safe and effective drug withdrawal in a supportive setting." Had a nice ring to it, like the "friendly skies." Good thing I never buy into ads. Just as the "friendly skies" are mined with turbulence and wind shear (but the quickest route from one place to another), the loony bin was the shortcut from dying to living. I ignored the "supportive setting" and got down to business—sweating, shaking, insomnia, nightmares. Curled up on my bed, I dared it to kill me. A shrink dropped in and advised me to cry. Standard shrink rap. I told her that you don't cry about the things you do to yourself. Then, just to be ornery, I told her that the next time I try to destroy myself I'll cut to the chase—Russian roulette. Click, click, *bang*, Forest Lawn.

I should have kept my mouth shut. She freaked.

Now the shrink, eminent Beverly Hills psychiatrist Dr. Karen O'Brien, who's also my mother, is convinced that I need an extended stay at her psychiatric facility. Her husband, Dunn Carlisle, who was bred on a stud farm for the purpose of servicing Mother, thinks I need to get laid. Dr. Morris Spellman, the shrink assigned to me by Mother at her dingbat emporium, has concluded that I need to see him every Monday, Wednesday, and Friday for the rest of my life. I've written to the president, soliciting his sage advice, but as yet he hasn't replied. When he does, I'll take all these options under advisement and the winner will receive an all-expenses-paid trip to Death Valley, plus a pair of my baby shoes, bronzed.

The truth is I'm done with destroying myself. My brain on drugs (sizzle, sizzle) accomplished what no broken heart can do. I forgot who I was.

My name is Demeter "Dutch" O'Brien. I'm female, thirty-one and a third, five feet seven, one hundred and twenty-four pounds, dark brown hair, green eyes, no distinguishing marks I care to talk about—and I was last seen skipping down the Yellow Brick Road.

I was, and will be again when I choose, a private detective.

I'm licensed to carry a gun, which I do, in a shoulder holster cradled just beneath my heart.

I stood around awhile longer, watching the crew set up for the next scene. Electricians, supervised by the director of photography, Bob Wolcott, cut the lights on Buck's Sassafras living room, a set with three walls, enough Early American furniture for an Ethan Allen blowout sale, and a fireplace so obviously constructed of cardboard and plaster, I was always amazed to see that on film the mantel looked like real wood and the fire itself—a special effect, hidden lights shining on tinfoil behind a paper log—looked like you could toast marshmallows in it.

Once I asked Bob how it could all look so tacky in real life and so pretty on television. He shifted his wad from one cheek to the other and winked at me. "Ruby dust, honey. We sprinkle it around and presto, we have magic."

I decided I should have met Bob sooner. If he'd sprinkled his magic ruby dust on my love affair, right now I'd be with Michael in an oceanside bed-and-breakfast four-poster listening to him tell me how good I taste instead of on Stage 53 watching electricians light Buck's kitchen—Early American overkill with pine furniture, pottery roosters, and wall-to-wall gingham. Only the Bradys and Cleavers could love it as much as Buck, who often sat there between scenes, sipping from a pink gingham coffee cup and thinking his Early American thoughts.

Instead, I was in the way of a guy pulling cable who said "Excuse me" in a tone that meant *vamoose.*

Vamoose sounded like a plan, so I headed for the stage door. Halfway there, someone tapped me on the shoulder, saying, "Hey!"

"Word is you're a real private detective," he continued, extending his hand. "I'm Steve Pierce. Camera operator."

"A *real* camera operator?" I deadpanned, but smiled and shook his hand to show that my teasing was all in fun.

"Got my own camera and everything," he said, and his grin got wider.

He was cute, all right, and he knew it: a brown-haired, blue-eyed all-American boy, the kind who plays the harmonica in war movies and gets his head blown off on his final mission. His eyes were Midwestern skies and his hair a wheat field and his grin Jimmy Stewart walking up the Capitol steps. Aw shucks and by gosh, it said, rub me under the chin, I'm a real puppy dog.

I wanted him.

Of course, for the past month I've wanted every man under eighty-five who doesn't have leprosy. I don't know what this means, but it can't be anything good. Then again, if I wait thirty seconds the wanting goes flat. My lust burns hot, but it doesn't connect. Nobody is Michael.

"I know where they make the best burgers in town," Steve said. "How 'bout lunch tomorrow?"

"Excuse me," I answered. Then I bent over and retied my Reeboks, something I do when I need time to ponder.

Yeah. Michael and I had started with "lunch," then the week after that "dinner," then the weekend after that "dessert at my place." That evening began with coffee, moved on to simultaneous orgasm, and ended with melted chocolate–chocolate chip eaten in bed.

After that we saw each other three times a week until both of us knew it was love, not just heat. For a while I waited for the false move that meant I should cut and run. But Michael never broke a date. He never lied to me. When I looked rotten he didn't tell me I looked great. He asked me what was wrong and then listened when I told him. He didn't tell me my job was too dangerous. He didn't seem to mind my gun on his dresser. He understood that all-night stakeouts were as much a part of my job as drawing up blueprints was his. He showed me his heart. He didn't want to improve me. He didn't snore. He showered before and after. He made me laugh. After a while I relaxed. He was mine. I was his. This was it.

No matter that my sharp detective's instincts were turning to goo. No matter that one night on a stakeout, my latest cheating husband slipped into the condo, sloshed his girlfriend around on the water bed, and then slipped out while I sat in the car daydreaming about Michael, the telephoto lens in my lap.

Gus chewed me out. I didn't care. I was full up and over-flowing with love. It leaked out my fingertips.

Then it started. Overnight, Michael turned evasive. About where he'd been, what he was doing, how he felt. Knowing, because I loved him, that he was troubled about something, I backed off, assuming he'd tell me when he was ready. He didn't. So I asked what was wrong. He said, "Nothing." I know the sound of a death rattle when I hear one, but I never give up. I pursued him.

Tell me. Tell me.

Nothing. Nothing.

Tell me, goddamn it!

Nothing. Nothing.

Do you still love me?

Yes, Dutch, I love you. My feelings haven't changed but I can't do anything about them.

What did that *mean*?

If he was terminally ill, I'd take care of him. If he was in debt to the Mafia, I'd go kill the Godfather. If he . . . if he . . . *what* did it mean?

While I was wondering, Michael left me. He stopped calling. When I called him, I got his answering machine. He might be there for every other call he got, but he'd decided not to be there for me.

I reached for Michael. My hand closed on a pill.

My Reeboks were tied and Steve Pierce was waiting, hunky and here. Maybe, I thought, I could take him for a test-drive, just to see how he ran, then return him to the lot, no strings attached. But I knew better. Steve's heart might be pro-grammed for meaningless flings, but mine was still grounded, attached to more strings than Pinocchio.

"Sorry. Can't," I finally answered him breezily. "Maybe some other time."

"Anytime." And he smiled. "I turn up every day, just like a bad penny."

And he ducked his head, looking like a pooch who's preparing to wait a long time for a biscuit. Then he threw back his head and smiled at me. "See you later."

He walked away slowly, easily, his hips swaying slightly, the gait of a thoroughly relaxed man with all the time in the world.

I looked after him, wondering. When he'd raised his head sharply, his light brown hair had flown back and I'd seen black roots at his temple and a minute hole where his right ear had been pierced.

*Hollywood* was my first thought. Then came the second. Maybe Steve Pierce was someone other than he wanted people to believe.


Outside, I quickly put on my sunglasses and headed for Building 35, a stucco bungalow that housed the offices of *Stone, Private Eye* and a meeting with the producers who'd hired me to ensure the show's authenticity.

L.A.'s sun is blinding, a sweep of halogen light that bleaches terra-cotta tile roofs to pale peach at noontime. It burned the back of my neck and the part in my hair. I hurried for shade.

"Hey!" a man's voice behind me called. "Hey, you with the black sneakers!"

That had to be me. I turned around, cupping my hands over my eyes to shade my sunglasses. Squinting through the glare, I saw Buck Stevens standing in the door of his trailer, waving at me.

"Come here," he called. "C'mon now. Won't take a minute."

I walked to the stairs of his trailer and looked up. "You want something, Mr. Stevens?"

He grinned toothily. "Mr. Stevens, hell. The whole country calls me Buck. Come on in."

He disappeared inside his trailer, obviously expecting me to follow. I did.

"Close that door, will ya?"

I did, then watched Buck curiously as he unbuttoned his shirt. "Gotta change for the next scene," he explained. "So, I've noticed you around the set. Who are you?"

"Demeter O'Brien," I replied, lowering my gaze as he emerged from his shirt. It's not that nudity offends me. Some of my best friends have been naked. But I've always assumed that once the aging process has progressed beyond a certain point, most of us would rather people not stare at us. Evidently Buck didn't feel that way. He paced up and down in front of me, soliciting my admiration for his pale, flabby torso with its wrinkled love handles and florid splotches. Since he wanted me to look, I looked—and decided that he could use a bra, about a C cup, underwired.

"What kinda name's Demeter?" he asked. "You some kinda Iranian?"

"I'm Irish," I told him. "Demeter's the Greek goddess of something or other. My mother was one of the founding feminists."

"Dykes, alla them," he snorted. "Bet your daddy took off."

In reply, I just grunted, allowing Buck to take it as *yes, no,* or *maybe.* He just grinned, not committing. I smiled in return. Buck Stevens may be ugly, but he isn't dumb. Not smart either, but shrewd like a ferret, eyes darting around and claws out. "I'm a private detective. Your producers hired me as a consultant, to make sure your scripts are authentic."

He grinned. "You're going to keep us honest, huh? A cute little girl like you."

He stepped closer and I knew what was coming. He'd either unzip his pants, then grab me—or grab me and try to unzip with one hand. Very quickly, but gently, I placed my palm on his chest and, still smiling, said, "You don't want to do that."

"Sure I do." He grabbed my wrist. "Just settle down. You'll like it."

"Buck, fair warning. I'm carrying an STD."

His hand fell. "A what?"

"A sexually transmitted disease," I said coolly.

"What kind?" Then his eyes widened and he stepped back. "Is it curable?"

"In time," I replied. "My doctor says to think positive."

He backed away slowly. "Good idea. Now, uh"—he cleared his throat—"is this thing catching?"

I smiled sweetly. "Not if we don't fuck."

"Good, good." He was very relieved. "You're sure I can't get it from breathing in the same room?"

"Positive. I'll put it in writing."

"No. I believe you. Anybody's got the nerve to admit something as shameful as that ain't gonna lie about it." He reached for his shirt and put it back on, forgetting that he'd been "changing for the next scene." "So, you say *my* producers hired you? And they never told me. Buncha snakes, alla them."

He whirled around and his eyes blazed pale blue fire. He poked his forefinger into my chest and thundered, "*I'm* Stone, Private Eye, and don't you forget it. You got any authenticating to do, you do it to me. You got any tricks of the trade gonna make me look smarter, you tell me first. Understand?"

"Perfectly."

"You don't go running upstairs to *my* producers, them sons a bitches, leeches sucking off my talent, lying, cheating assholes. . . ." Out of breath, he stopped and panted for a moment. Tiny beads of sweat burst like bubbles all over his reddened face, then ran down his neck in salty streams. I'd seen this before. With him. With others. Sooner or later, in one of these rages, something big, red, and ugly would pop in his brain. He'd gasp and choke and his eyes would bug out and someone would call 911. They'd arrive, maybe on time, maybe too late, and there he'd be, either alive with half his brain scooped out or lying somewhere cold with a tag on his toe.

"Would you like some water?" I asked.

"No, no." He sat down heavily and waved me away. After a moment or two of raspy breathing, he glanced up at me. "Ever seen a bull hump a cow?"

"No."

"You gotta. Awesome. All that screaming and snorting and her trying to get away. You'd swear he was killing her. But what you get out of it is one of God's miracles. Ever see a calf born?"

"No."

He nodded. "You will. I got a ranch 'bout a hundred twenty miles from here, up past Goleta. Raise Herefords. One a' these days you're gonna come up, have lunch, tell me about the PI business, and watch one a' my bulls screw one a' my cows."

"My pleasure."

"Yeah," he agreed. "You'll get a kick out of it. And"—he hesitated for a moment, then went on—"when your trouble . . . your female trouble clears up . . . you'll let me know?"

"You'll be the first," I assured him. "See you later."

And I backed out of the trailer wondering how it could

be so easy to feel sorry for a man who, this week, was going to make more money than I'd made in my whole life.

Not only easy. A treat.

I walked away, then glanced back, astonished to see the pale, anxious face of a woman with short curly hair looking at me through a back trailer window.

Buck's wife, Mary Lou, had been in the bedroom the entire time I'd been sparring with Buck.


Once, Michael and I set off to go water-skiing. I'd never learned and he was going to teach me. As we drove up Highway 1 toward Point Dume, Michael pointed out the beach houses he'd designed, each with the soaring roof that defined his philosophy. Architecture should uplift. The structure should provide safety and strength like the bones of a body. But the space within that structure should set the spirit free.

My hand, resting on his tanned bare knee, moved upward in soft strokes to his less-tanned thigh.

The next thing I knew, we were in a Malibu motel with blue sailboats on the sheets and the reflection of the ocean dancing on the ceiling, making urgent love with slow concentration.

But it was later, hours later, listening to his measured breathing that I leaned up on one elbow, looked down at him, saw in his wet, tousled hair and sleep-eased face the untroubled boy he'd once been, and knew that I loved him.

Dear God, dear Freud, dear Dr. Kevorkian, when will I stop thinking about him?

I will stop thinking about him.


Building 35, Suite 14, the executive office of *Stone, Private Eye*, looked like it was hatched in a Dairy Queen. Everything—the furniture, the walls, the computers, the drapes, the Sparkletts cooler—was shades of vanilla.

I wondered: Was the decor chance or design?

During my incarceration in Mother's nut haven, I'd asked why she'd done the whole place in greens, shades that ranged from mashed peas to slime. Mother explained that monochromatic color schemes prevent overstimulation and are soothing. Then she corrected my color identification. Her greens, she insisted, ranged from celadon to hunter.

Whatever. Martha Stewart I'm not.

Despite the office decor, tension crackled through the air like ozone before a rainstorm. I could smell it and feel it. It clung to my clothes. Definitely something brewing.

As always, the producers' assistants, Margo and Frances, greeted me warmly.

"Hi, Dutch, good to see you." Frances's brown eyes twinkled with suppressed laughter as though a joke someone told her a long time ago was still tickling the inside of her brain.

Margo's head swung around from the files, her red curls bouncing like copper springs. "The meeting's postponed. Richard's having back and neck X rays."

Richard was Richard Raymond, one of the show's two producers and writers.

I wasn't surprised. In the short time I'd been here, Richard Raymond had been X-rayed, tested, scanned, and scoped head to toe. He was spread all over Cedars from radiology to cardiology; his blood, bones, tissues, and giblets immortalized in pictures and reports.

There was much speculation about Richard's "problem," but no one dared to ask Richard and he didn't say. Margo thought he was dying and worried about him. Frances thought he was dying and worried, but with a twist. Richard's obit would be her pink slip.

My jury was out. The few times I'd seen him, he looked healthy enough.

Since most of the meetings Richard scheduled in the office were canceled at the last minute, Frances's announcement wasn't a shock, just business as usual.

Richard Raymond preferred working at home in what Frances described as his "beeyootiful" French Normandy mansion. There, surrounded by computers, fax machines, three separate phone lines, four television sets, two VCRs, and a juice machine, he ran *Stone, Private Eye* by voice and in absentia, like Saddam Hussein from the bunker. He came into the office only in times of emergency, such as a one-point drop in the ratings, a crisis that kept him in the office for round-the-clock meetings with short guys in suits three whole days in a row. Every six weeks he dropped by the set mostly to quell the persistent rumor that he'd died and been buried at sea. I'd heard him described as a "real television producer," whatever that means.

I scooped a handful of jelly beans from the jar on Margo's desk. "How's the screenplay coming?" I asked.

"Fine," Frances replied.

Margo frowned. "Mine's going nowhere."

"That's because you're trying to write like Quentin Tarantino," Frances told her. "What do you know about the seamy underbelly of American life?"

"As much as he does. I've seen every gangster flick from *Public Enemy* to both *Scarface*s, Raft *and* Pacino. My characters say *fuck* five times a page and shoot guys they work with." Margo's curls danced wildly, copper springs on speed. "And don't tell me you aren't copying Eszterhas because I saw your last scene in the computer." Margo closed her eyes and recited. " 'Daphne undresses slowly in front of the window, knowing the show she's putting on is twisting Joe's guts.' " Margo opened her eyes. "Please. He's a hack."

Frances shrugged. "Three-point-one mil for his last script. We should be so lucky."

Margo nodded. "Yeah, you're right. Help me with my story after work?"

"Sure." Frances smiled. "We'll go to my place, call Domino's. Want to come, Dutch? Pizza and plotting."

"Thanks, but I'm not writing a screenplay," I told her.

"Not now, but you will." Margo seemed certain. "Everyone does, sooner or later."

I'd never put writing in the same category as death and taxes, but then I'd never been in show business either. Maybe writing a screenplay was part of the drill, like taking meetings and doing lunch.

I was mulling over the screenplay I'd write when the door to Cassie Sayres's office opened and she sprinted into the reception area.

"Did I eat lunch?" she asked Frances.

Frances nodded. "Tuna salad, apple, and hot tea."

Cassie smiled. "Oh good. Low fat, high fiber." Satisfied, she turned and walked back to her office, her near-bony frame lurching slightly, as though walking was a skill she was still acquiring.

Frances shrugged. "She's a writer."

"I know what you mean," I told her just to be agreeable. Truth is, I've met a couple of television writers and they're no different from mechanics. All they want to do is fix the script, wash up, and go home. Not one of them can remember lunch.

"Sorry, Dutch." It was Cassie again, right beside me. "I didn't mean to ignore you. I just didn't realize I'd seen you till I got back to my office."

"Uh-huh." I nodded pleasantly. "Looks like our meeting is canceled."

"No, not at all. I mean, Richard's part is because he isn't here. But I need to talk to you. Okay?"

I followed *Stone, Private Eye*'s second producer and writer into her office. She sat behind her desk, brushed ashes off her black jacket, her black blouse, and her black skirt, then lit a cigarette and squinted at me through the smoke. "I need a poison that paralyzes."

"Curare," I offered.

"Great." Her dark eyes lit up. She scribbled it down. "I've used monocaine so often, people are asking their doctors to prescribe it."

"Monocaine?"

She nodded. "Causes LSD-type hallucinations, induces euphoria, depression, rage, agitation, coma, kills slowly, kills instantly, causes temporary blindness and the delusion you can fly."

"That's some drug." I was impressed. "Never heard of it before."

"I made it up." She ground out her cigarette. "Has Buck made a pass at you yet?"

Some instinct told me not to cop to anything till I knew her better.

I smiled. "Buck makes passes?"

"At everybody, including Amy Westin. *And* a crew member's twelve-year-old daughter," she said, then suddenly looked confused. "Or was that in a script I wrote?" She ran long nail-bitten fingers through her short black hair and muttered, "Was it Buck or Stone who took the teenager rowing and then . . . I can't quite remember. Well, it was either real life or 'The Case of the Lurid Lolita.' Yes, that's what it was. Well, who cares? Buck makes passes at everyone."

"In real life?"

"You'd better believe it," she said, relieved to have cleared that up. "Do you carry a gun?"

"Yes, but not today."

"Bring it in sometime. I'd like to see it."

"You're interested in guns?"

She leaned forward. "It is my personal conviction that all women should be armed."

"Why?"

She looked at me like I was stupid. "You know why. All women know why. You're a woman. You *must* know."

Her hands were shaking slightly. She lit another cigarette to cover.

"You have a point there," I said quickly.

"Damn right. We're a lot alike, you know. Living on the edge."

I would have told her that the edge she was on I'd already dropped off, but I didn't want to rattle her further. She resembled one of the characters in a movie I'd seen, where, for no reason at all, people suddenly looked tense, then their heads blew up.

Abruptly she stood up and extended her hand. "Your work has been excellent. Your comments are invaluable and your expertise makes my job easier. I'm glad you're here."

Sensing myself dismissed and knowing that fifteen minutes from now Cassie Sayres wouldn't know if she'd spoken to me or written me, I was about to shake her hand, when her door banged open and Richard Raymond stalked in and threw his briefcase on the couch. . . . "We're firing Amy Westin."

"What? Why? We can't!" Cassie leaped across the room and grabbed his arm. "Hello, Richard. Terrific suit. Are you nuts?"

"You haven't seen dailies today?" Richard asked, his long, lean face white with repressed anger. Though his voice was, as always, low and perfectly controlled, there was a thin film of sweat on his forehead and his light brown hair, usually slick Gordon Gekko, was flopping over his forehead.

"You know I watch dailies at night, Richard." Suddenly

Cassie's voice, normally fingernails on blackboard, deepened and softened to nearly maternal. She patted his lapel, removing imaginary lint, her eyes focused on his. "Now, dear, what is the problem?"

"My words!" he said furiously. "She won't say my words. The dummy ad-libs."

"A word here and there," Cassie agreed. "What's the harm?"

"The harm is she says whatever comes into her head. And she doesn't make sense. Then the scene doesn't make sense. Then the story doesn't make sense. Then the whole damned episode doesn't make sense."

"I know you're frustrated, dear." Cassie clucked sympathetically. "But don't you think you might be overreacting? Just a tiny bit?"

Richard shook his head. "Do you remember the scene I wrote where Stone's daughter unmasks the killer?"

"One of your best," Cassie said quickly.

"Wait till you see it on film," Richard told her. "In the middle of the scene, Amy turns to the victim's wife and says, 'You killed him because if you couldn't have him, nobody else couldn't neither.' "

Cassie looked confused. "That's ridiculous. Aside from the grammar, the wife didn't do it."

"Of course not," Richard said. "The brother did. But Buck went along with it. He turns to the wife and says, 'You're going over, honey.' And then he hugs Amy! I nearly had a stroke. How many days did we work on that story and that . . . actress . . . destroyed it." He took Cassie by the shoulders and looked into her eyes. "Don't you understand, Cassie? The audience will think we wrote it that way. They'll think we're morons."

"Forget the audience. The network will think so. Not a

good thing." Cassie frowned. "But why did Buck go along with it?"

Richard glanced at his watch. "He'll be here in a minute to answer that question."

So, I thought, there'd be a meeting after all, a bona fide emergency. I decided I'd better vacate the room before Buck arrived with the short guys in suits.

"Well," I said, heading for the door. "See you later."

"Stay where you are," Richard commanded. "I have scripts I want you to read. If you go, I'll forget to give them to you."

Okay. If Richard Raymond wanted me to witness this scene, who was I to question his judgment?

Cassie took Richard's hand and led him to her chair. "Sit here, Richard, behind my desk. When Buck comes in, don't get up. And don't offer him a chair. Make him wander around. That way, you retain the position of authority and he's looking for a place to park."

Richard blinked at her. "Is this really necessary?"

"Buck hates you. And loves Amy. If this desk isn't between you, he might strangle you."

For the first time Richard looked defeated. "I'll never talk Buck into firing Amy."

Just then, the door opened and Buck stomped into the room. "Fire that bitch Amy Westin," he bellowed, "or I'm quittin' the show."

Cassie and Richard looked at each other, astonished.

Richard cleared his throat. "Uh, Buck, why do you want us to fire Amy?"

Buck leaned over the desk and glared at Richard. "The bitch stopped sleeping with me! Yesterday. Right after we finished shooting. After I bent over backward to do that scene her way, the cunt cuts me off!"

"Oh." Since this scene had taken a turn Richard hadn't expected, he was fresh out of words.

Cassie picked up the slack. "Buck, as distressing as that might be, we can't fire Amy for not sleeping with you. She'd sue us."

Buck pounded on the desk. "Then fire her for being a bad actress. Fire her for fucking up my show!"

Richard leaped to his feet. "A brilliant idea! Why didn't I think of that!"

"Because you're so fucking dumb you probably squat with your spurs on," Buck said, but he smiled. He and Richard Raymond had just had their first meeting of the minds.

Cassie's phone rang. She snatched it up. "Yes, Margo." She listened. "Fine. Just give us a minute." Cassie hung up the phone. "Amy's just arrived. Now, here's what we do. We tell her that the role of Stone's daughter is being cut from the show because . . . because . . ."

"Because . . ." Richard continued, "we're going in another direction." He paused in midfabrication. "It's not our idea. We love her. The network is forcing us because . . . because . . ."

"They want Buck to have a major love interest," Cassie went on. "Which will . . . uh . . ."

"All take place in flashbacks in the Fifties before she was born." Richard finished with a flourish, then grinned at Cassie. "Does it work for you?"

"Let's shoot it." Cassie smiled, then buzzed Margo. "Send Amy in."

Buck looked from Cassie to Richard, smiling approval. "Hate to admit it, but you two can bullshit with the best when you need to."

They all turned to the door, waiting. As the door slowly opened they tensed.

Amy walked in, in costume, a white loose-fitting dress befitting Buck's virgin daughter. Over it, a fringed white shawl protected her slender shoulders. I felt sorry for her, an oblivious turkey being led to the block by three smiling executioners hiding axes behind their backs.

"Hello, all," Amy said softly.

"Amy, you look wonderful."

Richard approached her to bestow a Hollywood air kiss, but Amy evaded him, went around Cassie's desk, sat in her chair, and kicked off her shoes. "My poor little feet hurt," she complained, looking miserably at Buck. "I've been standing on the set ever so long, waiting for you."

"You can stop waiting," Buck began, cranking himself up to fire her, but Cassie put a restraining hand on his shoulder. Uncharacteristically, Buck shut up.

Cassie smiled sympathetically. "What Buck means is that we have . . . difficult news."

"We love you, Amy. We cast you. You're a very fine actress," Richard began. "But the network wants us to give Buck a love story which will last the rest of the season. . . ."

Cassie picked it up. "And which will take place in the Fifties before your character was born. So, much as we hate to . . ."

"You're firing me," Amy said flatly.

Buck couldn't resist. "That about cuts it." He headed for the door. "Gotta get back to the set."

"Wait." Amy's shrill voice stopped Buck cold. "You can't fire me."

"Like hell I can't."

"You listen to me." Amy leaned forward in Cassie's chair, the authority position Richard had vacated. "One, I'm the only demographic under fifty you've got. Until I started on the show, your audience was halfway between comatose and dead. I lowered the demographics. I brought up the ratings. Two, the network you've lied about loves me so much, they called my agent to tell me that next season they want half the stories to be about me."

"What!" Buck exploded. "You're lying, you bitch!"

"Check with *your* agent," Amy advised. "The network told him, too, but he's afraid you'll fire him, so he won't tell you." She turned to Richard and Cassie. "Three, fire me and next season *Stone, Private Eye* will have new producers because I'll tell the network you can't write for me. I might do it anyway. I hate your damned words." Then she turned back to Buck. "Four, treat me like gold, Buck, because if you don't, all the fans who think you're some down-home daddy are going to hear what a dirty old man you are. From *me*. On *Larry King Live*. I'll trash you, Buck, with a tear in my eye. Poor little me, a virgin from Georgia, taken advantage of by a big TV star."

With that, Amy got up, and with her shoes in her hand, sashayed to the door. "Have a pleasant day, all."

She opened the door and went out, slamming it behind her. For a moment there was silence.

"This remedial-reading dropout hates my damned *words*?" Richard was turning bright red. "She crawls out of the ooze and onto *my* show. *She's* going to replace *me*? Not while I'm breathing."

"I'll kill her," Cassie breathed. "In real life. I will."

"The crew's waiting for me." Buck went to the door, then stopped with his hand on the knob. "That woman's fucking with me. Just so you know, nobody fucks with Buck Stevens. Not nobody. Never." Then he opened the door and went out.

Cassie flew at Richard. "Richard, what will we do?"

Richard glanced at me, suddenly realizing that his habit of treating the "little people"—secretaries, production assistants, and technical consultants—in the same way the English treat servants might in this case not be wise. Though he assumed us to be deaf to what we heard, blind to what we saw, and dumbly loyal, I was a wild card. Temporary. Just passing through. Not concerned with my next job in the business. Out of here soon with stories to tell. Maybe even sell to the *National Enquirer*. Before he and Cassie dug deep into the what-to-do question, he wanted me out of the room.

"I'll get you those scripts."

"Terrific," I said, wondering if I should thank them for a lovely time or, better yet, decide that my time-out was over, quit show business, and go back where I belonged, to Gus and my own show: *O'Brien, Private Eye*. "I'll read them tonight."

Richard opened his briefcase, removed four scripts, and handed them to me. "The next four shows. If you have any thoughts, please let me know."

I took them. "I'll call you tomorrow."

I left the office without looking back. I sniffed for the ozone, but the smell was gone.

Storm's over, I thought. All that's left to do is clean up the mess.

God, was I wrong.

*Chapter 2*

My apartment is the standard one bedroom, one bath with a dining area and small kitchen. Instead of charm, I have plants, dozens of them, most in green pots set on wicker stands. I seldom invite anyone home. I'm sociable enough for a PI, which means I'm a virtual recluse; but beyond that, my decor is a secret. I've furnished my place from antique flea markets all over L.A., the Rose Bowl, Pasadena City College, Santa Monica, Pickwick, and a hundred others. If the cops and the crooks and the victims I deal with walked into my place, they'd see wicker and tapestry and ivory lace, a king-size brass bed, a collection of rose-covered straw hats—a bargain-basement version of a Victorian house. And they'd hoot. And they'd be right. Whoever heard of a female PI who lives in a place out of a Merchant-Ivory flick? A female PI with a penchant for pretty can't have any balls. Since tough is the name of the game I play, I've kept my place to myself. Except with Michael, who loved my apartment and me, under the antique quilt on my big brass bed.

Once inside, I dead-bolted the door and took off my holster and laid it on a mauve needlepoint bench. A quick trip to the refrigerator for lemonade, then into my favorite wing chair, a cushy old piece that seemed to hug me.

I scanned the *L.A. Times*, noting the alarming rise in ATM robberies and a new wrinkle called *ganging*—robberies perpetrated by gangs of twenty to forty unarmed young men who enter stores late at night, surround and intimidate on-duty clerks, then make off with cash and whatever else suits their fancy. Creative, I thought, and scary and maybe a taste of future anarchy seasoned with a dash of consumer confidence—maybe they weren't actually *buying* the goods but they *were* appreciating the quality of the merchandise.

When my eyes blurred on local, I went to national, flipping on my coffee table TV just in time to see Dan Rather deliver the news with all the gravity of Moses delivering The Law. While Dan discussed this week's national crisis, compared it with last week's national crisis, and anticipated next week's national crisis, I leafed through the scripts Richard Raymond had given me.

The first, about a circus coming to Sassafras, had one clown killing another because the second clown was having an affair with the first clown's wife. The suspects were the ringmaster, the second clown, and the guy who gets shot out of the cannon. Sam Stone solves the case with a brilliant deduction based on absolutely nothing that I could see. I made notes: *needs evidence for support* and *Stone shouldn't call each suspect a jackass—it's harassment.*

The second script, set in the Sassafras mortuary, had the first mortician killing the second because the second mortician was having an affair with the first mortician's wife. The suspects were the second mortician, the cosmetician, and the husband of a recently dearly departed. Stone, Private Eye, solved this one with yet another deduction almost as brilliant as that in the clown caper.

I was halfway through the third, set in the Sassafras Old Tyme Bakery, when the words and the suspects blurred together and I fell asleep.

I dreamed about Michael. As usual, I was begging him not to leave. I pleaded, sobbing that I couldn't live without him.

"Sure you can," he said, and his tall, slender frame began to fade until he was transparent. "You're a strong woman, Dutch. Get a grip."

My face was wet with dream tears when I woke, startled out of my sleep by someone screaming down the hall.

I shot out of my chair, reached for my gun, and headed for the door.


In the hallway I found the landlady, Mrs. Ramirez, pounding on the door of the apartment next to mine and screaming, "You son of a bitch! You son of a bitch!"

I grabbed her by her arm. "Hey, calm down. What's going on?"

She turned to me. "The son of a bitch! It took me five months and a lawyer to evict him for not paying rent and now he's back in the apartment again."

"How did he get in?"

"I don't know. I changed the goddamn locks." Mrs. Ramirez was distraught. "I called my lawyer and he said it will take another five months to evict him. I gotta go through all that hell again."

She was crying now, wiping her tears away with the sleeve of her bathrobe. "I give up. I give up."

I knew how she felt. I patted her on the shoulder. "Don't give up yet. You have a key for this door?"

She nodded, reached in her pocket, and pulled out a key. "But the law says I can't go in till he lets me."

I took the key from her hand. "The law doesn't say anything about me."

As I unlocked the door Mrs. Ramirez grabbed at my hand. "Be careful. Donald Miller is not a nice man."

I smiled at her and opened the door.

The inside of the apartment was dark, but since it was the double of mine, I knew where everything was. Keeping close to the wall, I moved toward the light switch and flipped it on.

He was lying on the couch, sound asleep and snoring. I approached him slowly, wondering how he could have slept through Mrs. Ramirez's racket. Then I saw—he was wearing earplugs. I stood over him for a moment, scoping him. He was thirtysomething and definitely strong. Biceps bulged the sleeves of his T-shirt. But they were gym muscles, evenly matched, the result of Nautilus equipment, not sports or hard labor. His hands were large but finely made and his nails were trimmed. Brown hair fell over his high, thoughtful forehead. He was a thinker, a planner, a yuppie turned rogue. Whatever I did, I'd have to do it fast. So I did it.

I picked up a heavy ashtray and dropped it on his stomach. By the time he yelped and sat up, I had my gun to his head.

"Don't move, honey," I said softly. "I'm going to kill you."

Donald Miller's eyes bulged. "Wh-why?"

"You're bothering my mother, Mrs. Ramirez," I whispered. "And that bothers me. Turn your head. I want to shoot you in the ear."

He began to shake violently. "What are you, crazy?"

I tapped the side of my head with my finger. "That's what everyone says, but I'm better now."

Now his teeth were chattering. "Look, lady, I'll go away. I won't bother your mother anymore. Honest to God. I swear."

I hesitated, seeming to think this over. "Get outta here. Don't come back."

I took one step back. He got up and raced for the door, opened it, and almost fell over Mrs. Ramirez, who was crouched at the keyhole.

He looked back at me and screamed, "Bitch."

Then he was gone and Mrs. Ramirez was kissing my hand. "Thank you, thank you."

"My pleasure," I told her. "Go to bed now. He won't come back."

I walked back to my apartment, wondering what had come over me. What I'd done was unethical, illegal, and could get me busted. If the squatter complained, I'd lose my license.

I never do things like that, never. I believe in rules. Following them is the only difference between the good guys and the bad guys, except that the bad guys have better guns. Why had I done this? What did it mean? Was this some sort of drug flashback behavior? Or had my recent attempt at better living through chemistry permanently chipped my brain? Was I, like jocks on steroids or my betrayed-wife clients, living in a fantasy that my life hadn't changed, that I would go on as I had until the universe collapses and reverses itself—and I disappear into the Big Bang?

As I rolled into bed I found another explanation. "Damn you, Michael," I muttered, "this is all your fault."

In the morning I woke thinking I might need a reality check. Since the Psychic Hotline was busy, I headed for Beverly Hills and the Karen O'Brien Clinic, known to me as Mom's Cuckoo Nest.

I wanted to see Dr. Spellman—not Mother, who'd see my questions about flashbacks as a disguised cry for help and whip out her admissions forms yet again. Since at this early hour Mother was usually at Christophe getting a blow-dry and drumming up business among the rich and twitchy, I thought I was safe. Not so. As I slunk toward Spellman's office I heard telltale high-heel tippy-tapping behind me. Then came the voice, so soothing to psychotics but somehow sandpaper to me. "Demeter, are you taking your antidepressant?"

"You betcha," I lied. "I sing. I dance. I kiss strange men in the street."

"Come into my office," Mother ordered, and I followed her dutifully, noticing that her short light brown hair was slicked back, not blow-dried, and her suit, a mud-brown wrap-skirted number, was last year's Donna Karan. Compared with her usual style, Mother was done up like a bag lady. Definitely something afoot.

Once in her office, Mother gestured me to the patient's chair while she sat behind her desk.

"You are still under my care," Mother said, speaking with the authority vested in her by the Menninger Clinic and the APA. "I insist you take your medication immediately."

"I don't see the difference between the pills you prescribe and the pills that got me here in the first place. I know you do, but that's because you peddle them. You don't take them. The guy who sold me grass on the street did it for money. You do it out of conviction. Either way I get high." I talked fast, knowing she wasn't listening, just waiting for me to stop. "I don't get high anymore. It's too damn hard to get clean."

"Then I'm admitting you to the hospital," Mother said, her well-modulated voice rising ever so slightly.

I got up. "Go ahead. Fill out the forms. All you'll have to show for it is an empty straitjacket in an empty room."

"I don't use straitjackets." Mother was irritated. "Sit down."

I remained standing. "I'm over twenty-one. You can't make me stay here. You can go to court and try to have me committed, but by the time they even schedule a hearing, I'll be applying for a PI license in a foreign country. So give it up,

Mother. Go find some crazy people to impress or, better yet, grab your husband and romance him in the linen closet. Just leave me alone."

Mother frowned just slightly. The line between her eyebrows deepened. She was shifting gears. I braced myself.

"Demeter, darling," Mother cajoled, "I know that you've had a very bad time. I know that Michael broke your heart. I know you can't see a future without him . . . but please . . . you must know I'm worried about you. Come home. Live with me."

I couldn't help it. I smiled. "I'll bet you say that to all your patients."

Mother sighed. "At least tell me your address."

"You have my phone number. That's enough."

"You're too damned old to be rebelling" was Mother's opinion.

"You're too damned smart to say that" was mine. Then I noticed a stain, probably red wine, on the lapel of her outdated suit. "What's going on, Mother? Something's wrong. What is it?"

As usual, when I turned the spotlight on Mother, she dove into it headfirst. "Not wrong. New. And exciting." She paused for dramatic effect. "I've been working round the clock and I'm about to open a clinic with Dr. Humbolt Moldavi, the brilliant plastic surgeon. Together we are creating a climate for pioneers in the Cosmetic and Rejuvenation Rights Movement."

Okay. My cue. "Mother, what's that?"

"It's the movement to combat the rampant ageism and lookism sweeping the country."

"Lookism?"

"Discrimination against people because of the way they look," Mother snapped. "Demeter, I know that you have never been an ardent feminist, but even you must see what's happening out there."

"Maybe your 'out there' is a different place from my 'out there.' And nobody except Phil Donahue could be as ardent a feminist as you."

"You don't try, Demeter, and do you know why? Because you and your generation take feminist gains for granted. It's *my* generation that fought all the battles, my generation that invented itself. I was raised to be a housewife, not a psychiatrist. I had to fly in the face of family tradition, the medical establishment, and the sexism of colleagues. I fought, I persevered, I—" Mother stopped, staring. "Why are your lips moving?"

"I'm reciting, Mother. I know this by heart."

She glared at me. "Then why haven't you fallen into line?"

"It's your line, Mother. You fall."

Mother's face softened. She smiled. "God knows I understand your rebellion far better than any lay mother could, but—"

"Feminism isn't the issue," I interrupted. "Until you answer The Question, we have nothing to talk about."

"It's not a reasonable question."

"That's not a reasonable answer."

"If I told you why I can't tell you, you would know instantly that I'm right. But I can't, so you'll have to trust me."

I leaned over her desk. "What would Freud say about this?"

Mother shrugged. "Freud is passé."

Oh, great. The old mom/dad/kid triad inventor was suddenly as outdated as Mother's brown suit, just when I needed his goofy theory to squeeze the truth out of Mother. I decided on the direct approach. "For the one millionth time and this is for the jackpot . . . *who* was my father?"

There was a long pause. I could hear Mother thinking, trying to decide which approach would be more effective:

maternal/empathetic ("Sweetheart, I'm only trying to protect you.")—or maternal/objective ("Didn't we agree not to discuss this?").

Mother ahemmed, then: "The identity of your father is none of your business."

Ouch. She'd gone right for maternal/obliteration.

"Gotta run, Mom. My apartment's on fire."

"Wait." Mother was on her feet and coming around her desk. "You asked me about my new enterprise. I want to tell you."

I could leave. Or I could listen. I split the difference. I backed slowly toward the door. "Go ahead. Shoot."

"All right." She spoke quickly, hoping to hook me. Not wanting me to go. Wanting her own way. She went on. "Since freedom from ageism and lookism is a basic human right and the general population is aging, Humbolt and I have devised a program to enable people to exercise their cosmetic and rejuvenation rights. I do the counseling and he does the surgery."

"What surgery?"

"Cosmetic, Demeter. Haven't you been listening?"

Suddenly I understood what she was saying. Almost. "But I thought you always said that plastic surgery is an antifeminist fraud perpetrated on insecure women by a sexist pseudomedical fashion-industry cartel."

There was dead silence. When Mother spoke, her voice was a whisper. "Jane did it."

"Jane?" I was puzzled, then I got it. "*Jane!* Really? What did she do?"

"Breast implants. Face-lift. Cheekbone implants, I think. So if Jane did it . . ."

"It's got to be PC," I finished for her.

"Exactly." Mother's voice warmed. "Demeter, darling, please come home. I do miss our before-dinner chats. You're my only child, you know."

"Are you sure, Mother?" I interrupted. "Are you sure I don't have a sibling somewhere who's also none of my business?"

Suddenly Mother looked at her watch and I knew what that meant. Now *she* wanted *me* to leave and was looking for an excuse. "I have an appointment, Demeter. I'll be gone for a few days. But reachable by phone. You have my pager number?"

"I got your number," I assured her. I didn't ask where she was going. I might be curious, but if I asked her and she answered, then, when she asked me, I'd have to answer and that was the road back to childhood. Where are you going? Out. Now neither of us asked and neither answered. We were two grown women treating each other with respect and totally screwed in case of emergency.

Mother walked me to the door. "Would you like to see Dr. Spellman?"

"I'm late for work," I told her, intending to stop at the nearest pay phone and see if the Psychic Hotline was finally free. Or forget my flashback theory.

We said goodbye. She closed her office door behind me.

As usual, I was angry at her but also as usual, admiring. As always, she knew how to change with the times. So this was the new rap. At thirty you accept yourself exactly as you are. At forty you work out for strength and health. But at fifty, with the onset of sagging and bagging and with wrinkles popping out like middle-aged acne, you chuck acceptance and health to throw yourself under the knife. I could see Mother now, counseling aging feminist boomers, supporting their secret desire to "do it," shouting her battle cry, "ageism, lookism," and giving permission to lift, tuck, and implant. After an hour of Mother at her counseling best, these women would fling themselves into Humbolt's waiting arms and beg him to carve them up.

Was Mother wrong? I didn't think so. After all, she and her generation *had* fought, *had* persevered. And true to their history, my mother and Jane were still inventing themselves.

As for me—since Mother had refused to answer The Question since I'd first asked it at four, I'd had no choice but to invent the half of myself that was my mysterious father. And that half, an obsessive-compulsive private investigator, would never stop asking, or looking.

I arrived early for my script meeting with Richard and Cassie only to find Richard was having a laparoscopy, whatever that was, and Cassie was at her computer trying to outrace the next episode's deadline. I interrupted her anyway.

"You can't imagine my surprise," I told her, "when I discovered that the second baker murdered the first baker because he was having an affair with his wife."

Cassie punched the save key then looked at me. "Our audience doesn't want to be surprised. They're old. They want to be mildly entertained and lulled to sleep. Now go away. Unless you know a new way to smuggle diamonds into the country."

"In a corpse," I offered. "Make it look like an autopsy, but bury the rocks just behind his stomach."

Her fingers hesitated on the keyboard. She squinted into deep space. "I wrote that last year. Or maybe I read it in the *Enquirer*. Or maybe it happened to Richard's uncle Harry." She looked up at me. "Richard's uncle Harry's cadaver was kidnapped from the Smith Mortuary and used to transport . . ."—she squinted—"I forget. Or maybe it was Stone, Private Eye's uncle Harry. You don't have an uncle Harry, do you?"

I shook my head no.

"Good." She sat back and lit a cigarette. "In life and in art Uncle Harrys are nothing but trouble." She smiled. "Up to teaching our star, Amy Westin, that consummate bitch, how to hold a gun?"

"That's what I'm here for." I nodded.

Cassie puffed her cigarette. "I'll pay you big bucks if you'll load it."

"Sorry. I'd lose my license."

"Worth a try." Cassie shrugged. "Richard's idea is to send Amy to an ATM machine and pray for a drive-by."

"Inventive. But too dependent on luck."

"Richard's religion is luck. He believes that when it's running, you go with it. When it's tapped out, you lie low until it comes back or go chase it. But you don't let anyone change it."

I understood. "Just like his *words*."

"His luck and his words. Don't tamper with either." Cassie nodded. "Other than that, Richard's the most rational man I know. Calm. Measured. A terrific dresser. He can blow like a whale but never with me. I love Richard's words."

Interesting, I thought. Symbiosis. Like Gus and me. Partners. I filed it away.

"Richard's out sick again," I said. It was a question, but she didn't know it.

"He's not sick," Cassie said quickly.

"What is he, then?"

Cassie thought for a moment, writing dialogue in her head. "Richard's in a state of transition." She turned back to her computer. "Tell Amy she'll be getting the next script this afternoon."


Steve Pierce won five hundred dollars in the state lottery and took everyone to lunch. I sat next to him, which was a mistake. By the time lunch was over, I had heartburn and finger-shaped bruises on my thigh. Between the soup and the salad, he grabbed me and squeezed hard. I pried his fingers off my thigh, then reached between his legs and squeezed equally hard.

Steve's face drained white with shock. Maybe where he comes from, nice girls don't give what they get, but I've always believed that no expression of affection should go unreturned.

While I was squeezing, Steve was moaning, loudly. As everyone at the table stared at him he slithered sideways off his chair and fell to the floor curled up like a ball. I went to his aid.

"What's wrong?" I asked innocently, bending over him.

Finally he managed to wheeze, "Nothing."

Good sport that I am, I helped him to his feet. He staggered back to the table and sat down. When his eyes focused again, he leaned over to me and whispered, "How about dinner?"


Early that evening, after the day's shooting was finished, I knocked on the door of Amy's trailer. When I heard her faint "Come in," I opened the door.

Amy was sitting on the trailer couch in her underwear scribbling in her script.

"Hi." I stepped in. "What are you doing?"

Amy looked up at me, grinning. "Rewriting this piece of shit."

I sat down beside her. "I didn't know you're a writer."

She laughed. "Put a hundred monkeys in a room with a hundred typewriters and they'll write the Bible. Anybody can write. Better than Richard and Cassie. And who knows the character better than me?"

"Who indeed." I took my .38 out of the holster. "You wanted to learn how to hold a gun."

Amy's eyes gleamed. "Is it loaded?"

"Not today." I handed the gun to her. She grab stood up, and pointed it at me. I swung at her hand, knocking it to one side. "Never do that. Even unloaded."

For a moment she looked angry, then decided against it. "You ought to know. Show me what to do."

I showed her the standard cop shooting stance and how to hold the .38. She tried it a few times, then grinned. "I got it." She examined the weapon, then said, "This makes me feel taller."

"Gun'll do that," I told her as I left.

On the way back to the office I tried to slip by Buck's trailer when the door slammed open. Buck stood in the doorway, his clothes disheveled and his wino hair standing on end. Thinking he'd electrocuted himself with his hair dryer, I walked toward him, saying softly, "So, Buck, what's new?"

He looked in my direction but somewhere past me, trying to focus his eyes but weaving too badly. Then he grinned. "I'll show ya."

He reached in his mouth and took out his teeth, put them in the palm of his hand, and set them chattering.

"Nice," I commented, and walked away.

It wasn't much of a drunk trick as drunk tricks go, but obviously the only drunk trick Buck knew.


That night I was in my apartment eating Hershey bars and watching CNN. It was a slow news day, so they just kept repeating the same three stories over and over. Fire, flood, and breast implants. Fire, flood, and breast implants. I immediately thought of Jane and her silicone protrusions and wondered how this news would affect Mother's new business. Perhaps Mother's unfortunate victims of *ageism* and *lookism* would have to exercise their cosmetic and rejuvenation rights only from the neck up.

I was about to change channels when there was a knock at the door. It was Mrs. Ramirez carrying a very large box.

"A messenger in a uniform delivered this." She was clearly impressed.

She handed me the box, which was heavy, then closed the door.

I carried the box to my bed, tore open the wrapping, and found a cardboard carton. Inside the heavily taped carton was a flowered hatbox scented with roses.

A sudden chill raised the hair on my neck. I opened the hatbox. Inside it, wrapped in pink tissue, was Amy Westin's head.

*Chapter 3*

I screamed. And immediately clamped my hand over my mouth.

I don't know how long I stood there riveted, seeing nothing but Amy's staring blue eyes. They were fixed and wide with sudden shock as though someone had just told her she was about to die.

Then my automatic pilot took over and I moved to the phone, never taking my eyes off Amy. Her baby-doll lips were parted slightly and gray. I dialed, half expecting to see Amy's mouth open, to hear her last scream.

Emergency 911 connected me with the nearest police station, where the officer on duty immediately put me on hold. I waited. When I noticed that my knees were shaking, I sat on the floor, then glanced over at Amy. From the floor all I could see was the top of Amy's blonde head with an inch and a half of black roots showing. I stood up. I had to see her whole head so the part of my brain obviously in shock wouldn't hallucinate its rising from the bed of pink tissue and floating toward me.

When the officer on duty finally came on the line, I gave him my name and address and reported Amy's murder, all in a voice so calm it surprised me. The officer instructed me to wait where I was. He was sending a car immediately.

Forty minutes later Detective Beauregard Hart was at my door, apologizing for the delay.

"I would have been here sooner," he said, grinning cheerfully, "but I was interviewing a suspect I'm sure's going to leave town and I figured a head in a box isn't going anywhere." Then he looked stricken. "Jeez, I'm sorry. Is the deceased a relative . . . or friend?"

I shook my head no. "I work with her."

Hart looked relieved. He joined the gangly uniformed officer who, at the moment, was staring fascinated at Amy's head.

I liked Hart's breeziness. A long time ago I'd realized that if I was going to go into the heartbreak, murder, and mayhem business, I'd have to develop a few useful defenses against emotional involvement. So I went to the source, Mother, who'd let her breakfast eggs grow cold while she retreated into thoughtful silence. I waited, not knowing if Mother was considering my question from all possible angles or planning her grocery list. Finally, she said, "Humor is good. And just remember that no matter how terrible any single case might be, it's happening to someone else, not to you."

I'd nodded. Good advice. Screw empathy. Full speed ahead.

Then Mother added: "Would you like grilled chicken tonight?"

I'd been right on both counts. Mother had decided both defenses and dinner.

• • •

A half hour later my apartment was full of "the boys," Hart's description of forensics and homicide.

While the boys went about their manly duties, Hart questioned me.

"The victim's name?"

"Amy Westin. She's an actress on the television show *Stone, Private Eye*."

"Do you know her?"

"Yeah. From the show. I work there, too."

"Actress?"

"No."

Hart looked me up and down. Checking me out. "You could be. I'd watch you. What do you do?"

When I explained my job and my background, he laughed. "You! *You're* a PI?" Then he looked embarrassed. "Not that you shouldn't be. Or couldn't be. Or aren't good at it."

"Thanks. If you didn't approve, I'd quit."

"You're kidding."

"You got it." Now I knew his MO. First he'd say whatever came into his head, then hearing himself, stop and backpedal like crazy, trying to be sensitive. Macho cop versus Nineties sensitive male, the fight of the century going on inside his post-Christmas sale blue suit. But he was cute, tall, sandyhaired, blue-eyed, a little too square-jawed, and WASP—but definitely cute. Looking at him, I felt the familiar yearning stir then quickly fade like new jeans in Clorox. Cute, maybe even sexy, but he wasn't Michael.

He consulted his notes. "Were you on good terms with the deceased?"

"As far as I know. We were acquaintances, not friends."

"When was your last conversation with Miss Westin?"

"Earlier this evening."

"Concerning . . . ?" He looked at me, waiting.

"I showed her how to hold a thirty-eight."

He looked confused. "She wanted to know how to fire a weapon?"

"No. She wanted to know how to look good firing a weapon. You know, authentic."

"Maybe. And maybe she knew someone was after her and wanted to learn to protect herself."

He waited, hoping I'd spring loose with some gossip or wild speculation that would make his job easy. I could tell what I knew. He'd write the names—Sayres, Raymond, and Stevens—into his book and be off in a second, jumping to a conclusion I'd gift-wrapped for him. But I didn't want to do that. I never jump to conclusions. I follow the evidence that presents itself, point A to point B, until the case is a series of logical steps leading somewhere. Let Detective Hart dig for his answers.

He got tired of waiting. "Do you know of anyone who might have wanted to kill Amy Westin?"

"I only know her at work. I know nothing about her personal life."

"I didn't ask you that." He was growing impatient. "Do you know anyone *at work* who might have wanted to kill her?"

I shrugged. "Amy wasn't easy. She rubbed people the wrong way. But that doesn't mean any of them would actually kill her."

"What people?" He jumped on that. "Who was she rubbing?"

I dug in my heels. "Look, I know how this works. You've got a caseload that won't quit, backed up five years. If I give you names, you won't look any further. You'll just chase these leads down and forget the big picture."

His pretty eyes narrowed. "Now *you* look, Sherlock. You

give me those names or my first bust on this case will be you. For obstructing justice."

"Okay," I agreed immediately. This wasn't worth the loss of my PI license. "Write this down. Richard Raymond."

He pulled out his black book and commenced scribbling. "Who's he?"

"Exec producer, *Stone, Private Eye*."

"Amy Westin was giving him trouble?"

"Threatened to have him replaced."

"Who else?"

"Cassie Sayres. Exec producer, *Stone, Private Eye*. Same motive."

"This is more like it. Who else?"

"The star of *Stone, Private Eye*. Buck Stevens."

That got him. He looked up from his notebook, startled. "You mean kindly, wisecracking Buck Stevens, one of America's enduring folk heroes?"

"You talk like the *National Enquirer*."

"That's where I read it. But I've been a fan of Buck Stevens for years. Hell, I grew up watching him on *The Buck Stevens Good Time Roll Along Variety Show*. And I'll bet you did, too."

"Every Saturday night," I lied. If this cop loved that show, then I'd love it, too, until I saw which way his investigation was leading. So I smiled and rolled out the nostalgia. "Didn't you love the way the show started every week with Buck in his Sassafras living room playing his banjo and telling funny stories?"

He grinned, replaying his adolescent favorite in his mind. "Yeah. And then he'd wander out of the house and all over town . . . my favorite place was the Koffee Kup Diner . . . and all his friends and neighbors would sing and dance and Carol Burnett and Dick Van Dyke would drop in. And Buck would do a double take, like it was a big surprise."

At that, he made a face that so perfectly imitated Buck's trademark *lookee here!* openmouthed expression that I grinned.

Then he looked self-conscious. "What can I say? I know the show was corny, but Buck made me laugh. It must be great working with him."

"A real laugh riot." I smiled sincerely.

His eyes flicked his notes. "But you're telling me that Buck Stevens is capable of murder?"

"I didn't say that. I said he had problems with Amy." I enjoyed his look of astonishment. Served him right for believing everything he saw on TV.

"Okay. I'll talk to him." He made another note, then looked at me curiously. "Now, why do you suppose the killer sent you Miss Westin's head?"

"I've been wondering about that myself."

"Did you see the person who delivered the box?"

"No. The landlady, Mrs. Ramirez, answered the door." I quickly added: "Please don't tell her what's in the box."

"But she's gotta know something's wrong. How often do you have eight cops in your apartment at three A.M.?"

"I'll tell her it's a slumber party. C'mon, she doesn't need to know everything."

"Okay. Just leave it to me."


Of course I didn't. When he interviewed Mrs. Ramirez, I was standing right next to him.

"Mrs. Ramirez," he asked, "can you describe the messenger who delivered the box?"

Mrs. Ramirez looked at me. I nodded. She turned to the detective. "He was a nice, polite young man wearing a blue uniform."

"Any logo?" he asked.

Mrs. Ramirez looked puzzled.

"Was the name of his messenger service on his shoulder or his hat?" I interjected.

Mrs. Ramirez shook her head no. "Just a plain blue uniform on a very nice young man."

Hart persisted. "Did this nice young man ask you to sign anything?"

"No," Mrs. Ramirez replied. "He handed me the box and went away."

"Great. Dead end." Hart walked off.

Mrs. Ramirez frowned at me. "Did I do something wrong?"

"No, no," I assured her. "You did fine."

For a moment she seemed relieved, then suddenly very worried. "What was in the box?"

"Supposed to be jelly doughnuts," I lied. "For the slumber party. But the box was empty. And you know how cops are about their doughnuts. They don't get 'em, they get crazy."

Mrs. Ramirez smiled, then frowned. "But the box was heavy."

"Bricks," I said quickly. "A cruel hoax on the cops."

"I'd send 'em bricks, too," Mrs. Ramirez whispered, and I sensed that once again, she was about to launch into the story of her brother-in-law, Ramon the coyote, who'd been busted by the INS for shepherding nineteen illegals across the border at Calexico. I said good night in a hurry and chased Detective Hart down the hall.

"Hey, Beauregard, wait up."

"Call me Buddy," he ordered. "Everyone does."

"Not on your life," I said, grinning. "I never knew anyone named Beauregard and I'm gonna use it. How many slaves did your family own?"

I must have really hurt his feelings because he wrapped

up our interview in one second flat, then left with a sour look.

By this time the boys had gone, taking Amy's head with them. I closed my apartment door behind me, got into bed, and lay awake, seeing Amy's wide dead eyes staring at me. Finally I got up, put on a raincoat, and drove the streets aimlessly until I came to the Farmer's Daughter Motel.

Ten minutes after checking in, I was lying in a strange bed staring at a strange ceiling, thankful that Amy's eyes hadn't followed me here.

Now questions were beginning to buzz through my head. Who killed Amy? Where was the rest of her? And why, damn it, *why*, had the killer sent her head to me?

Next morning, back at my place, I was handed the answer to one of my questions when Beauregard Hart appeared at my door. "We removed the head from the box," he told me. "And found this underneath."

The hair on the back of my neck stood up. "Do I guess or do you tell me?"

He handed me a note. "This was wrapped in plastic to keep the blood from soaking it. No fingerprints on the note, the plastic, or anything else. The killer wore gloves."

I'd figured as much. I unfolded the note, certain that its contents wouldn't make my day.

I read, *Dear Miss O'Brien. You're next.*

I made certain I was poker-faced before I looked up at Beauregard, who shrugged apologetically. "Sorry."

I was more than sorry. I was pissed.

## Chapter 4

A half hour later Beauregard and I were sitting in my kitchen, drinking bad coffee, which is the only kind I make.

I had been listening carefully while Beauregard explained, in unwarranted detail, how I should protect myself from a death threat. "Don't answer the door unless you know who it is. Check your rearview for cars following. Stay in crowds; no walking alone. Stop jogging." He gave my body a quick up-and-down. "You do jog, don't you?"

"Only when someone's chasing me." I gave him the little-woman smile I learned from watching Cathy Lee flummox Regis.

His helpful hints weren't anything I didn't know, but I listened like a woman who'd never learned to protect her tail. Why? First, because Beauregard was a man and men deflate like leaky balloons if women don't let them do their macho thing. And second, I wanted him to feel flattered because I was about to hit him with a demand he wouldn't like. I even tried batting my eyes at him.

"Got something in your eye?" he asked, concerned.

"No. I'm fine," I said quickly, adding, "Thank you." So much for eye batting. Obviously, I'd been absent in school the day they taught womanly wiles.

He finally ran down, then shut off.

"Do you understand everything I just said?"

"I think so," I replied. "But in case I forget, may I call you?"

"Anytime," he said, smiling warmly.

Bingo! I had him. So I went for it.

"Beauregard, I want in on this investigation," I told him.

"No." His response was automatic. And expected. I tried again.

"I'm the one being threatened. I'm a licensed PI. I carry a gun. I can interview suspects. I run a six-minute mile and can bench-press three times my weight." I looked at him expectantly.

"Not on your life." He got up, dumped his coffee in the sink, and straightened his tie. "I'm outta here."

"Beauregard," I began.

"Miss O'Brien," he interrupted, then stopped. "What's your first name?"

"Call me Dutch," I answered.

He smiled, a slow lizard smile. "Uh-huh. What's your *name?*"

"Demeter," I replied, hating the immediate gleam in his eye. "My mother has a thing for Greek mythology."

He laughed. "Great name, as in 'Cabbie, Demeter is running.' "

"Thanks."

"Demeter, Demeter," he chanted. "You sure know how to set yourself up."

"You noticed." I couldn't help it. I grinned. He had me. But now for the kill. "Let's arm-wrestle."

"What?"

"You win, I not only shut up about the case, but I'll call you Buddy," I promised. "I win, and from now until we collar this creep, I'm your shadow."

He thought about it. "You'll call me Buddy?"

"Affirmative." I nodded.

He sat down at the kitchen table, rolled up his sleeve, and plunked down his arm. "Life is short. Play hard."

I sat opposite him, taking the same stance. We locked hands and glared at each other.

Each of us tried for a quick win and failed. Thirty seconds later, with the sound of groaning and the smell of sweat filling the room, we were deadlocked, with clasped hands straight up at twelve o'clock high.

In competition, time either stretches or collapses, fast-forwards into a blur, or slo-mos into infinity. Unfortunately, the time was stretching. My arm, shoulder, and neck were on fire. I could smell muscles burning. But it did give me time to think. By all rights, Beauregard should win. He was bigger and stronger than me and with a man's superior upper-body strength. But in this game I held the wild card. Ever since I can remember, when I've really needed to win, I've told myself that I *would* win—even if I had to die for it. And I've meant it. I didn't care if my arm broke or my neck snapped or I had a stroke. I wasn't going to give in. And I didn't. Finally, thirty seconds or maybe a year later, Beauregard, who was sweating like a pig and grinding his teeth, whispered, "Time's up," and released my hand.

"Time's up?" I protested. "What the hell do you mean, time's up? We didn't set a time limit."

"A minute and a half—that's an arm-wrestling time limit," he insisted. "Everyone knows that."

"Bullshit," I said succinctly. "I was beating you and you quit."

"Like hell," he yelled. "I had you wobbling when the time was up."

"You son of a bitch. What a cop-out."

"Cop-out, my ass. Quit whining."

I got up, took my cup, and tossed it in the sink. It shattered. "Look at me, louse," I said quietly. "I'm on the case."

He looked at me. After ten seconds he blinked, then
looked away. I had him.

He looked back but avoided my eye contact. "You'll call
me Buddy?"

"I'll call you Your Majesty if that's what you want."

He got up. "Okay. It's a deal. But no investigating on
your own, only when you're with me."

"No good. I've got a license, remember. I'll investigate
whatever, whenever I want."

"A lot of jerks have licenses. How do I know you're any
good?"

I looked him in the eye. "Okay? How about this. You're
thirty-four, have an ex-wife and two kids living somewhere in
the Valley, and spend most of your time with your cop buddies drinking and lying about the women you've laid. You
worry about losing your hair, you don't sleep well, and your
stomach's beginning to burn when you eat pizza. Your marriage broke up when your wife caught you cheating after you
swore you'd never do it again. But she calls you when she's
lonely or a toilet gets stopped up. Want me to continue?"

"No!" he said quickly. "How did you know about the
ex?"

"I'm a good PI and good PIs are observant," I answered.
Of course, I've also read everything Joe Wambaugh ever wrote
and had taken a gamble that my buddy, Beauregard, fit the
Wambaugh cop profile, but I wasn't about to tell him that.
"This is my case and I'm on it."

"Only when you're with me." He stuck out his jaw. "I
mean it."

I smiled at the jaw but took heed. Men do that only when
they're ready to go to the mat but hope they won't have to.
Truth was, I didn't need his permission to investigate with or

without him and he knew it. But I did want to know every-thing he knew, every step of the way, something I couldn't do unless he invited me in. "Agreed," I said, letting him off the hook fast. "Where do we go first?"

"To talk to America's enduring folk hero." He smiled. Hollywood cops love hassling celebrities. "C'mon, honey. De-meter's running."

"Hey!" I protested. "What's with Demeter?"

He shrugged. "I won."

"Bullshit."

He was still shrugging and I was still bullshitting when I followed him out the door.

Buck's house in Brentwood was a version of Scarlett O'Hara's Tara, movie-star big but neglected. The exterior needed paint, and in place of a garden, there was a brown stubby lawn and dead azalea bushes.

"I've never seen bushes with cobwebs before," Buddy noted as he rang the doorbell. "And what's that stuff all over the porch?"

"It's a veranda, not a porch. And that's mold."

The door opened slowly. For a minute we thought no one was there, but then Mary Lou Stevens's small, heart-shaped face appeared, half-hidden in the house's deep shadows. Her eyes, or the eye we could see, widened when she saw me. "Miss O'Brien," she whispered, "have you heard about Amy? We heard it on the news this morning. Katie Couric seemed upset, but that Bryant Gumbel, he wouldn't turn a hair at World War Three."

"Amy's death is why we're here," I told her, then intro-duced Buddy. "This is Homicide Detective Hart of the LAPD."

"Good morning, ma'am." Buddy did a Joe Friday. "I'd like to speak to your husband if he's available."

"Buck!" Her whisper ended in a squeal. "Why?"

"He knew the deceased, ma'am," Buddy explained. "May we step in?"

Mary Lou glanced apprehensively back over her shoulder. She wavered, wiggling the door in a fit of indecision. "Well . . ."

From behind her, a familiar voice called, "Mary Lou, why are you standin' there with the door open invitin' flies into my house?" It was Buck.

Buddy nodded at me. We stepped in, walking past Mary Lou, who was still undecided.

We found Buck in the entryway, looking down-and-grungy, like an Erskine Caldwell tobacco farmer, wearing his usual at-home overalls.

I introduced Buck to Buddy. "Homicide Detective Hart, this is America's enduring folk hero, Buck Stevens."

Buck glanced sideways at me, suspecting I was putting him on, then shook hands vigorously with Buddy. "Pleased to meet you, Detective, though not under these circumstances. I assume you're here to find out if I know anything about the death of that poor unfortunate woman."

"Yes, sir," Buddy answered. "You worked with Amy Westin?"

"Indeed I did." Buck shook his head sadly. "A great actress. A true professional. And charitable? She was always downtown with Dennis Weaver at that LIFE thing of his, handing out canned goods to the down-and-out."

"Admirable," Buddy agreed. "When was the last time you saw Miss Westin?"

"We worked yesterday," Buck told him. "Then we wrapped, said good night, and we all went home."

"Did you notice anything unusual?" Buddy asked.

"Yeah, might say that," Buck offered. "She was all gussied up like she had a date, you know—dress cut down to here, jewelry, the works."

"That was unusual for her?" Buddy pulled out his notebook and started scribbling.

"Yeah. Mostly she hung out in old shirts and jeans." Buck hung his head. "Sensible girl. Salt of the earth."

Buddy glanced at me. I could almost hear him thinking.

"So, you saw Miss Westin leaving the studio dressed for what you assumed was a date."

"That's right," Buck said, then leaned closer to Buddy. "News said that whoever killed her lopped off her head and mailed it to someone. That true? Who got the head? You can tell me."

"I'm sorry. I can't discuss that." Buddy glanced at me and I knew what was coming. He was about to do a Columbo. "Guess that's it. Thanks for your cooperation."

Buck nodded graciously. "Glad to help."

Buddy turned away, hesitated, then turned back. "Almost forgot. I have one more question."

Buck immediately bit. "What's that?"

I chewed the inside of my mouth, trying not to laugh. Investigators love doing Columbo. I've done it myself.

Now Buddy stepped in closer to Buck, who was shifting uneasily in his shoes. "Rumor has it that you threatened Amy Westin."

Buck's face went purple, and when he spoke, it was thunder. "Detective Hart, I'll have you know I'm a Christian!"

"I've heard you say that in many an interview and I believe it," Buddy said. "But still, I have to ask. Is it true that you felt Miss Westin was fucking with you and you said, quote, nobody fucks with Buck Stevens, end quote?"

Suddenly, Buck grabbed me by the arm and pushed me forward, straight into Buddy's arms. "*She* put you up to this, the lying bitch. She has it in for me. She's been chasing me since her first day on the lot, and when I turned her down flat she started spreading lies about me. I'm a Christian, Mr. Hart, a Christian!" He turned to Mary Lou, who was hidden in the shadow of the stairs. "Don't listen to this, honey. Remember what I told you."

"All great men are persecuted," Mary Lou whispered. "I remember, Buck."

I winked at Buddy, meaning, *Told you so, baby.*

Buddy gently set me out of his way. "Then you categorically deny any personal animosity toward the late Amy Westin?"

"Bet your ass."

Buddy scribbled. "All right. Now, one more question. Where were you last night between seven and eleven P.M.?"

"Right here with Mary Lou, eating dinner and watching *Predator 2* with that German fella and going to bed 'round ten P.M." Buck smiled his America's-enduring-folk-hero smile. "Ten's late for a country boy, you know. Where I come from, we get up *before* the chickens so we can catch the eggs warm." He chuckled and I could see Buddy respond. *This* was the Buck he grew up with. But Buck wasn't through. "And having been both a private eye and a sheriff, I know you'd 'preciate a witness. So, tell this good detective what we did last night, honey."

From behind us, Mary Lou whispered, "We ate dinner, watched *Predator 2* with that German fella, and went to bed 'round ten P.M."

I turned to look at her and gasped. Mary Lou had stepped out of the shadows. The eye she'd hidden at the door was purple and swollen, as was the left side of her jaw. I could feel Buddy beside me, scribbling in his notebook as I stepped toward Mary Lou. "What happened, Mary Lou? That's one hell of a shiner."

"I tripped over the cat and hit my face on the doorjamb on the way to the bathroom in the middle of the night," she whispered in one tone. At that moment I realized she was either stoned or on trancs or still in a tripped-over-the-cat daze.

"Anything I can do for you?" I asked gently.

"Thank you kindly. No," she whispered.

"Poor little thing never even woke me up to tell me she'd had an accident." Buck shook his head sadly. "I never knew till I woke up this morning."

Buddy shut his notebook. "Where's the cat?"

Buck sighed. "I shot 'im and buried 'im in the backyard. Shouldn't have, I suppose, but the sight of my sweet Mary Lou looking like she lost a round with Mike Tyson just took me right out of myself."

"Can't blame you for that," Buddy said agreeably, then glanced at me. "Well, thanks for your cooperation, Mr. Stevens. We'll be going."

Buck walked us to the door. "Come back anytime," he invited. "And let me know what you find out. Ain't nobody safe in L.A. these days, 'specially if you're famous. Kooks and cranks just comin' from everywhere. And most of 'em can't speak English." He suddenly laughed, a short, unpleasant bark. "Know why the war on poverty failed?"

"No," Buddy said, playing straight man.

Buck's eyes twinkled. "Because they didn't shoot enough poor people."

Buddy blinked, as Buck guffawed, then slapped him on the back.

"Go ahead," Buck urged. "Laugh. It's okay. You won't find no liberals hiding in my closet."

"Didn't think so, sir." Buddy shook hands with Buck and we left, but not before I whispered to Mary Lou, "Call me if you need me."

Once outside, with Buck's door closed behind us, I demanded, "Why didn't you tell him to show you where he buried the cat?"

"I'd need a warrant for that."

"Get a warrant."

"I have no probable cause." Buddy smiled at me. "This isn't TV, Demeter. But you're right about Buck. He's slime."


Richard Raymond was next on Buddy's list. Knowing Richard, I called the office the following day to see if he was in. When Frances told me he was at Cedars having an MRI, I wasn't surprised.

"We'll catch him later," Buddy decided.

"No. When he's at home, he never answers the door. You'd need a warrant just to talk to him. If we go to Cedars, we'll catch him off guard."

Buddy, who evidently has a thing about hospitals, finally agreed, but only after I promised to have dinner with him. He seemed to think this was some sort of victory, but I thought, What the hell, I'll take my own car, we'll split the check, and after dinner go in separate directions.

Cedars's MRI unit, a right turn off George Burns Boulevard, is in a Quonset hut–type structure attached to the hospital proper by a rickety bridge. We stepped carefully in the shadow of Cedars, where all movie stars go to die.

"If you don't need an MRI when you get here, you will when you leave," Buddy observed. "Watch it. The plank is loose."

We stepped into the hut. Buddy flashed his badge at the technician, who not only wasn't impressed but seemed thrilled to tell us that Mr. Raymond was already in the MRI and we could go whistle for the next hour and a half. And we would have, except I heard Richard's voice cracking over a speaker from the inside room. When I looked through the glass separating the rooms, I saw familiar shoes sticking out of the ten-foot, tunnel-shaped tube. Richard was saying, "With a cost of one-four and a license fee of nine, we have a deficit of five and should seek a foreign partner."

"That's him," I told Buddy.

"Who's he talking to?" Buddy asked. "And what's he talking about?"

I pointed at the state-of-the-art tape recorder hanging by a Velcro strip over the entrance to the tube. "See that recorder? It's voice-activated. He dictates stuff and sends it to the office. And I don't know what he's talking about. All producers talk like that, only most of them slower."

Buddy nodded, thinking I must know. "Are you sure that's him?"

"Yeah." I pointed. "Those are his shoes, custom-made in Italy. I saw boxes of them once in the office. He orders them from Milan two dozen at a time."

"No scuff marks on the bottom," Buddy observed. "They must be brand new."

"Not necessarily," I countered. "He seldom walks anywhere. Mostly he lies down and has tests."

Buddy turned to the technician. "There's a mike in that tube?"

"Cylinder," the technician corrected. "Sure there's a mike. A lot of patients get claustrophobic in there. When they start screaming, we pull them out."

"Thoughtful," I said. "May we talk to Mr. Raymond?"

The technician sighed. "If you have to. But be careful. If he starts moving around, we have to start over."

Richard Raymond didn't move. He never even twitched. He answered Buddy's questions in a calm, measured voice and in great detail, beginning with Buddy's first: "Did you know Amy Westin?"

At that, Richard Raymond launched into a strangely unemotional but sincere expression of what Amy's loss would mean to the show, then continued with a flat but detailed evaluation of her talent, potential, and career—and finished with what could only be described as an eloquent eulogy.

Buddy was impressed. And the technician was bowled over. "Shit!" he exclaimed. "I've never heard a spiel like that."

Buddy continued the interview. At the important part— "Where were you, etcetera and so on"—Richard Raymond described the industry dinner he'd attended last night, naming the people with whom he'd shared his table, the various speakers and their topics, the orthopedic backrest he'd brought with him, and the muscle relaxant he'd taken one hour before. "Looperol, one quarter grain."

Though Buddy went into a scribbling frenzy, he couldn't get everything. I could have told him, but didn't, that he was wasting his time. I knew that like every other word Richard Raymond uttered, this, too, would be captured on his Dictaphone, sent to the office, transcribed by Frances, and in the blink of an eye, sent to the station marked *cc: Homicide Detective Beauregard Hart.*

Let Buddy scribble, I thought. Serves him right for calling me Demeter.

Eventually Buddy thanked Richard Raymond and motioned at me. Time to go. I went, but reluctantly. I would have preferred to wait until Richard slid out of his tube just to check his eyes for the usual signs.

But I followed Buddy. After all, as irresistible a mystery as Richard was becoming, finding a maniac who wants to cut off your head takes precedence any day.


Buddy's idea of dinner was takeout Chinese at his place with me scooping noodles onto plates and him opening wine.

Okay, so he got me, and okay I was pissed, but I tried to be cool about it. If he knew I was on edge, he'd have the advantage. So I'd eat some Chinese, swallow some wine, thank him for dinner, and split. I'd be a buddy to Buddy, and after I left, before he could make any moves, he could rewind the evening and play it backward for all I cared.

"There's something missing." Buddy stopped me as I was about to sit down. I looked at the table. Since he'd ordered everything on the menu, I couldn't imagine what could be missing.

"Candles," Buddy explained, jumping up from the table and rummaging through drawers. While he tore things apart, throwing unpaid bills on the floor, I ate all the egg rolls. Finally, he yelled, "Aha!"

He came back to the table, holding aloft four small birthday candles. "Not exactly an Olympic torch, but they'll do." Buddy lit the candles, poked them into a wilted philodendron drooping on the table, smiled, and said, "Perfect." Then he sat and attacked the Chinese food like a man who hadn't eaten in a month.

Buddy told me about his ex. "Linda, thirty-two, five-three, one hundred eleven pounds, strawberry blonde, would like me to fuck off and die." He shook his head. "She's soft and round and cries at sad movies. She should never have married a cop."

I reached for a sparerib. "No one should marry a cop."

"Hey," Buddy protested. "It's just the way I make my living."

"Sure, like the Mafia's just the way a wiseguy makes his." I shrugged. "Cops are bad news. They come home late for dinner, sometimes with bullet holes in their backs."

"What about you?" he challenged. "PIs don't spend their days smelling the flowers. You could wind up just as dead as a cop."

"You don't see me married, do you?" I asked, and attacked the moo shu mystery meat.

"No exes?"

"Not legal," I said, recalling Michael, and suddenly the memory took me back to the day Michael had shown up unexpectedly at my place with twelve dozen roses. Twelve dozen! Just because I'd told him I'd always wanted to make love in a bed covered with rose petals. He'd chilled the champagne and stripped the roses, then taken me to bed, where he made love to me with a tenderness I'd never experienced. "You're my lover, my father, my friend," I'd whispered, then later wondered if any other woman had ever held all the love she'd ever felt in her life in her arms, all at one time.

"Hey! Hey!" It was Buddy, waving a noodle-laden fork at me. "You stoned out on MSG?"

"No, I'm here." I waved my fork back at him, then wished I hadn't. Pork egg foo yung flew everywhere. While I was cleaning it up Buddy asked me how I got into the PI business.

"I was in law school. Second year. Dating another law student, six-one, one hundred eighty, brown hair, brown eyes, no priors, and not really serious. I took him home to meet my mother, because, in law school, that's what I did. She and Jeff hit it off. She loves to give advice and he had a habit of asking everyone he met what they thought was the most lucrative branch of law. So the two of them would sit there and talk bucks and I would get bored and wander off until one or the other noticed I was gone and came looking."

"So you became a PI because your boyfriend was boring."

"Smart-ass. No. After a few months I got curious about why Jeff never mentioned his family. So I asked him. About thirty-seven times. Finally he told me that his father lived in L.A. I was curious. I wanted to meet him."

"You mean check him out. To see what Jeff might be in the future."

"Something like that. Anyway, Jeff finally took me downtown to meet his father, Gus Whitlow, an old-time PI with an office that smelled like stale beer. I liked Gus. He'd look you straight in the eye, or as straight as he could through all the cigar smoke, and tell you who you were and what you were down to the color of your underwear. The man had an eye and instinct, believe me. He also had a gambling problem, but nobody's perfect. Anyway, Gus offered me a summer job doing legwork since both his legs were in casts, the aftermath of a visit by guys named Rocco and Louie who'd been sent by someone named Mort who figured Gus should pay him money he'd lost on slow ponies. I did legwork all summer and never went back to law school. How could I? Gus said I had the calling, and if anybody knew, it was Gus."

"And Jeff?"

"He graduated, went to work for Ivan Boesky, got busted with him, did three-to-five, and the last I heard of him, he was working in one of those Italian restaurants where all of the waiters sing opera. Mother thinks it's a tragedy, but I heard that when Jeff sings *Pagliacci*, all the customers cry in their rigatoni."

Buddy unscrewed the wine and poured. "You don't like to be bored," he observed.

I nodded. "Gets me in no end of trouble."

By the time we'd eaten everything, the candles had melted all over the philodendron, which wouldn't live till morning. Buddy rose slowly and winked at me. "Let's leave the dishes."

"Good idea," I agreed. Now for my jacket, purse, and a quick getaway.

I was about to thank Buddy for the lovely evening when he grabbed me by the shoulders and kissed me. "I'm crazy about you," he breathed in my ear.

"You're half-right," I told him. "Get away from me or I'll deck you."

Buddy took one step back but held on to my arm. "You're attracted to me and you know it. So why are you doing this dance?"

I looked him straight in the eye. "Are you going to rape me, Buddy?"

"God, no." Buddy was appalled. "Rape. I mean, I wouldn't . . . ever . . . anybody . . . jeez . . ." Then he stopped and took another step back. "*Now* what are you pulling?"

"I don't want to sleep with you, Buddy," I said evenly.

"Okay. Okay. You don't want to, that's it." He took one step forward. "But I've been six inches away from you all day, and I know something's happening between us. You can't say you don't feel it."

"Right now all I feel is indigestion," I said, then admitted: "And maybe a small attraction. Or maybe not."

He looked hopeful. "So kiss me. See if your bell rings."

"No way," I insisted. "Look, Buddy, last night I got a head in a box. This morning I got a death threat. And under those circumstances, how can I know how I feel about you or anything else?"

"That's probably true," he agreed. "But, if we'd met under other circumstances, by now we'd be in there." He pointed toward the bedroom.

"No, we wouldn't. This is the Nineties, Buddy. You don't jump in bed with people. Have you had an HIV test?"

"Sure."

"Good. Where is it?"

He shrugged. "It's negative, but I don't carry it on me."

"I do." I picked up my purse, got my billfold, fished under my driver's license, pulled out the report, and showed it to him. "Negative, four months old."

"That's great." He was really happy. "My medical stuff's at the station. I'll get it tomorrow." He stepped toward me.

I stepped back. "Forget it."

"Okay, here's what we'll do." He bargained. "We'll practice safe sex. I've got condoms. Wait here."

He ran off and I could hear him rummaging through the bathroom medicine cabinet. Something glass crashed to the floor, then something else, then silence. I could have left while he was busy, but I didn't. If he wouldn't take no for an answer, I had my karate black belt to fall back on. Besides, I was determined to make him acknowledge that my no really meant *no*.

In a few minutes he was back, looking glum. "No condoms."

"What a surprise," I said, but he missed the sarcasm.

His face lit up. "I know, I have Saran Wrap. I'll just Saran Wrap the sucker."

I stared at him. "You're out of your mind."

"Or maybe you'd feel safer with aluminum foil. I've got the heavy-duty stuff, the kind you use to cook turkeys."

He couldn't be serious. But he was. His eyes were on fire with his brilliant idea.

I laughed. It started as an amused chuckle, then grew to a laugh that exploded into a rowdy and uncontrollable shriek, even as I tried to stop it.

I didn't like seeing the eagerness on Buddy's face deflate into disappointment, embarrassment, and finally humiliation, but I couldn't help it. I continued to howl.

All Buddy had done was want to be closer to me, as I'd wanted to be closer to Michael. At least Michael, for all his cool determination, had never once laughed at my feelings.

Clearly, I must be a bitch. A hard bitch. A cold bitch. A stone bitch.

I tried to concentrate on hating myself, but even that didn't work.

This was like laughing in church, all guilt and giggles.

Finally, when I started hiccuping, I knew it was over. "I have to go home."

Not surprisingly, Buddy handed me my purse and opened the door, not bothering to tell me to drive safely.

*Chapter 5*

*I*n my dream, I poured out my love to Michael, who mumbled "Just the facts, ma'am," then turned to smoke and went slip-sliding away. Lost again. Lost for the thousandth time, lost. For the thousandth time lost without telling me *why.*

I called, "Michael, Michael," but he didn't come back. A black chill ran through me. I heard my heart pounding in my chest, in my ears, until I woke in a sweat, realizing that the pounding was at my door.

I stumbled out of bed mumbling, "Damn you, Michael," which seemed to have become my morning prayer.

"Keep your pants on," I shouted at the door, then opened it to Buddy, who was carrying a huge box and wearing a contrite expression.

"You had to say that, didn't you?" Staggering past me into the apartment, he dumped the box on the floor. "I acted like a jerk last night," he said.

I thought about my guilt and giggles. Okay. So I'd been a bitch. But he *had* been a jerk.

"You got that right."

Reaching into the box, he began pulling out Saran Wrapped paper plates, three, four, a dozen. "I was selfish, self-centered, self-obsessed, self-delusional, self-absorbed—"

"What are you doing?"

"I'm apologizing, for Christ's sake. Don't interrupt."

"Okay. You're a creep, a weasel, a louse. Now that we've both beaten you up, what the hell's with the plates?"

"Breakfast. I've been up since dawn making breakfast."

Buddy unwrapped plates and presented them to me. "Waffles with strawberries, blueberry pancakes, Western omelette, lox, onions and eggs, cottage-cheese-and-fruit plate, homemade granola with dried raspberries, steak and eggs . . ."

Caught up in a culinary frenzy, he continued unwrapping and presenting while I gaped at an array that looked like an explosion at Denny's. Not since Mother had sent me to Nature and Self-Realization Camp in the Berkshires, a touchy-feely summer "experience" run by a sinister shrink cartel for their kids, had I seen such a spread of cold, congealed food. But I knew that if I didn't accept the apology this nightmare buffet represented, not only would Buddy be devastated, but rumors of free food would quickly spread through the cockroach grapevine and within the hour my apartment would be inundated with bugs carrying knives and forks and wearing tiny bibs around their necks.

"This is wonderful, delightful, delicious. Thank you." I pointed at the granola. "I'll start with that."

He handed me the granola and I commenced munching and wondering why men are so crazy.

In Mother's opinion, it's womb envy. According to her, men realize they can't give birth, so they run around accumulating money, building skyscrapers, manufacturing wars out of border disputes, writing symphonies, and throwing paint on canvas—anything to forget their bottom-line lack: When it comes to creation, the force isn't with them.

At least, that's what Mother says. Personally, I think that men are just born crazy out of the box, crazy and complicated and needing cuddling and scared silly that women will find out.

Now that I was eating, Buddy calmed down. "Any thoughts on the Westin case so far?"

I shook my head and reached for the omelette. "We're right back where we started. Buck Stevens has no alibi. One look from him and poor Mary Lou would testify that he was busy that night changing water into wine and curing the lepers. Richard Raymond may be able to quote the guest list, the speakers, and the topics at that dinner he attended, but that doesn't mean he was there all evening. He could have come in, schmoozed around enough to make his presence known, slipped out and killed Amy Westin, then slipped back in in time to make the rounds for good nights. I think we should check with the valet parkers. They'd know if he left, then came back."

"My thoughts exactly." Buddy nodded solemnly. "I'm on the valet parkers."

"Baloney," I said, reaching for the waffles. "You wrote Raymond off the minute we walked out of the medical center."

"How do you know?" Buddy was more curious than defensive.

I grinned. "His recital bored you, so you shrugged him off. How could anyone that painfully precise and detailed be involved in anything as messy as murder? Especially this murder. He didn't strike you as the type who'd cut off a head and wrap it in pink tissue, did he?"

"Okay. Okay. Maybe you have a point. But I don't know the man and you do. What's he like?"

I reached for the pancakes. "Do you know the old joke about the four blind men describing an elephant? One describes the trunk, another the tail, another the leg, another the tusk. Each description is accurate but none is an elephant. Well, Richard Raymond's that elephant. He's volatile, charming, reclusive, and attends every important dinner in town. He's arrogant, insecure, and tall. Everyone agrees on that one. He's tall."

Buddy took out his notebook and flipped it open. "We'll reinterview Raymond." He looked at me. "You'll notice I said *we*. I'm being sensitive to your feelings about staying involved."

"Sure. And even more sensitive to my black belt in karate. But hey, giving folks the benefit of the doubt is something I'm good at and you're definitely folks, so you have it your way."

Buddy glared. "If you're finished stuffing yourself . . ."

I was already throwing paper plates into the box. "Let's review. Somebody does a John the Baptist on Amy and has her head delivered to me. Probably just a messenger. Mrs. Ramirez wouldn't notice a uniform logo if it was in neon. I unwrap the head, scream, call 911. You finally arrive and we meet cute. I give you the names of work people who hate Amy, but advise you to look into her personal life. Then you find a note threatening me. How am I doing?"

"So far we've seen the same movie," Buddy agreed.

"Okay. So we can forget Amy's personal life."

Buddy nodded. "The only connection between Amy and you is *Stone, Private Eye*." He picked a muffin out of the box and nibbled the edges. "That's what I said in the first place. Sayres, Raymond, or Stevens."

"Or someone else we don't know about yet." I had an idea. "Maybe someone on the show who's also involved in her personal life. Maybe a boyfriend she dumped or was about to."

Buddy picked up the box. "We're not going to find out standing here. Where's the trash?"

"Out back." I pointed in the general direction of the door. "I'll call the studio for a drive-through for you. We'll take separate cars."

Buddy's eyes lit up. "I got it. You don't want anyone to know we're investigating together. I'm the cop, you're the consultant. That's very cool."

"Thanks, but the truth is I'm taking my own car to avoid that awkward moment when you bring me home tonight and chase me around my apartment waving Day-Glo condoms."

"What the hell do you think I am?" Buddy shouted, then reached in his pocket and pulled out a package that he threw in my lap. "Day-Glo? You think I'd buy *Day-Glo*?"

I glanced at the package of perfectly ordinary latex condoms, then smiled sweetly at Buddy. "I rest my case."

Stepping into the office was a trip into virtual reality. Everything was the same but it wasn't. Frances and Margo spoke in shocked whispers and no one had brought in jelly doughnuts. They were poised, on tiptoe, ready to run. Murder in the house will do that.

Even though Margo and Frances hadn't known Amy as a person, they mourned her as a peer, a young woman approximately their age, horribly murdered at the start of her life. Murder was sad, always frightening, never deserved. But there was another truth about murder, a truth no one, including me, liked to admit. Murder was exciting, damned exciting, and I could see their excitement in Margo's twitchy fingers and Frances's sparky eyes. The office was awash in adrenaline.

"Are you all right?" Frances asked. "I mean, I've heard rumors."

Of course she had. So had I. The guard at the gate, who didn't know me by sight, had told me that both Amy Westin and the show's consultant . . . me . . . were dead. I didn't correct him.

"I still have my head," I told her, then was shocked when her eyes filled.

"Don't take it so lightly," Frances begged. "I'm worried about you."

"Don't be. I can take care of myself." Her concern made me uncomfortable. Why would she worry about me? And did that mean I had to worry about her? All of a sudden we had a relationship. For a moment I was afraid she might follow me home. Then, dismayed with myself, I made a mental note to ask Mother someday, after she'd answered The Question, why the kindness of strangers, or anyone, makes me want to scream and jump out the window.

"Frances, where's Cassie Sayres?"

Frances pointed. I looked.

Cassie Sayres was where she always was, in front of her computer in a cloud of blue smoke.

"She knows about Amy?" I asked Frances.

Frances rolled her eyes. "I told her, but . . . who knows."

I nodded, getting it, then stepped into her office.


Cassie never looked away from her computer. "The scripts I gave you—they're all right?"

"I didn't finish reading them. I was interrupted by Amy's murder."

That got her attention. She punched the save button, then turned to me. "I am personally devastated."

Sure, I thought. I decided to level with her. "Look, Cassie, save the bullshit for *Daily Variety*. I was sitting right here when Amy put the screws to you, Richard, and Buck. I'm the PI you offered to pay to give Amy a loaded gun. I know how you felt about Amy, so since we're alone with the door closed, cut the crap. Okay?"

Cassie glared at me. "What bullshit? Have you any idea what a disaster this is?"

She looked sincere enough, three quarters crazed instead of the usual half. "You think Amy's murder is a disaster?"

Cassie got up and started pacing. "So would you if this week's script was half-shot and you'd been here since dawn writing her out of so many scenes the whole episode won't make sense. That bitch, nothing but trouble, alive *and* dead!"

Now I could understand the personal devastation. But something rang false. "If I remember correctly, you wanted to fire her."

Before she could answer, Buddy walked in.

"Detective Beauregard Hart, LAPD," he said, flashing his badge. "I'd like to ask you some questions, Miss Sayres."

Cassie barely glanced at Buddy then went back to her computer, squinted at her screen, and started typing. "Detective Hart. I didn't like Amy Westin, but I didn't kill her."

"Oh." She'd caught Buddy off guard before he could ask the question. "Then you won't mind telling me where—"

Cassie interrupted. "Last night I was at a movie screening. *Three Men and a Teenager*. The parking stub's in my purse."

"Oh." Buddy looked at me quizzically.

"She writes mysteries," I told Buddy. "There isn't a question you're going to ask she hasn't written a hundred times."

"Two hundred," Cassie corrected. "This is my third mystery series. And my worst. And most likely my last. Our ratings are going down. Every week our audience dies off by the hundreds and there aren't enough sixty-five-year-olds to replace them. I hate going out a *failure*." Suddenly she turned her computer off, no save button, nothing, just blip and gone.

She turned toward me, looking very depressed. "To answer your question, yes, I was going to fire Amy. She was a nuisance, a bore, and a bad actress. She was also the kind of stupid, shrewd bitch who likes to mangle people and would have, once she got her own show. But . . . and this is a big but . . . I'd never kill anybody. I know I said I would, but I didn't mean it. I kill people on paper, not in real life. Do you believe me?"

"I'd like to," I told her. "Have you anything else to say?"

"Yes." Cassie sighed, looking exhausted. "Where's Richard?"

"At Cedars," I answered.

"Why did I even ask?" Cassie switched on her computer then stared at it as it hummed into life. "You'll know where to find me, Detective. I'll be here in this chair going out of my mind."

"Thank you, ma'am," Buddy said, then gestured at the door. "Miss O'Brien."

I had no reason to stay, so I followed him out. As we went Buddy whispered, "Woman's a nutcase."

Once outside, Buddy made notes. "I'll check out that screening."

"She probably went to that screening. But unless she went with someone who can testify that she didn't slip out when the movie began, then back in before the lights went up, we have to figure she could have killed Amy."

"She could have," Buddy agreed. "I'm also checking out messenger services."

"Go ahead, but she probably didn't use one."

Buddy stopped scribbling. "That's my instinct, too. What do you think?"

"I think that in a town full of unemployed actors who own blue shirts and pants and who'd be thrilled to make fifty bucks delivering a package, the killer'd be crazy to go on record with a messenger service."

Buddy looked at me appreciatively. "Not bad. Same conclusion I reached when I talked to your Mrs. Ramirez. I have one reservation. Do you think that the killer's that smart?"

I thought about that. "A head in a hatbox is real Manson stuff—witchy, schitzy, LSD trippy—but the note was wrapped in plastic and there weren't any fingerprints anywhere. I think the killer's shrewd, maybe smart, savagely angry, controlled, a borderline personality currently decompressing, homicidal, suicidal, and disintegrating."

Buddy closed his notebook. "How do you know that?"

"Years of dinner-table shrink talk, overhearing conversations about the weird, the perverse, the whacked, the bizarre." I laughed at the surprised expression on his face. "Yeah, shrinks talk about this stuff in front of their kids. It's only shoptalk, like you talk about the busts you've made and the perps who got away. You think Cassie Sayres is a nutcase? My mother would love her and what she'd love most are the kinks that make her a nutcase. Shrinks get bored only when the patients get better."

"Then I'd bore the hell out of your mother." Buddy was certain. "I'm the most normal guy I know."

"You're a cop. Cops are psychopaths with delusions of normalcy. Everybody knows that. But if you want to kid yourself . . ." I walked away from Buddy. "Come on."

He caught up to me. "Where are we going?"

"I have a hunch."

"About what?"

"Steve Pierce. He's a real cameraman."

We crossed the lot, heading for Stage 53.

As we passed the Company Store, where everything— sweatshirts, jackets, T-shirts, ashtrays, crackers, cigarettes, wrapping paper, aspirin, disposable razors, tampons, *and* the clerks—bore the studio logo, Buddy's head began to swivel.

"What's that?" he asked at a corner, pointing down a street.

"What's it look like?" I replied.

"New York. But not now. Maybe fifty years ago."

"That's what it is," I told him. "Three New York City blocks circa 1943. This is the set for that TV series—*The Boys Came Home*. And about forty major motion pictures over the past twenty years. Look behind you."

Buddy looked and laughed. "A Western town complete with hitching posts in front of the saloon."

"You've seen it in Western movies since Hopalong Cassidy. Someday when we have time, I'll show you the whole lot. There's a lake around here somewhere where *Jaws* got blown into bait chips."

Just then two cowboys walked by with Dracula. Buddy's head spun full circle. "Jeez."

"I know. First time I saw actors in costume going to lunch, I walked into a wall. Luckily it was a flat, a fake wall, and I broke it instead of it breaking me. This place is a trip, isn't it?"

"Certainly is." Buddy grinned, watching cops and mobsters, men in tuxedos and women in feathers, dashing from stage to wardrobe or on break, strolling under the blazing sun lapping at Sno-Kones while their makeup ran off their chins.

"What do you know about Steve Pierce?" Buddy asked, sidestepping a midget on roller skates who tipped his hat and rolled on.

"To begin with, he projects all-American boy, but he isn't. There's a hole in his head where an earring should be, his roots are dark, there's a pentagram tattoo on his right inner elbow, and he's a dedicated sexual masochist."

That got Buddy's attention. "You know that from personal experience?"

"Yes, but not the kind you think. He put his hands on me without an invitation. I hurt him. He came back for more."

Buddy frowned. "Why didn't you tell me? I would have taken care of him for you."

"You're going to fight my battles for me?"

Buddy squinted at me through thick sunshine. "I could if you'd let me."

I thought about it. So Buddy wanted to take care of me. Deep inside, the part of me that needed taking care of jumped up and down yelling, "Whoopee!"

Another minute and that needy part, which I always pictured as a little girl with an anxious smile, would fly into Buddy's arms, murmuring, "Daddy."

So, as always, I told her to sit down and shut up.

"Thanks, Buddy." I smiled, hoping he'd know I liked him even though I was rejecting his idea. "But if I let you take care of me, sooner or later I'd forget how to take care of myself. Then, when you aren't around anymore, I'd be helpless. Frankly, I'd rather be dead."

Buddy flinched. I'd hurt his feelings. But he didn't give up. "What do you mean 'when I'm not around'? Who says I'm going anywhere? What if I stay?"

"Nobody stays." I patted his cheek. "That's life, honey. No big deal."

I walked on ahead of him but slowly, giving him a moment to burn off his anger. When he caught up with me, he muttered, "You're really screwed up, Dutch. You know that?"

I kept going. "I wish you hadn't told me that, Buddy. I thought I was perfect." As we approached the stage door I saw the red light flashing. I grabbed Buddy's shirt. "We can't go in yet."

"Oh yeah?" Buddy's jaw jutted. He didn't like the word *can't*. "Why the hell not?"

"They're filming. We go in now, they'll throw us out." Buddy reached for his badge. Throw the LAPD out? Not damn likely. "Two minutes, Buddy," I said quickly. "Wait two minutes and people will answer your questions. Okay?"

Buddy hesitated, torn between macho and common sense. Finally he relaxed, pulled a pack of chewing gum from his breast pocket, and offered it to me. "Juicy Fruit?"

I slid a stick from the package. "Thanks."

We leaned against the wall, chewing companionably.

"You catch that movie last night on TV about the Jurgens kidnapping in Des Moines?" Buddy asked.

"No. I can't hook into that true-crime crap, some actress with a two-hundred-buck hairdo and perfect makeup playing a trailer-park mom whose kid has been snatched. Like the first thing a woman does when she finds her kid missing is put on mascara."

"I didn't notice the makeup, but I know what you mean." Buddy popped a second stick of gum in his mouth. "Those ripped-from-the-headlines things come off phony."

"Made up. Like a camel. It isn't a horse. It isn't a cow. It's something in the middle with a hump in its back," I said, noticing a couple walk by. Man and woman, their heads inclined toward each other, their bodies separated by a careful, discreet distance. Lovers, I thought. One's married, one's not. They think nobody knows. Everybody knows. It's written all over them like a tattoo.

Buddy glanced sideways at me. "So, what *did* you do last night?"

So that was it. Buddy wanted to know what I did after I left his apartment. He was frantic to know if I was out doing what he wanted to do with me. "I read a book."

"What book?"

"Anne Rice."

Buddy stopped chewing. "You like vampire stuff?"

I was surprised. "You've read Anne Rice?" Then I laughed.

Buddy's jaw was a perfect square. "What's so funny about that?"

"She writes women's books, Buddy."

Buddy unwrapped a third stick of gum. "You're nuts. Women don't like reading about blood and gore and mangled corpses."

"You mean about a man who drives women mad with desire then makes love to beautiful young men? You bet. Women like it even more than *Good Housekeeping* and you know how nuts we are about recipes."

Buddy jammed the gum in his mouth. "I only read one book and I didn't finish it. I got pissed off at that vampire guy Lester."

"Le*stat*."

"Whoever. Rich, good-looking, gets to live forever, and always pissing and moaning about something."

I laughed. "Being a vampire isn't easy."

Buddy shook his head. "Come on. He couldn't die."

"He paid a big price for that."

"Wouldn't you?"

I thought about that. "He had to drink blood to live."

"No problem." Buddy shrugged. "I'd go to a blood bank."

That irritated me. Buddy was making sense. "Buddy, he sold his soul."

Buddy grinned. "Gotcha. If he sold his soul to the devil and he was going to live forever, then the devil would never collect. Right?"

Just like a cop. Figuring the angle. But he had me. "Right."

Buddy nodded, satisfied. "If I could make a bargain like that, I'd sell my soul in a minute, wouldn't you? If there was something you really wanted?"

I couldn't answer. Michael. Michael. Would I? For Michael? After all I'd been through? What would I tell the devil I wanted? To forget I'd ever known Michael? Or to be with him forever? "I don't know if I'd sell my soul, Buddy, but I'd sure as hell lease it."

"Thought so." Buddy grinned, happy I'd sold out in theory right along with him. "My favorite writer's Stephen King. Man's a genius."

"You got that right," I agreed. "*The Stand*'s my all-time favorite book."

"Yeah!" Buddy was thrilled, certain that the Stephen King connection was karmic and meaningful. "Who's your favorite character?"

I knew, but I didn't want to tell him. "You expect me to say Frannie because she's a woman."

"No," Buddy said quickly. "You're not like most women. I mean, you are but you aren't. I'll bet Stu's your favorite. Or Larry. Come on, tell me."

Why not? "Frannie . . . because she's tough."

Buddy looked confused. "But you just said . . ."

I glanced up at the stage door. The red light was off. "Light's off, Buddy. Let's go."

No one on Stage 53 could tell us where to find Steve Pierce. We'd just about given up when Steve appeared, brushing dust from his jeans and grinning.

"Hey, Dutch, we finally on for dinner?" he greeted me, then scowled at Buddy. "Your friend here better leave. You know how Buck feels about strangers on the set."

"This is Homicide Detective Buddy Hart. He's investigating the death of Amy Westin. Detective, this is Steve Pierce, one of the show's cameramen."

Steve's attitude changed instantly. He shook hands with Buddy. "Nice to meet you. But not like this. Poor Amy. Nice kid." He paused, a beat of respect for the dead. "How can I help you?"

Buddy flipped open his notebook. "Tell me what you know about Amy Westin."

"Okay." Steve thought a moment. "She had skin you could light from any direction and had no bad angles. She was usually on time and knew most of her lines." He glanced at me. "I only knew her professionally."

Buddy looked to me for confirmation. I shrugged, not knowing. I turned to Steve. "Just for the record, where were you on the night Amy was killed?"

Steve laughed. Buddy scowled. "What's so funny about that?"

Steve continued to laugh. "If Buck heard you say that, he'd shit bricks. Every week the script has him asking that question, oh, maybe four or five times. And Buck always takes the line out. Says it's so boring it puts him to sleep."

Buddy was curious. "Then how does he ask the suspects where they were when the victim was killed?"

"Sometimes he tells them where the victim was killed and they say they were somewhere else . . . sometimes he doesn't ask at all . . . says the audience doesn't know the difference. And sometimes he just grunts and spits on his shoes and the actor playing the suspect pretends he asked the question and answers it. But he'll never say, 'Where were you on the night the victim was killed?' "

While Buddy wrestled with that one, I repeated, "So, Steve, where were you on the night in question?"

He glanced at me, a quick flip of his left eyeball. "Want to beat it out of me with a rubber hose?"

Buddy took over. "Mr. Pierce, please answer the question."

"I was with a friend."

"Who?"

"A lady."

"The lady's name?"

Steve looked at the ceiling. "The lady's married."

"We're investigating murder, not adultery, Steve. What's her name?"

"Lulu."

I smiled. "That's a start. Lulu what?"

"The lady didn't say." Steve grinned. "All she said was that she was married, madder than hell at her husband, and rarin' to take it out on somebody."

Buddy and I exchanged glances. Buddy persisted. "Where did you meet Lulu?"

"The Monkey Club on Pico and Frontera."

Buddy closed his notebook. "Hope for your sake this checks out."

Steve nodded. "Me, too. Nice to meet you, Hart. Catch you later, Dutch." Then he strolled off, trying to look cool, but I knew better. His neck was rod-rigid and he'd forgotten to affect his John Wayne gait.

"What do you think?" I asked Buddy.

"He's not as weird as the midget on roller skates" was Buddy's opinion.

"Midgets aren't weird. They're short. And he was on roller skates because . . ." I stopped, wondering why I was doing this. "I'll be right back."

"Where are you going?"

"Ladies' room."

"I'll wait here."

"Then we'll check out the Monkey Club."

On the way back from the ladies' room, I heard Steve's voice coming from behind a flat. I tiptoed up to the flat, peered through a crack, and saw him speaking into a cellular phone. "We've got trouble," he was saying. "The bimbo PI and a cop are checking out my alibi for the night Westin packed it in." He listened. "No! I gave them a song and dance." He listened. "See you in twenty minutes."

I slipped away from the flat and hurried toward Buddy. "Change of plans," I announced. "We've been tapping our toes to the wrong song and dance."

"What?"

"C'mon. I'll explain on the way."

By the time I explained and Buddy got it, we'd followed Steve's pickup deep into Chinatown, which isn't that deep, because in L.A., Chinatown is basically two square blocks. After that you run smack into Olvera Street, where the spring rolls are deep-fried and called chimichangas. We pulled up in front of Sum Low's Seafood Restaurant and followed Steve inside.

Inside, we zigzagged our way through Anglo tourists from column A and the Chinese regulars from column B. Dodging waiters pushing carts of dim sum, we scooted beyond screens painted with cranes, checked both rest rooms, and found each other in front of a jade-green Buddha gazing benevolently at the cash register.

"We lost him," Buddy groaned.

"He lost us. On purpose." I pointed at the two exit doors and the door to the kitchen. "That's why he came in here. A crowd and two back doors."

"When *I* follow suspects, they don't know it," Buddy protested.

"Sure. Be right back." I headed for the ladies' room, where I knew there'd be a phone for the convenience of women who find it necessary to call a getaway cab in the middle of dinner.

When I returned, I found Buddy at the cashier, paying for a takeout. "*So?*"

"I called the office. Frances said she'd let me know when Steve returns to the set."

"She didn't ask why?"

"After six years with Richard Raymond, Frances is the perfect assistant. She never asks why, just does as she's told." I laughed. "But she has a wicked gleam in her eye. Come the revolution, Frances will be the point man."

"Which revolution?" Buddy sighed. "According to the last community-affairs briefing we had at the precinct, L.A.'s working on at least six. Anything else?"

"Yeah. I got a parking ticket. Seems that I parked my car under an elm tree which is where the studio's new chairman, Mr. Yokomoto, likes to park. So the studio rent-a-cops towed me to a landfill in the back lot. Frances has my spare keys. She said she'd go move my car after lunch." I glanced at the take-out. "Speaking of lunch . . ."

"Assorted dim sum. We'll eat in the car."

The weather outside had turned gloomy—gray sky, thick sticky air, and a strange stillness that made me feel I should tiptoe. Buddy squinted upward. "Earthquake weather."

"Tornado weather," I disagreed. "Or maybe flood or fire or Armageddon."

Behind me a woman's cracked voice hissed, "Miss . . . Missss . . ."

I glanced over my shoulder. An ancient Chinese woman wearing a long red dress and a black cape covered with inscrutable symbols stood in a doorway beckoning to me.

Buddy glanced her way and muttered, "Fortune-teller." He kept going.

I hesitated. The woman's eyes bore through mine straight into the back of my head. And in the back of my head I felt a door open, a door I saw in my mind's eye. The door was black. The thin laserlike line of light streaming through it was gold.

"I'll be right back," I told Buddy, and walked toward the woman, who disappeared into her booth knowing that I would follow.

Ten minutes later Buddy looked up as I approached the car.

"So?"

"I am the universe. Magic surrounds me. All I need do is believe and summon it. I should be careful what I pray for because I'll get it." I glanced at the empty carton in Buddy's lap. "You son of a bitch. You ate all the dim sum."

"Serves you right. Get in." Buddy opened the door and I got in.

I didn't say word one on the way back to the studio. Buddy thought I was stiffing him over the pot stickers, but the truth was the ten minutes I'd given the Chinese lady shaman had scrambled my brain cells. Her piercing eyes had zapped me senseless, her hissing had hypnotranced me, and the words she'd spoken had slithered out of her mouth and straight into my brain. When finally she'd pinched the back of my hand and told me to go, I'd come to shivering, feeling the magic closing around me, powerful, impatient magic.

I sat very still, feeling myself teetering on the edge of my future. One step and I'd be there, ready or not.

As we stopped at a red light I told myself that I must heed the shaman's warnings to be careful what I prayed for. Immediately, the hair on the back of my neck stood up straight and prickled. And I knew without knowing how I knew that it was already too late. Between the second my brain had shattered and the second it had reassembled there in the shaman's hot, dark room, my hungry heart had tossed up its prayer.

Whatever it was, it would happen. Whatever it was, magic was having its way with me.

I wondered what Mother would say about this.

As we drove through the studio gates an explosion rocked the back lot.

Later everyone would say that their first thought was that some special-effects guy had gone for the big one and the studio would have his ass. Special effects are supposed to thrill audiences, not rain dirt and small rocks onto executive hair transplants and Armani lapels.

Fifteen minutes after that first thought, everyone would know that the fireball hanging over the studio was all that was left of my car and Frances, who'd been doing me the favor she'd promised.

I hadn't really known Frances, so all I could miss was that secret wild gleam in her eye. But since that was more than I'd miss in most people I knew, I'd really miss Frances.

And I'd sure as hell never let anyone, anywhere, ever do me a favor again. Ever.

Waiting for the bomb squad with Buddy, I wondered what the hell kind of magic it is that saves you from a murder attempt but blows apart someone else, someone innocent.

Not any magic *I* wanted to mess with.


Two days later Cassie Sayres, Buck Stevens, and I gathered around Richard Raymond's desk. In the middle of Richard's desk his speakerphone held court. We all stared at it, mesmerized, looking like the apes in *2001: A Space Odyssey* staring at the obelisk. And just like the apes, we jumped at The Voice.

"Miss . . . uh . . . O'Brien," Richard's voice floated out of the phone. "I hope you're all right."

I leaned forward. "Fine." Then as an afterthought: "Thank you."

Buck scowled. "Frances is dead. Blown to smithereens."

"I know. Her death is a considerable personal loss to

me." Richard's voice was steady. "I'll notify you of the funeral arrangements when I've completed them."

Cassie frowned and blew her cigarette smoke at the phone. "Frances had a family. Why are *you* making the arrangements?"

"Her family is understandably distraught," Richard offered. "I thought I could be helpful."

Cassie suddenly jumped up and leaned over the phone. "Richard, if you want to be helpful, you'll get your ass out of your bunker and in here. This two-part story I'm working on is mush in the middle and Buck's story arc is going nowhere."

Buck turned on Cassie. "What the hell you mean my story arc's going nowhere? It's my show and my story. If I'm going nowhere, then you better haul your smoky ass back to your office and get me going somewhere. You hear?" He turned and yelled into the phone. "Where the fuck are you anyway, Richard?"

"I understand how upset you must be, Buck," Richard said smoothly.

"He's ballistic," Cassie interjected. "Foaming at the mouth."

Buck sneered at Cassie. "Look here, you weird little bitch. . . ."

Cassie stared, then shrieked, "Wait, Buck! Don't move your face." She opened her purse, yanked out a mirror, and held it up to Buck. "Look at that sneer and the way your eyes pop. You look absolutely crazy."

Buck looked. "Yeah."

Now Cassie was hopping around the room. "I got it! I got it! Your best friend gets killed and you go temporarily wacko and run around doing things out of character."

Buck squinted warily. "What kind of things?"

"*Interesting* things! *Dramatic* things! *Emmy Award–*

*winning* things! Things that will make your audience sit up and say, 'Hot damn, I never thought old Buck had it in him!' " Cassie was rolling.

Buck's eyes widened. "Think I can kill somebody?" He wheedled. "Without wrecking my character, a' course." He turned to me. "Audience stops loving ya, you're dead."

Cassie puffed rapidly, then stared at some vision only she saw in the smoke. "If I do it right, *Stone, Private Eye* can waste a carload of nuns."

Delighted, Buck clapped his hands. "Well, don't just stand there, girl, git to it."

Cassie was out of the room in a second.

Buck looked at me. "Somethin's *wrong* with that woman." Before I could say anything, he was hunched over the phone. "Now you listen here, Richard Raymond. Maybe you can git away with hiding out at home like some muley-eyed weasel, but I can't. I'm here on this lot with a show in decline and a killer on the loose. And it's clear to me if it's not clear to you that this maniac's after my ass."

"Yours!" My head spun around. "This guy is trying to kill me!"

"You're a prop!" Buck yelled. "He killed Amy, he killed Frances. Now, what does this mean?"

"You tell me." I waited.

Buck circled me slowly. "He's killing people on my show, cutting a swath of death around me, that's what it means. And why? He's inching his way to the core, charging full bore at the mother lode, heading for the source and who's the source? Me!"

"Wait a minute," I protested. "We have no evidence. . . ."

Buck waved his arms over my head. "You think I'm gonna stand here and wait for evidence till I wind up with my head in a box on the desk of some hack at the *National En-*

*quirer*? This fucker's out to git me and the rest of you guys are rehearsal!"

"Thanks." I sat back, realizing that Buck was fighting to stay center stage in a play where he wasn't the star. "I'm sure this guy killed Amy and Frances and tried to kill me only to scare you."

"Well, he's done it. Done it good."

The phone crackled, then Richard's voice floated. "How may I help you, Buck?"

Buck and I both whirled, surprised to find him still there. Buck hunched over the phone. "You can't help me, Richard. And you sure can't hurt me. Until the police find this fucker, I'm shutting down the show."

There was a slight pause, then Richard continued: "I think if you'll look at your contract you'll find it clearly states—"

Buck interrupted. "I'm not looking at nothing. This is what I'm doing. I'm doing it now, and I'm doing it for Mary Lou."

Sure, I thought. This old baby's found a situation he can't control, so he's going to bang on his high chair until everyone listens, then pick up his toys and go home.

Richard Raymond cleared his throat, sending his speakerphone into spasms of static. "I can understand how you feel, but I'm sure your wife wouldn't want—"

Buck pounded on the desk. The phone didn't budge. "You fucking dare to tell me how my wife feels? You fucking *dare*?"

"I didn't mean—"

"You bet your ass you didn't mean. You don't fucking know!" Buck screamed. "You want to know how my wife feels, I'll tell you. She's scared shitless something's going to happen to me. Right this minute I got a nurse with her, sitting beside her holding her hand. I got a doctor prescribing four kinds of pills and a minister holding a prayer meeting in my living room. And it's still not enough." He took a deep breath and his voice lowered. "My Mary Lou is not a well woman. Not that she's sick . . . no . . . she comes from good stock. But she's . . . fragile."

No shit, I thought. The speakerphone crackled, evidently thinking the same thing.

Buck continued. "Her daddy was a mostly unemployed meat cutter who ran moonshine through Appalachia. Her brothers worked for him. Their job, besides stokin' and drivin', was to ride around dead of night blowing up other folks' stills. Mary Lou's mama died young and she was the only female around who didn't run her daddy and brothers off with a shotgun on sight. Now I don't have to tell you that country folk is mainly plain, good-hearted, and no bullshit, but good to the bone. But the dumb ones and mean ones . . . well . . . you don't fuck with 'em. They take what they want and what they took was Mary Lou. And that's where I found her when my car broke down about a mile and a half from their house—penned up inside like some kind of animal, broken down by her daddy and brothers. Broken down and used up. So I took her right out of there. Gave her daddy all the cash I had on me, eleven hundred dollars, and took that poor child and lit the hell out. I been looking after her ever since. Only thing ever sets her back is when she gets worried about something happening to me. Then that poor little girl just falls apart." Buck glanced at the phone, then at me. "I know what both of you are thinking. If old Buck cares so much for his wife, why doesn't he keep it in his pants?"

Bingo, I thought. Good question.

Buck went on solemnly. "My daddy couldn't, his daddy couldn't, and his daddy before him. Don't know why, but once we're half-grown and come into season, it just never stops. It's kinda out of our hands like a goddamned tornado."

Despite myself, I smiled. Only Buck Stevens could make chronic screwing around sound like an act of God. Funny thing was, I heard truth in what he'd said. How much and what part, I didn't yet know. But truth, at least a few grains in the bullshit he'd shoveled.

The phone crackled. "Buck, if you'd like, I can recommend an excellent psychiatrist—"

Buck interrupted. "See him yourself, Richard. The show's down till I say so."

With that, Buck walked out of the room. I waited a moment, then spoke at the phone. "Buck's gone."

"I thought so." Richard sounded thoughtful. "In my personal opinion, the killer is after you. May I suggest that you leave this to the police and get out of town until we resume production."

"I'll think about it," I said, planning to call Buddy immediately. "And you?"

Richard chuckled. "I'm holding a full house. I'll stand pat."

"Uh . . . good," I replied, wondering what he meant. "Uh . . . goodbye?"

"Nice talking to you." The speakerphone crackled, then the volume suddenly went up just before he hung up, but not before I heard a familiar sound. Wherever Richard was, planes were taking off.

I called Buddy. "You'd better check on Richard Raymond's whereabouts, Buddy. I think he may be on the run."

"Shit." Buddy's anger was immediate. "I should have slapped that son of a bitch in handcuffs."

"Issue an APB."

"I might." Buddy sounded uncertain.

"*Might*? Buddy, why so coy?"

Buddy hesitated, then sounded embarrassed. "Okay. I issue an APB. Some cop somewhere spots him, hauls him back cuffed. He's a rich, well-known man, Dutch. This is L.A. The first thing Richard Raymond does is call Robert Shapiro. Then Shapiro charges the LAPD with false arrest. Also harassment. There's a twenty-million-dollar lawsuit the city has to defend. And while the city's defending, I'm pounding a beat in Pacoima."

I understood. "You need more evidence."

"You got it." Buddy sounded weary. "Enough to nail him. But . . . I'll find out where he went."

"If I hear anything, I'll tell you."

"Dinner?"

"No . . . thanks," I said. "I'm going to take everyone's advice and lie low for a while."

"Are you going somewhere?" Buddy asked, sounding anxious.

"I'll keep in touch."

*Chapter 6*

Three weeks later, with Frances's funeral over and the investigation at a crawl, I decided to go home. After all, I had everything I needed for the trip—a car, a suitcase, my mother's address, and a bad attitude left over from childhood. So I called Buddy.

He approved. "I was going to suggest that you go somewhere and lay low for a while, but I was afraid you'd bite my head off."

"Me?" I asked, dumping my underwear drawer into my suitcase. "Why?"

"You know." Buddy sounded nervous. "You're working on the case. And then there's the, uh . . . feminist thing."

"Oh, that." I dumped socks on top of the underwear. "You mean that if you tell me what to do, I'll tell you you're being a paternalistic macho pig?"

"Yeah. Right." Buddy sounded relieved.

"Buddy." I mashed a plastic Savon bag full of makeup into the cotton/spandex heap. "You *are* a paternalistic macho pig, and nothing you say or don't say is going to change that."

"Shit, Dutch, gimme a break."

"Not in this life, Buddy. Bye."

"Gimme your mother's phone number?" Buddy shouted. "Dutch!"

I hesitated, then recited: "1-800-555-6262."

"Your mother has an 800 number?"

"Bye, Buddy." I hung up.

If Buddy called the number I gave him, he'd be offered his choice of a Whiz-o-matic Veggie Grater or a Bamboo Barbecuer, each on sale for $19.95. He'd thank me later.

I snapped my suitcase shut, turned out the lights, and slammed the door behind me. To hell with Buddy Hart, Buck Stevens, and a maniac on the loose. I was headed for the Far Country.

Halfway home, I stopped, pulled over, and tore the wrapping off an Almond Joy. As I munched I looked back. The lights of the San Fernando Valley were doing their famous Christmas-tree thing—twinkling and blinking through the pollution, a thousand points of blight in the smog. Overhead, a full moon, free of the smog, brilliantly key-lit the scene.

Looking down, I knew I was supposed to be pondering the dramas being played out in the Valley—the lives and loves being lived and lost beneath each flammable shingle roof and inside each stucco bungalow. In *Stone, Private Eye* this was the moment when we'd hear Stone's voice-over with some wry, pithy observation about human nature or some deep psychological insight, all written by Cassie Sayres with a Kool Light hanging out of her mouth, then printed phonetically on cue cards for Buck, who claimed to be dyslexic but just plain couldn't read.

At the moment I didn't care about drama or insight. Or about the people living in the Valley. I had once, and not so long ago either. During my Michael days we'd often driven up here, stopped, looked down, and hoped that the people those lights represented were happy or at least content. Michael, in particular, had empathized, but then Michael is nicer than I am.

Since the abrupt, unexplained end of my Michael days, my own heart had gradually dried up and sealed off. There was little warmth left in it for anyone—strangers, friends, or myself.

I chewed the last of the candy, knowing that Mother would identify my hardened heart as a symptom of depression. Maybe. Hopefully. A symptom can pass. But until it did, even I knew that a heart without warmth is dangerous, hair-trigger, ready to pop. The person who owns a dead heart can wound, even kill, and never look back.

I threw the wrapper out the window, started the engine, and headed for Beverly Hills.

As the car ate the curves on Coldwater I glanced in the rearview and wished I'd worn makeup. Without my eyeliner/blush/mascara mask, Mother would take one look and know I was still mourning Michael.

If you take San Simeon, shrink it two thirds, and set it on top of the Beverly Hill known as Bel Largo, you have Mother's house. Like Hearst, Mother's taste is eclectic. The house itself is two-story stucco, sand-colored with a subtle hint of pink, a color Mother mixed herself after driving two battalions of stucco men crazy with her demand for a shade the exact color of the Lady Montbatten rose.

To get to the house, you drive through the wrought-iron electric gate set in a ten-foot-high curving concrete wall. To the right of the gate is a tiled plaque with the street number and legend VISTA DEL MAR, something of a misnomer, since no one's been able to glimpse the ocean through the smog since 1951. There is, however, an excellent view of the Beverly Hills fire station, a real comfort to Mother, who gets edgy in September at the beginning of fire season, in November at flood season, and during any week when there have been more than two earthquakes.

Once inside the gate, a broad driveway circles up to a red brick pathway that leads into a Spanish courtyard inlaid with yellow-and-blue Moroccan tiles. Then it's over the tiles and into the house, stepping directly into a great circular entryway two stories tall with a Baccarat crystal chandelier hanging overhead and a grand staircase spiraling off to the right. From the marble-floored entryway, it's three steps down into the pine-floored living room, a pastel expanse roughly the size of Union Station. From there the house just flows with bedroom suites, studies, a library, a sunroom, and a kitchen with magnetic doohickies that pop small appliances up out of countertops decorated with hand-painted tiles depicting Greek goddesses at play. Everywhere are French doors looking out at gardens surrounding the house. In the north-side garden is the swimming pool, Olympic-sized and blue-tiled, which Mother had built for her husband, Dunn, who enjoys rippling the water with his rippling muscles as he backstrokes and ogles the maids.

For me, coming home is like visiting a well-run luxury hotel where the surroundings are elegant, the service impeccable, and the cost a piece of my soul. I know Mother tries, really she does, but she's more a natural shrink than a natural mother, so time spent with her is less like a homecoming and more like a Vulcan mind probe.

The minute I drove through the gate, I wished I'd called ahead. Instead of the empty courtyard and still nighttime beauty of Mother's house, floodlit from all directions like Grauman's Chinese, there were valet parkers everywhere and white twinkling lights blinking from the shrubbery. Damn! Mother was having a party.

As I negotiated the driveway, then turned to the right, heading for the five-car garage, two valet parkers pursued me.

I stopped the car, got out, and waited as they huffed to my side. "We're supposed to park you," the pudgy blond kid panted.

I unbuttoned my jacket, flashing my gun. "Forget it, boys, I'm security."

"No problem." The Mexican kid backed off fast, then turned and ran, followed clumsily by the blond. I grinned then felt guilty. So I'd intimidated two eighteen-year-olds who were working for their money instead of running with gangs or robbing ATM customers. So I should feel ashamed. Some tough guy.

I went around to the back door, thinking of Frances and the favor she'd done me. She was young. She had a life. It was gone. Because of me. Shit.

The back door, bought by Mother from a farm couple in Tuscany, then shipped and rehung by Jorge, her Peruvian carpenter, was unlocked. I entered, stepping into the sounds of a party and the smells of a catered affair. Three Hispanic women working in the kitchen looked up briefly, nodded politely, then went back to arranging cold shellfish on platters.

I speared a chunk of lobster, popped it in my mouth, reached for another, then stopped. I felt guilty. And wondered. For scaring the parkers—sure. For Frances—definitely. But for lobster—forget it.

There was only one explanation.

The guilt that I always felt under my mother's roof, even in her driveway, had sensed I was coming, then awakened and slithered out to wrap itself around me like a boa constrictor. It's not that Mother had ever worked at making me feel guilty. She hadn't. She didn't need to. It was there in her eyes, the critical tilt of her head, the sad squeeze of her well-toned arms.

I am her disappointment. Me. Her only child. Disappointing. To her, a good mother. In the name of all humanity and mothers everywhere, a curse should be placed on my head.

I grabbed another chunk of lobster and swallowed it whole. If you can't beat it, feed it.

Opening the kitchen door, I peered out into the dining room, where party guests were milling, casing the buffet table. Mother wasn't among them. Easing my way through the dining room, I noticed that the crowd was typically Beverly Hills—corporate moguls and entertainment mavens—not "the talent"—actors, directors, and producers—but studio heads and their top executives, all accessorized with gilded wives.

The wives startled me. So many of them were wearing quilted dinner suits in peacock colors draped with gold chains that for a moment I thought they must belong to some secret feminine army that issues padded uniforms in unflattering colors. Then I looked closer and saw that the identical purses they carried all sported interlocking gold Cs and I knew that this uniform was, as always, only the latest collection from Chanel.

But still—beyond the uniform the women themselves looked eerily similar. Most were blonde, ash or gold, with platinum streaks placed artfully around their faces. Among the blondes was a sprinkling of the rosewood-magenta hair color found only in Beverly Hills, rumored to be the invention of a famed colorist currently mixing his potions for his fellow patients at the Betty Ford Center. And here and there in the crowd were women whose jet-black hair seemed to be making a statement; but about what, who knew?

Even hair didn't explain the wives' Stepford similarity. It was . . . I concentrated. Hadn't I convinced Buddy that I was a master at observation? And here I was, seeing something in front of me, knowing that what I was seeing meant something else, but unable to put it together.

Next to me, a blonde suddenly sneezed, delicately rattling

her chains. She quickly pulled a lace handkerchief from somewhere in her bosom and gently dabbed at her nose.

And I had it.

All the women in this room had the same nose—small,
narrow through the bridge, and slightly upturned. And most
of them had the same face—skintight, jowls nonexistent, set
above necks that looked twenty years older than their faces.
Below the necks, their breasts billowed up toward their collar-
bones, all tightness and tautness and perkiness, all theirs because they had paid for them.

So *these* were Mother's victims of ageism and lookism,
the avant-garde revolutionaries who'd stood up for their cosmetic and rejuvenation rights.

Tempted as I was to congratulate the sneezing woman on
her revolutionary courage, I knew if I did she'd kill me. So I
mingled, looking for Mother and snatching gooey tidbits from
trays as I went.

"I can get you more crabmeat if you want," a young
waiter whispered, grateful that finally someone had taken a
morsel from his packed tray.

"Thanks, no. Maybe later."

"Nobody eats anything in Beverly Hills," the waiter complained. "The food comes in, goes around the whole house,
then goes out again, just like the guests. Makes you wonder
what good it is being rich if you ain't allowed to eat nothing."

"Pack up the food and take it home," I advised, then continued looking for Mother. I finally spotted her across the
room, dressed in a red quilted trench coat draped with enough
gold braid to embarrass an admiral. She was deep in conversation with her hunky husband, who was practicing his chosen profession: looking more handsome than any man in the
room while gazing at Mother with desire in his eyes. Dunn's
performance, as always, was impeccable, worth every penny.
As I approached her I noticed that Mother's hair was longer

and blonder, done in hey-look-at-me, I'm-a-blonde-goddess waves that would have made Ivana Trump or Marla Maples proud. Beyond that, the face peering out from the golden cascade was almost, but not quite, familiar.

"Hi, Mom," I greeted her. "Where's the rest of your nose?"

"Shhh," she hissed, then embraced me warmly, raising her voice so nearby guests could hear. "Demeter, darling. What a wonderful surprise!"

Heads turned. A half-dozen quilted women with Mother's nose whispered explanations into their mates' ears. I could hear the words *daughter, detective.*

Mother held me at arm's length, scrutinizing me. "You look better," she said, sounding relieved. "How are you feeling?"

"Better," I told her. And I was. At some point in the process of being stalked by a crazed killer, I'd switched my focus from self-pity to saving my ass.

Dunn draped a proprietary arm over Mother's shoulder, then looked me up and down from my black turtleneck to my black jeans and boots. "Hi, Dee. I guess nobody told you we were having a party or you wouldn't be dressed like a ninja assassin."

"See what happens when you buy your own clothes." I smiled at him sweetly. "Lucky for you Mother picks out your wardrobe and pays for it, too."

Dunn's face darkened. Quickly Mother turned to him. "Dunn, darling, would you?"

As always, Dunn knew what was expected of him. He kissed her cheek tenderly then immediately began mingling, spreading his charm like Cheez Whiz over the crowd.

Mother glared at me. "That was uncalled for."

"No, Mother. He called for it. I never shoot at him unless

he fires the first shot. Wouldn't be sporting. He's such a sitting duck."

I noticed a short, smirking man wearing Armani and with newly planted hair plugs polka-dotting his scalp moving up behind Mother.

"Weasel to starboard," I warned her.

Mother turned slightly, then smiled brilliantly. "Humbolt! Come meet my daughter."

So this was Mother's new partner, the plastic surgeon who'd made off with half of her nose.

He offered his tiny hand. "Delighted to meet you, Demeter. Your mother's told me so much about you, I feel that we're old friends."

I couldn't help it. I laughed. Humbolt was perfect, slick as an oil spill and sincere as Jimmy Swaggart.

Mother glowered.

"Sorry," I apologized, shaking hands. "Mother will tell you I have an odd sense of humor."

"Reaction formation," Mother whispered to Humbolt, who nodded understanding. Suddenly one tiny hand reached out and his forefinger, the size of a gherkin, poked my face. "I can do something about this," he announced.

I recoiled. "About what?"

Mother looked at me curiously as Humbolt leaned closer. "Your chin. It's insufficient. I'll do an implant, a small one. You'll look just like Raquel."

"Just what I've always wanted." I bit the inside of my mouth to keep from laughing. "But I'm not sure that'll do it. I have an overbite. If you build up my chin to meet my overbite, I'm going to look like an orangutan."

"No, no," Humbolt protested.

But Mother interrupted. "I think she's right, Humbolt. She does have an overbite. It's genetic. And if you enhanced her chin, I do believe that her jaw might take on a . . . um . . . simian quality."

"Thanks, Mom. You're a peach," I said, seizing on the clue. Since Mother's jaw was classic WASP perfect, clearly my father had been the one with the overbite. Now all I had to do was round up every guy in the country over fifty who could slurp up a shake without using a straw and ask each where he was the night nine months before my birth.

"You can borrow something from my closet if you like." I came out of my reverie to find Mother staring at me and Humbolt gone.

I shook my head. "Thanks, but if I wear one of your outfits on the street, I'll get picked up for being AWOL."

"Military themes are *in* this year, Demeter." Mother smiled and her nose wobbled ever so slightly to the left.

"I know," I told her. "Among the homeless, everybody who is anybody is wearing army-navy surplus with fleas."

Mother leaned closer. "Don't start with me, Demeter. Unless you want grief."

I leaned even closer to Mother. "Are most of these people your patients?"

"Some of them. Why?"

I nodded knowingly. "I thought so."

"You thought so," Mother said, working herself up to something. "Why did you look at my guests and see patients?"

"Isn't it obvious, Mother?" I said, knowing I was driving her crazy. "I mean, really."

Mother's eyes narrowed. "You're testing me." She turned away.

I threw the bait at her back. "I dreamed about you."

Mother turned, grabbed me by the hand, and without her social smile or a single excuse, dragged me out of the living room, up the spiral staircase, down an endless corridor, and into her suite. She slammed the door behind us. "Tell me."

So I made up a dream, a nice one, a real mother-daughter fantasy with a sunny day at the beach, a picnic, and a boat that took us to Oz.

"Bullshit," Mother said at the end of my recital. "Even you can do better than that." But she smiled as I knew she would. "You've been seeing a therapist, haven't you?" She put a hand on my arm. "Sorry. You don't have to answer that. It's none of my business. But it's just so . . . well . . . clearly, you're better." She patted my arm, a gesture that might have been comforting if her nails had been shorter. "I saw on *Entertainment Tonight* that an actress on your show was murdered." She shook her head. "Random violence. It's a growing national concern and the subject of a lecture I'm giving in New York this September. I'm discussing root causes and possible solutions."

"Great. If we can keep the guns out of kids' hands till September, you'll have the problem licked."

Mother's eyes narrowed, but she didn't bite. "He isn't from the Valley, is he?"

"Buddy?"

Mother blinked. "You call your therapist Buddy?"

"What therapist?"

A banging at the door ended our mutual confusion. We heard a muffled voice. "Darling. Our guests are asking for you."

It was Dunn, anxious as always that Mother might be forming an actual bond with me.

"A moment, darling," Mother called, then turned back to me. "One more thing, Demeter. I'm sure it thrills you to make fun of my friends. They're rich. They're privileged. They're easy targets. Not only do you get to laugh at them behind their backs, but your laughter is politically correct. I say Chanel. You say homeless. And that makes you a better person. When you go out there, take a good look at these rich people. Besides money, they have depression, failing marriages, dysfunctional families, and cancer. Give them a break, will you?" Then Mother opened the door and went out.

I picked up Mother's brush, an antique Art Deco mother-of-pearl number inset with sapphires, and began brushing my hair. Mother had a point. People were people. All people have problems. But since poor people's problems also include poverty along with Mother's laundry list of personal woes, I couldn't work up much sympathy for people who live like white Russians. Besides, they didn't need me to give them a break. If I ever presented them with a problem, they'd simply throw money at me.

I looked in the mirror. My hair—dark, chin length, and straight as a snake—was standing on end all over my head. I looked at Mother's brush. Sure her Art Deco brush had Art Deco bristles, worn to nubs through sixty years of brushing, but that didn't explain the static electricity lifting my hair.

Then I heard it, the sound of a freight train rumbling toward the house. Earthquake!

I headed for the door, the roaring getting louder. Too late. The first sharp jolt and the room raised abruptly, then bounced, knocking me off my feet. I hit Mother's Oriental rug face-first with a clunk. A second later the shaking started, a rapid-fire tremor that felt like Charles Barkley was dribbling the room. With the walls creaking around me and the ceiling swaying above, I crawled toward Mother's English four-poster. From experience I knew that in the next five seconds, the shaking would either abate or get worse.

It got worse.

As I crawled under the bed Mother's paintings, a collection of customized faux classic oils depicting Mother and

Dunn as a Roman god and goddess, fell from the walls. Her hanging light fixture, a swag of porcelain Cupids purchased in Florence, crashed to the exact spot where I'd fallen. From the bathroom came the sound of glass shattering on marble. And still the shaking went on, only now I felt the floor beneath me shift and slide. I held on, expecting to fall into a hole any minute.

Overhead, the ceiling creaked ominously, then cracked with a sound like an ax hitting plywood. A moment later a large chunk of ceiling came crashing down and hit Mother's bed square in the middle, cracking the frame.

As the section of box spring to my left hit the floor next to me, I rolled to the right, knowing that if the rest of the ceiling came down, I'd be squashed flat as my shadow under the springs.

Lacing my fingers across the back of my head, I said the only prayer that came to mind. "Hey, stop with the acts of God already. Who needs this shit? Amen."

And I knew that if this didn't stop in less than ten seconds, I'd be dead. Everyone in the house would be dead. Everyone I knew and cared about would be buried in rubble somewhere in L.A. Buddy floated to mind. Where was he? And Cassie Sayres. And Buck. And whoever it was who'd killed Amy Westin and Frances. The killer could get away with two murders simply by dying in an earthquake. I'd never know who the killer was. Or why Michael had broken up with me. Or who the hell my goddamned father was.

"Shit!" I yelled, and it wasn't a prayer. Why had I spent so much time brooding and moping and reading the papers, combing through flea markets for that very special Victorian something that really meant nothing once I got it home. Why had I pursued all life's *little* things with such energy and determination and left all the *big* things to some mythical future when I'd have enough time to sort them all out?

Why? Because I was an idiot, a stone fool.

Well, no more. With my nose full of dust I vowed that if I ever got out of this room alive, I'd track Michael down and force him to tell me why he'd left me. And I'd take Mother by the heels and hang her upside down over her second-floor balcony until she told me about my father.

The shaking stopped. The earthquake was over as abruptly and shockingly as it began. And the silence it left in its wake was as eerie and thick as the dust in the air.

I moved carefully, simultaneously inching my way from under the bed and checking out my body. Neck, back, limbs, head—all seemed to be working.

Once clear of the bed, I started to my feet then thought better of it. Though the moonlight streaming through the windows provided just enough light to outline large objects, the floor was dark and undoubtedly covered with dangerous debris. I stayed on all fours, patting the floor in front of me as I crawled toward Mother's closet, where I knew I'd find one of the four earthquake survival kits Mother had stashed all over the house. Luckily, the closet door was neither obstructed nor jammed. I found the kit, a large black nylon backpack, unzipped it, fished around, and pulled out a flashlight.

As I flicked on the light the heavy gilt mirror over Mother's dresser fell from the wall glass side down, onto the Oriental carpet.

One last salute from the departing disaster, I thought, then looked closer. Taped to the back of the mirror was a medium-sized envelope faded brownish with age.

I ripped the envelope from the mirror and tore it open, knowing that whatever was inside was a secret, carefully hidden a long time ago by my mother. This was the box and I was Pandora, snatching a secret to which I had absolutely no right.

I pulled out a picture, looked at it, and knew. The tall,

lanky man in the yellowing picture, the man with my light
eyes, my overbite, dressed in a white long-sleeved shirt and
black pants, was my father.

"Oh," I said softly. "Oh, God."

In the picture he was standing in front of a small white
frame house with a modest porch, smiling at the person taking
the picture.

Mother, I thought, leaping to the sentimental conclusion.

Then my PI mind kicked in. Not necessarily. Anyone
could have taken this picture, including my father himself,
with a delayed-action camera. Except this picture was obviously old. Did they have delayed-action cameras twenty, thirty
years ago? I'd find out. About cameras. About my father. I'd
find out. I'd find my father. Or I'd find his grave. If his grave,
I'd mourn him. But if I found him alive, I'd look into the eyes
identical to mine and ask him how he could have fathered a
daughter then walked away without looking back. Like a
daughter was trash you leave on a lawn for someone else to
dispose of. How could he?

I slipped the picture in my pocket, hoping it wouldn't
crease until I put it in my briefcase. I wouldn't tell Mother I'd
found the photograph. Who knows what lies she'd feel com-
pelled to tell me, what obstructions she'd put in my way. This
was my father. My case. I'd solve it.

Picking up the kit, I opened the bedroom door and
stepped out, suddenly aware that the house was filled with the
sounds of panic and pain.

Earthquake aftermath. I ran toward the living room,
thinking, *Gas!*

In the living room, candles flickered everywhere. Besides
Mother's finest beeswax set in the candleholders she collected,
there were short, thick emergency candles in water glasses,
vases, any handy container. Along with the candles were
lightsticks from various earthquake kits, some placed high on

the mantel, some leaning against the walls on the debris-covered floor. Someone had worked very fast to provide illumination.

Frantic people were making their way to the front door, stepping carefully, the men holding the arms of the women. Most of the women had removed their high heels and were carrying them, opting for mobility and a chance encounter with glass underfoot over the need to teeter on shoes useless to feet.

From the outside, I could hear car engines starting. After an earthquake the first instinct of everyone not injured is to go home, if only to see if *home* is still standing.

I looked for Mother and saw her immediately, kneeling beside a blue-quilted woman. She was taping the woman's arm to a long piece of wood, a leaf from the dining-room table.

"Where's the wrench?" I asked her.

"Gas is okay. I put in an automatic shut-off valve." She continued to wrap.

"You okay, Mom?"

"Fine." Mother finished wrapping, patted the woman's hand, then looked up at me. Her nouveau nose looked like a squash and bruises were beginning to form under her eyes.

"Your nose is broken." I stated the obvious.

Mother stood up and began checking me out. "It's only a nose, Demeter, not a liver or kidney. Humbolt will fix it."

She turned my head to the right, then the left. "Any pain?"

"I'm okay. Really. How's everyone else?"

Mother ran her fingers over my shoulders and down my arms. "Fortunately, mostly bruises and contusions. A couple of fractures, both clean." She moved around behind me and placed her hands on my waist. "Bend over."

"My back's fine," I protested but I bent over. "See?"

"Good. Outside of the shiner you'll have in the morning, you're in one piece."

"Shiner?" I tapped both eyes. The right one was tender. I grinned at Mother. "Mother-daughter shiners. How chic."

Mother didn't smile back. "Will you give me a hand over here, Demeter?"

"Sure." I followed her to a corner where three survival kits were lined up on the floor. "Pull everything out, sort it out, and let's see how much water we have."

"Okay." Just as I knelt beside the kits, Dunn appeared, transistor radio in hand.

"Cal-Tech says it was a six-point-one. Epicenter is right here in Beverly Hills, maybe under this house!" Dunn's face was red with excitement. "Aren't earthquakes supposed to happen in the desert?" He turned to Mother. "Darling, let's go to the beach house in Malibu."

"No." Mother was blunt. "I'm taking care of the injured here, then you'll help me see that they all get home safely. Then I'm going to the clinic to check on my patients."

Dunn wasn't about to give up. "But, sweetheart, I just know that the water and electricity will be on at the beach house."

"Dunn, stop whining and make yourself useful," Mother snapped at him, then walked away.

Dunn stared after her, looking confused. "She's never talked to me like that before. She must be in shock."

"Anything's possible," I said, pulling survival food from the kits. "If you want to see water, go fill the bathtubs. There's plenty of water still in the pipes. Then get whatever containers you find and drain the water heaters."

Dunn looked at me disdainfully. "Me? Aren't there people you can hire to do that sort of thing?"

I turned my back on him. Eventually he wandered away. I finished the survival kits then headed for the bathroom to fill the bathtubs.

Mother finished tending to her last bruised and contused guest just as dawn was making its entrance. She'd worked all night, stopping occasionally to call the clinic on her cellular phone.

I'd watched her, fascinated. Though I'd grown up seeing her as a psychiatrist, *always* a psychiatrist in fact, I'd never seen her function as an MD. She was skilled—focused, quick, reassuring, and tireless. She was a *doctor* I could admire, and had all night, watching her with my father's picture still in my pocket.

As dawn lightened the day I went looking for her and found her in the entryway, pushing shattered fragments of chandelier into a corner with a broom.

"Nothing else for me to do here, so I'm going," I told her, then looked down at the broken crystal. "Too bad. I'm afraid besides this, you've lost the Italian chandelier in the bedroom and every Baccarat and Lalique in the house."

"It's only *stuff*, Demeter." Mother looked up briefly. "Thank God no one was standing under this when it fell."

Only stuff? My mother, to whom *stuff* is the soul of life? For one crazy moment I wanted to hug her.

So because I'd just learned life is short and at any given second can get a lot shorter, I did.

Which surprised the hell out of both of us.

*Chapter 7*

Ten minutes later I was heading over Coldwater, taking a chance that the canyon road would be open.

I should have been tired, but I wasn't. Every time I started to fade, a fresh pump of adrenaline zapped through me, jolting me into a hyperawareness I felt in the tightening of muscles and a tingling all over my skin. I was a cat at a mouse hole ready to pounce the moment the mouse appeared.

So far no mouse. Just emergency vehicles, fire trucks, police cars, and ambulances moving in all directions in response either to specific calls or to an emergency master plan.

Master plan, I decided. The movement of vehicles seemed random and chaotic, a sure sign that once again, some L.A. city disaster plan, probably a masterpiece on paper, had burst apart at the seams during the actual emergency. Later newspaper headlines would shout WHY WASN'T L.A. PREPARED FOR THE SEMIBIG ONE? The answer would be that the computers storing the master plan had gone down with the first shock and, other than the name of the plan, Operation Rock 'n' Roll, no one in city government could remember any details.

I punched buttons on the car radio, looking for updates. A few stations were off, but finally I found the all-news network.

The announcer, his own adrenaline surging, was gasping out breathless headlines. "So far the death toll is nine, including two heart attacks, remarkable considering that L.A.'s latest, but not largest, earthquake has taken place in a densely populated area. It could have been worse."

By the time I reached home, I'd learned that area hospitals were full of the bruised and contused. Most everyone's *stuff* had been shattered, splintered, and smashed. The stores on Rodeo Drive—Fred Hayman's, Chanel, Versace, Harry Winston's—had taken a heavy hit, made heavier by area impulse shoppers who were climbing through broken windows to make off with merchandise that was suddenly free.

I shouldn't have laughed at that but I did, picturing looters dressed like Mother's guests in quilted suits and gold braid, accessorized with diamond tennis bracelets and genuine crocodile pumps.

Once home, I knocked on Mrs. Ramirez's door. She opened it, looking dazed.

"You okay?" I asked her.

She made a vague gesture before she spoke. "Want some coffee? I got General Foods International Coffee's French Vanilla Café."

"Maybe later," I answered, and walked into her apartment. "Look, Mrs. Ramirez, you're in a mild state of shock. Most people are. It'll pass. Just sit down here and rest while I check out the place."

Obedient as a well-disciplined child, Mrs. Ramirez sat facing the television set, which was off. I flipped it on, happy to see that power wasn't dead everywhere, then watched for a minute as a young female anchor wearing no makeup gave updates. "Could have been worse," she was saying, making it official. Could Have Been Worse would be this earthquake's theme, its leitmotif, its subtext. In L.A., where every event is theatrical, "could have been worse" would become the catch-phrase, like "Hasta la vista, baby" and "Make my day." By tomorrow it would be everyone's mantra, repeated with solemn shakes of the head. No one would say, "Hey, it could have been better," or even "Who needed this in the first place?"

At least "could have been worse" was positive and even sort of cheery, a Girl Scout reaction to being scared into shock and a lot more fun to repeat than its predecessor, L.A.'s former phrase fave: "Shit happens."

I checked the apartment. Water and power on. Bedroom ceiling and walls in the bathroom cracked. *Stuff* everywhere, not all of it broken. In the kitchen the floor was a mass of canned and packaged goods. But . . . it could have been worse.

I returned to the living room, where Mrs. Ramirez was staring at the anchor, who was still at it, updating.

"You're in reasonably good shape," I told her. "Just stay where you are. When you feel like it, eat something. I'll check with you later."

Mrs. Ramirez turned to me, her smile unexpected and glowing.

"In Koreatown, the outline of the Virgin has appeared on the side of a dry-cleaning store," she whispered. "It's a sign. Everything's going to be all right."

I patted her shoulder. "Praise the Lord."

I got her a glass of water, drank one myself, and left.

I was unlocking my apartment door when I suddenly panicked. The picture! Where was it?

I fumbled in my pocket, felt the edge of the picture and, one second later, a flood of relief. I had it. I hadn't lost the picture. I held it up to the light, staring at my father's face, so fine, so full of energy and humor, the eyes and the mouth so much like my own.

I'll have copies made, I decided. Two, five, a dozen. Now

that I have him I can't lose him again. And when I find him ... if I find him ... no, I *will* find him. I will.

I unlocked the door and went in.

My apartment was a duplication of Mrs. Ramirez's stuff explosion. Flea-market treasures were everywhere, bent, broken, busted. I might have spent time reflecting on how fast both secondhand lamps and Baccarat chandeliers can be transformed into junk, but my answering machine was blinking.

It was Buddy, his voice deep with concern. "Dutch? You okay? Honey? You there? Baby doll, it's Buddy. Honey, are you—" *Beep!*

Baby doll! I laughed. That's probably what he'd called his ex in the Valley right before she called her lawyer.

The bitch in me wanted to let Buddy stew, but the rest of me, only intermittently bitchy, knew that he'd think I'd been hurt in the earthquake, and letting him worry was mean. So I called the precinct.

Once Buddy knew I was safe, the excitement flooded into his voice. "This place is a fucking madhouse. Even Homicide's on emergency duty."

I was curious. "You have shoot-to-kill orders on looters?"

"Hell no," Buddy responded. "Word is, let them loot." He lowered his voice. "I just heard that everyone who can walk is in Beverly Hills, helping himself. Not just the people you would expect, but housewives and kids and old folks and homeless." He laughed. "I was thinking I'd drop by Van Cleef and Arpel's and pick you up an engagement ring."

"Earrings, Buddy," I told him. "Nothing gaudy. Small diamonds with maybe some pearls."

"Damn it, Dutch. I just proposed to you and you're shining it on." Buddy sounded disappointed.

"Don't worry, Buddy. Proposals made during earthquakes

and full moons don't count. Too much weird energy in the air." I thereby let us both off the hook. "I gotta go shower. Talk to you later. Bye."

I hung up, knowing that I was cutting Buddy off—but not caring. I did have to shower. I had someplace to go.

Two hours later I was knocking on the door of Michael Jamieson's house, a white Cape Cod in the Hollywood Hills.

I waited. He had to be home. His car, a four-year-old black Mercedes, was parked in the driveway. We'd driven to Big Sur and back in that car, with the weekend between coming and going devoted to passion at the Ventana Inn.

It had been more than passion, larger and deeper. A complete connection that had surprised both of us. "I hadn't expected it to be this intense," Michael had whispered. "If I'd met you years ago, my life would have been different."

I'd looked up at him wondering how this had happened. "Michael darling, I got here as fast as I could."

He and I had become we. And nothing would ever change that. He knew it. It was absolute truth like the sun coming up in the morning. We had nothing to say about it.

The door opened. Michael's housekeeper, Maria Flannery, peered out, looking exhausted, her head wrapped in a bandanna. "Miss O'Brien! What a surprise!"

"Maria." I smiled at her. "It's been awhile, hasn't it? Is he here?"

She glanced over her shoulder. "He's out on the patio, sweeping up glass."

"May I?" She nodded. I stepped in. "I know the way."

She smiled. "I'll get you some tea. I'm boiling all the water, just in case."

Maria turned toward the kitchen. I went in the opposite

direction through Michael's living room, with its whitewashed walls and spare, almost monastic furniture. Michael's whole house was like this—simple, full of light, and serene.

I found him, just as Maria had said, sweeping glass on his patio. He looked up, startled.

"Dutch!" He took one impulsive step toward me, then stopped. "I was just thinking about you, hoping you were okay. And here you are."

"Be careful what you pray for, Michael." Since he'd stopped, so had I. By now his arms should have been around me, but there we were, standing ten feet apart, staring at each other, Michael bound by some unknown restriction, and me, bound as always by Michael's desires. When Michael's desires had taken me to bed, I'd gone. When they took him out of my life, I let him go. Michael's desires. More important to me than mine.

Michael smiled. "I didn't say I was praying. I said I was hoping."

"And wishing," I added. "Wishing is praying."

"Now you know everything," he said, then turned away, setting his broom against the wall.

But it was too late. I'd seen the light in his eyes when he first saw me, seen the impulse that had moved him toward me. He loved me. Nothing had changed.

I started toward him, knowing that when he next looked at me, his face would be friendly, that's all. I was right.

He motioned to me. "Look at this."

I walked to the edge of the patio, stood beside him, and looked out. "What am I looking at?"

"Down there." He pointed. "The Hollywood sign. Part of it collapsed."

I looked. The entire middle of the sign was gone. It now read Ho-----od. *Hood.* I laughed. "Bull's-eye. This town's a bandit with a license to steal."

"Not all of it," he said softly, as always imagining the best.

While he surveyed the sign I surveyed Michael. At six-foot-five and slender, he cast a long shadow. His black hair was short and neatly trimmed, but always tousled because of his habit of running his fingers through it. His eyes, green flecked with brown, were warm with humor and inherent good nature. Michael was kind. To everyone, everywhere. Except maybe to me.

"I thought about you during the earthquake," I told him, noticing his eyes flicked sideways at me while his head never moved. "I heard that in the Hancock Park area, for no reason anyone can determine, bank ATM machines began spitting out twenties like slot machines. Did you hear that?

"Michael." I reached for his hand. "Please. Look at me."

He turned toward me reluctantly, his eyes asking me not to say what I was thinking. I ignored the look.

"Michael, I *must* know. Why did you stop seeing me?"

He tried to turn away, but I held him. Finally, he looked at me with sad, tired eyes. "There's no point to this, Dutch."

"There is to me." I moved closer, deliberately crowding him. "Is there another woman, Michael?"

"Stop!" He pulled his hand away and stepped back. "I'm not talking about this."

"Yes, you are," I insisted. I wanted what I'd come for. To *know*. So I could put him behind me. So the nightmares would stop. So I could look at other men without seeing Michael. "You're going to tell me."

"I'm sorry. I have an appointment." He started away from me, moving toward the house. In a moment he'd be inside, then out the front door and into his car. Gone. Like the last time. And then what? More loss? More pain? More drugs? More rehab? Or maybe this time, a quick overdose, the Russian-roulette threat I'd thrown at Mother. Why had I done this? Why, on a day of disaster, had I rushed to Michael just to replay the biggest disaster of my life?

Just then, Michael stopped at the patio door. Without looking my way, he murmured, "I didn't mean to hurt you, Dutch."

In a second I was beside him, my fingers gripping his arm. "What's that supposed to mean? That you didn't mean to hurt me, so I shouldn't feel hurt? What am I, Michael, a casualty of war? What are you, friendly fire? Hey, that's the breaks?" My fingernails dug into his arm. I was hurting him and I didn't care. It was my turn to inflict pain, and he seemed to know it. He didn't pull away. "I know you, Michael. You do what you want. You did what you wanted with me. You wanted to leave me and you did. And never looked back."

Michael's face went stony, his eyes blank. His voice was flat. "I never stopped caring about you."

"Then tell me why you left me."

"It wouldn't change anything." He stood very still. Finally, he looked down at me. "I have to go."

I released my grip. And stepped back. This was it. The endgame. I'd cried for six months. I'd cried enough. I pulled my gun. "Michael," I said sharply. "Stay where you are."

His eyes widened at the sight of the gun. "You're joking."

"I'm dead serious." It was true. "You're going to talk to me, Michael. For the first and probably the last time you're going to tell me everything."

He shook his head, disbelieving. "I know you. You couldn't hurt me."

"Trust me, Michael. I've changed. Right here and now I could fucking kill you and not blink. . . ." I stepped up beside him and pressed the gun to his side. To his credit, he didn't even wince, just waited quietly for whatever would happen. "Michael, my love, we're outta here."

I turned him toward the door. "Go on."

"Where?" came the quiet question.

"I'll tell you when to stop."

We were halfway through the house when Maria appeared, carrying a tea tray. Before I could say anything, Michael said, "I'll be gone for a while, Maria. Please take the rest of the day off."

Maria looked startled. "But there's the tea, and the cleaning-up."

"It's all right, Maria," Michael assured her. "I'm sure your own house needs some attention and this'll wait. I'll see you later."

Then we continued. Out the door. Into the driveway. We stopped at my car.

"Get in," I told him. "You're driving."

An hour later I was unlocking the front door to Mother's beach house in Malibu.

"Are you hungry?" I asked him. Michael didn't respond.

He was angry and I couldn't blame him. For hours he'd been sitting five feet from me, tied hand and foot in a William Morris pineapple-print chair. Every hour or so I asked him a question to which he replied with a stony stare.

"You can't keep me forever," Michael observed.

"Who's going to stop me? Nobody's looking for either of us or knows where we are. I'd say you can pretty much bet on forever."

"You can't do this. I won't let you."

"This isn't your call." I got up and stretched, keeping the gun in plain sight.

"You have no right," he fumed, "no right at all to force me to tell you anything I'd rather not."

"That's true," I acknowledged. "I have no right. What I'm doing is wrong. I wouldn't want anyone to do it to me. But I'm doing it to you. So, talk to me."

"Or you'll kill me?"

"Exactly."

He glanced away. "Maybe I don't know you as well as I thought."

Good, I thought. Now he's wondering. And maybe he's right. He knows what I was. But not how he changed me. "Maybe you don't know me at all," I said amiably. "Now I'm going to ask you some questions. Easy questions."

I waited to let that sink in. This was standard lie-detector technique. But he wouldn't know that. His work was blue-prints, everything to scale and precise. My work was lies and deceit. "Where were you born?"

He sighed. "If it'll make you happy, Connecticut."

"Really." He'd never told me where he was born or any-thing much about his family. I knew his father was living and that was about it. "Your family has money?"

He glanced at me. "We don't talk about money."

"Your family has money?" I repeated. It was important he answer each question.

"Yes."

"You started your company with family money?"

"Dutch," he began, then closed his eyes briefly. "No."

"How did you start your company?"

He yawned. "Excuse me." He glanced around. "It's get-ting dark. Turn on a light."

"We don't need light," I decided. "How did you start your company?"

"I invented a bilge pump, patented it, and went into part-nership with a manufacturer." Michael sounded annoyed. "Untie me and I'll draw you a diagram of the pump."

"Not necessary," I told him. "How did you invent the pump?"

"You'll laugh."

"I could use a chuckle. How did you invent the pump?"

There was a long silence. Then he said softly, "I dreamed it. I was traveling on a boat. I went to bed. I dreamed that the boat was much bigger, a freight carrier. In the dream I walked into the engine room and there was a pump. It was a design I'd never seen—simple, efficient, cost-effective. While I was studying it I woke up. It was just after three in the morning. I wrote the design down. I knew I had something."

"You dreamed it."

"That's right."

I sat back down, thinking of the old Chinese shaman and the powerful, impatient magic she'd set swirling around me. So Michael had experienced the inexplicable, too. And it had made him a fortune.

I glanced at Michael, barely able to see his outline in the lowering dark. "I believe you."

"It's not something I tell people."

"I know. When did you have this dream?"

"Five years ago."

That surprised me. For some reason, I'd assumed that Michael's business was older than that. "You were thirty-three when you dreamed this?"

"Yes."

"How did you make your living before that?"

"I taught."

"What?"

He paused. I knew from experience he would either lie or say something evasive. "A branch of philosophy."

"What branch?"

"Dutch, you know this is ridiculous—"

"What branch?" I overrode him.

"Theology."

"Theo . . . !" I stopped, hearing the astonishment in my voice. I'd have to watch it. Kick back and be cool. I couldn't let him hear any emotion in my voice. I had to hook him, not let him hook me. So far I'd played my hand right. He was discussing matters he didn't normally discuss. Now I'd give some space, some time to brood, then switch my probe from his history to his feelings. Still . . . theology? Why? Before this was done, I'd know that, too.

I stood and stretched again in the darkness. I was hungry. That was good. I knew Michael must be hungry, too. Well, I'd offered him food, deliberately early, but the offer'd been made. The Geneva Convention would be proud of me.


Stretched out on the floor with a pillow cushion under my head, I wondered what time it was. After midnight certainly, perhaps closer to two. Time to start again.

"Michael," I said softly, thinking he might be asleep.

"Yes."

He was wide-awake.

"Tell me about your mother."

"Dutch. No."

"Tell me about your mother."

"This has to stop."

"Tell me about your mother."

He didn't respond.

"Tell me about your mother."

A long sigh, then: "She's dead."

I didn't know why, but I wasn't surprised. "What was she like?"

A long pause, then: "She was a good woman."

"Were you a good son?"

"I tried to be," he said, with a catch in his voice.

"Did you disappoint her?"

"Yes."

"On purpose?"

"No." He inhaled sharply. "I could have done better."

"How?"

"Dutch, this is private. I won't talk about it."

He was tired. I wasn't. I was breaking him down and he knew it, and had spent considerable energy trying to fight it. I knew I was close and my adrenaline pumped.

"What did you do to disappoint your mother?"

"That's none of your goddamn business."

"What did you do, Michael? What terrible thing did you do to your mother?"

"Dutch, for God's sake!"

"Did you beat her? Kill her?"

"I . . . I . . . Jesus Christ, what do you want from me?" It was almost a wail. "Back off. I can't talk about this."

"Say it and I'll untie you. You can go home."

"No."

"What terrible thing did you do to your mother?"

"Do you want me to hate you?"

I stood up and stood over him, looking down. "I don't care, Michael. Say it."

"My God."

Suddenly I shouted, *"What terrible thing did you do to your mother?"*

He threw his head back. "I broke my vows."

"What vows?" I felt his pain, but I couldn't relent, not now. "What vows?"

"The priesthood," he whispered. "I was a priest."

I stood immobile, listening to his ragged breathing and trying to control my own. I hadn't expected this. But what had I expected? Hadn't I always known that Michael's invisible wall was a secret hidden deep in his heart? Now he'd said it. The secret. In one sentence. The way killers finally break and say, "Yes, damn it, I killed her." After that, it's bring in the stenographer fast, because after that sentence, the secret, all the rest just tumbles out. They talk and they talk, the killers. Killers and Mother's patients. I had to go on. "What happened?"

"I was teaching theology at Boston College. For some time I'd been questioning my commitment to the priesthood. Like a lot of us, I still loved my faith but had become disillusioned with my church. Then I met a young woman, a graduate student. She seemed full of mischief and very irreverent. And smart. And nice. All those qualities. What I didn't know until later, much later, was that she had been raised a very strict Catholic and that hellfire-and-brimstone Catholicism was still coiled in her heart like a snake. We'd talk after class, first for minutes, then hours. When we started meeting for coffee before class, I knew we were falling in love. I could have stopped then. At least, that's what I told myself later. Maybe not. But . . . I was selfish. I didn't. Six months after we met, I left the priesthood. A month after that we were married."

I leaned against the back of his chair, my mind tumbling. "Where is she? Where is your wife?"

"She became pregnant. It went badly for her. At seven months she delivered a stillborn, a boy, who was also deformed. She . . ." For a moment he was unable to speak. "That's . . . when her strict upbringing, the snake in her heart, woke up and struck. She became convinced that the baby's death was God's way of punishing her for marrying a priest. I . . . couldn't dissuade her."

"Where is she, Michael?"

"In a psychiatric hospital in Northern California. She's been there for more than six years."

"I see." I touched the side of his face. It was wet. "What's her name?"

"Claire," he answered. And began to sob, low, painful sobs like a boy who'd rather be caught dead than crying.

I slipped my penknife out of my pocket and quickly cut the ropes. Then I knelt in front of him, pulled off my shirt, and used it to dry his face.

"There, there," I said, pulling him close. "It's all right. It's all right."

He came into my arms as though he'd been born there, and let me cradle him, rocking him gently and murmuring for what seemed like forever. Finally, when he was quiet, I whispered, "Come on, Michael. You're tired."

I helped him to his feet, put my arms around him, and led him into the bedroom.

I led him to bed. "Sit down."

Obedient with exhaustion, he did. I knelt and pulled off his shoes. "Now stretch out."

He did, with a sigh of relief so deep, I knew he was already half-asleep. I took a quilt from a chest at the end of the bed, spread it over him, then lay down beside him.

His eyes were closed, but his breath was irregular and shallow. I stroked his arm, then his shoulder, then his chest.

He stirred under my fingers, then whispered, "I'm sorry."

"I know." I felt my own eyes tear and my heart dissolve. He was sorry. About Claire. About me. About his broken vows. Sorry and guilty and determined to bear it alone. "I know."

I rose on one elbow, leaned over, and kissed him.

"Dutch." He pulled away. "I can't."

"Then I will." I kissed him again, a kiss that lingered. This time he didn't pull away. He lay motionless as I kissed his mouth, his cheeks, his forehead, over and over. Then slowly I sensed his arms raising around me, then felt his hands resting lightly on my back. He was pressing me closer, kissing me, erasing the distance between us, the months, the grief, the loneliness, with his body, his mouth, and his need.

"I love you," he whispered. "I can't help it. I love you."

"Shhh. It's all right," I murmured. "I love you, too."

Eventually, we slept. Drifting down in the last second before blackness, I knew that the nightmares were over. I knew.

"I can't see you again," Michael said. He was standing looking out at the ocean. The sun was already high in the sky.

"Yes, you can." I put my arms around him. "We love each other."

"You don't understand. I can't marry you."

"You don't think I know that, Michael? You have a wife. You'll never divorce her. And God knows, you shouldn't. But that hasn't anything to do with us."

"It *does*. You deserve a husband, a marriage, a real life and family."

"I want you. I want to be with you. I don't care about anything else."

"You would. In time."

I smiled. "You're telling me what I deserve, what I should have, and how I'm going to feel?"

He nodded. "I'm trying to take care of you, Dutch."

"Thank you, Daddy." The words popped out automatically. I flushed, immensely embarrassed by what Mother would call a breakthrough.

Michael shrugged. "You think I'm paternal? Well, I am. It's my nature."

"I know." Of course he was paternal. Priests are paternal.

All those souls to be guided, those rules to be enforced, that power to be wielded, not to enhance the priest's power but the power of God; dictatorship for the "good of the soul." The benevolent fathers, the fathers who, though remote, are always there.

Of course I loved Michael. Along with everything else, he delivered "Daddy." In a way I hadn't realized until now, Michael had stepped into my heart's deepest yearning, supplied what was missing, and made me whole. The bond that tied my soul to Michael's would never be broken.

For a moment the revelation scared me. *Never* meant forever. Forever meant never walking out the door. Then I looked at Michael and felt what I'd chosen spreading through me like wildfire. Michael was my passion. And life, despite Mother's psychoanalytic theories and "underlying dynamics," was too short not to choose passion.

That didn't mean that I planned to be the adoring student worshiping the all-wise priest. What's Daddy for, if not rebelling against? What's a girl for, if not becoming a woman? And then where would I be, this girl gone through rebellion, this woman fired with passion but with a mind of her own? Standing next to Michael, his partner.

"I don't mind that you're paternal," I told him. "In fact I like it. But I'm not a child. I'm thirty-one and a third. I know what I want. I want you. You tell me I'll want the conventional life, marriage, and children. Based on what? Something I've told you? Something you see? You're describing someone else, Michael, not me. I'm not like most women. I carry a gun."

He smiled. "I noticed." Then he turned away. "But someday you may feel differently. And someday . . . Claire may get better."

"Someday!" I turned him around to face me. "You want

me to walk away because someday I may change or you may change or your life may change. What if someday never comes? What if there's another earthquake and we both die here and now? Or what if we walk away from each other and nothing ever changes? What if I love you and you love me until the day we both die without seeing each other? What if Claire never gets better? What if we lose each other when we've just found each other because someday something might happen? I can't live for *someday*. I can only live for now. We love each other, Michael. Don't do this to us."

For a long while the only sound in the room was the blue muffled roar of the ocean. Then Michael turned toward me. "You aren't wrong," he said softly. "Let me think about this."

Stooping, he kissed me first gently, then harder.

It was almost dark again when we left Mother's beach cottage.


As we pulled into Michael's driveway we saw Maria on the porch, waiting.

I cut the engine and turned to Michael, who'd been silent most of the way in from Malibu. "I know I should apologize for what I did to you, but I can't."

Michael kissed my cheek. "I have no regrets, Dutch. You shouldn't either." He opened the car door. "I'll call you."

Then suddenly his arms were tight around me. "I love you. Nothing will change that. Ever."

Then he was gone, out of the car, up the steps, smiling at Maria.

I started the car and backed out of the driveway, then looked back. The front door was open, Maria was inside, and Michael, still as the moment between heartbeats, was watching me go.

So now I know. For Michael, the operative word is *soul*. And soul would remain his ultimate concern for himself and for me.

Once home, I checked on Mrs. Ramirez. Just as I thought, her mild shock had passed and she was full of information.

"There's twenty million in damage. A tenth person died. A looter."

"The police shot him?"

"No. He got in a fight with another looter over the last big-screen TV, and the other looter brained him with a portable radio. Dumb people doing dumb things, 'steada bein' home lookin' after their families. . . . But the looting's all over. Lotta important people, you know, basketball players and actors, went down and did some kinda talking with the looters, and the looters, they just got 'shamed of themselves and went home. Nothing much left to loot anyway. I gotta go. The bus from St. Martin's is taking us down to Koreatown to look at the Virgin."

"Have a good time," I told her. "Say one for me."

"I pray for you alla time. You're not a happy girl." Mrs. Ramirez patted my hand. "Oh, there's a man waiting for you. That friend of yours, the guy who you hang out with."

"Buddy?"

She shrugged. "He came and asked me where you were last night. He looked very worried."

"Try nosy."

I found him sitting on the floor outside my apartment, looking tired and grumpy.

"Hi, Buddy."

He looked up at me sourly. "What am I, Dutch, some kind of goddamned sidekick you call when you need something and ignore the rest of the time?"

I unlocked my door. "Someone put a burr up your ass?" I asked pleasantly.

He scrambled to his feet. "You did! I called you every ten minutes until four this morning. Where the hell were you?"

Buddy followed me into the apartment, through it, and into the kitchen. I reached for the broom and started sweeping up my smashed stuff. "That's none of your business."

Buddy yanked the broom from my hands. "Like hell. Someone's trying to kill you. I'm trying to protect you. How can I protect you if I don't know where you are?"

I yanked the broom back. "I take care of myself, Buddy. I always have. I always will. And I don't need you."

Buddy lowered his head and glared at me so pugnaciously, I expected him to start pawing the ground. I glared back, choking my broom in a death grip and willing myself not to blink.

Buddy blinked first, then glanced away, then back at me. "That's what they all say until they're lying on a slab in the morgue."

"You'll be right there saying 'I told you so,' Buddy. Now, tell me. What's happened?"

Buddy smirked, preparing to shock me. "Two guys from the precinct found Amy Westin's leg in a Dumpster behind Steve Pierce's apartment. Pierce has disappeared." Buddy smiled. "He's somewhere out there, baby doll, waiting for you."

Buddy had succeeded. I was shocked. But my face never showed it. I dropped the broom. "Then why are we standing here? Let's go get him."

*Chapter 8*

Buddy had a couple of leads he was too mad to tell me about. It didn't matter. I knew that all I had to do was shut my mouth, buckle myself into his passenger seat, and keep breathing, and before long I'd know everything he knew.

Even though Buddy was steaming, he didn't take his mad out on the road. He drove smart—focused, alert, and buckled up. I liked that.

I also liked the solid clench of his jaw and the way his curly hair flopped down on his forehead. No doubt about it. Buddy was cute. I wondered how many women had told him that. Probably one too many for his ex in the Valley.

On Formosa Street in Hollywood, Buddy pulled up in front of a bar called Raves. "Steve Pierce hangs out here."

I followed him into Raves, expecting to find the kind of dark and funky industry bar where gaffers and grips hang out and the second AD is top dog.

I was wrong. Inside, Raves looked like New Age meets French bistro. Synthesized music drifted over small groups of people, most postyuppie young, dressed like old pictures of flower children and seated around small pine tables. The bartender, tall, late twenties, wore a loopy grin and an orange jester's cap with bells. Signs on the bar advertised SMARTEN-UP $3.00 and INTELLI $2.00.

"What is this?" I asked Buddy, who looked equally puzzled by the place.

"Hollyweird."

"Glad to see you." The bartender beamed at us. "What'll you have?"

"What have you got?" Buddy's tone was casual, but his eyes darted around and his nose was doing its cop twitch, sniffing the air Doberman-style.

The bartender laughed. "Chill out, Officer. We're legal."

"Sure." Buddy scowled, not happy to be so easily made.

I gestured at the signs on the bar. "Humor us. We're tourists."

"Right." The bartender crossed his arms and leaned on them. "What we sell here is smarts, memory boost, cognitive blast, concentration, alertness, problem-solving ability, a bridge between the right and left brains across the old corpus callosum. Our drinks are a mix of smart pharmaceuticals—choline, ephedra, phenylalanine, tyrosine, ginseng, Gingko Biloba, and hydergine."

Buddy laughed. "Great. Another New Age scam."

"Not New Age, brother," the bartender disagreed. "New Edge. You want to upload your memory, upgrade your hardware, broaden your bandwidth, really live long, and prosper with all of your cylinders firing, you've come to the right place. I'll mix you a nice Smarten-Up: choline, phenylalanine, ephedra, and a dash of caffeine. Lemon or lime?"

"Pass," Buddy decided. "People actually bring dates here?"

"Not you, Buddy," I told him. "One Smarten-Up and she wouldn't go home with you." I grinned at the bartender. "Lemon."

The bartender shook various powders into a blender, then

zapped it. Ten seconds later he was pouring a frothy concoction into a glass.

I drank the stuff down. It tasted artificial, like a lemonade-and-tinfoil shake. "Now what happens?"

"Your brain'll wake up." The bartender grinned. "We get a lot of cops in here. Cops like having an edge."

Buddy wasn't buying it. "A year from now some government agency will decide all this crap causes cancer and you fruitcakes will be out on the street selling maps to the movie stars' homes."

"An enlightened attitude," the bartender said. "Sure I can't mix you a Smarten-Up?"

"You can tell me if you know a man named Steve Pierce." Buddy cut to the chase. "Tall, light hair, a cameraman."

"Sure." The bartender nodded. "Steve's a regular. Likes the serotonin boosters." He turned to me. "Mood elevator, natural brain chemical. Loss or depletion causes depression. We have pharmaceuticals that promote linkage with serotonin receptors."

I nodded, wondering what he was talking about. "Is Steve Pierce depressed?"

"No." The bartender shook his head. "He's balanced but looking for the door to euphoria."

"Know where he lives?" Buddy asked.

The bartender shrugged. "Nope. I just know the basics: what he does, what he drinks, his take on the mind-body problem."

"Know any friends of his?" I asked.

"He usually comes in with a guy named Calico who runs the Blue Buddha Tattoo Parlor. You might try him."

"Thanks." I put a twenty-dollar bill on the bar, then headed for the door, knowing that Buddy was following.

Once outside, Buddy caught up with me. "Ever hear such crap in your life?"

I smiled at him. "The square root of six million ninety-two is sixteen."

Buddy's jaw dropped. "It works!"

"Gotcha." I gave Buddy a tap on the arm and got in the car, slamming the door on his mumbled, "Shit."

Smart pills. Sounded great. But I wondered. If everyone got smarter and smarter, would life get better and better or would we just find cleverer, more complicated ways to make the same old mistakes?

We found the Blue Buddha Tattoo Parlor in a Malibu minimall, jammed between a surfer shop and Videobusters.

The inside of the shop was a dark pit. Buddy's Doberman nose went into overdrive. "Cannabis." He sniffed. "Primo."

"Anybody here?" I called.

The red paisley curtain separating the back of the shop from the front parted and a skinny figure dressed in cutoff jeans slithered through. The man took one look at us and bolted. Buddy sprang after him.

After some crashing and bashing in the back room, Buddy reappeared through the curtain, his arm around the skinny guy's neck in a hammerlock.

"This is Calico. I grabbed him before he flushed his stash." Buddy thumped the wiggling Calico on the head. "Hold still."

"Hello, Calico." I nodded his way.

Calico's stringy body was just that, a neck-to-ankle calico of tattooed scenes with the predominant motif being movie stars. Marlene Dietrich lolled on one shoulder, while on the other, Elizabeth Taylor peeped coyly around a shrunken bicep.

"Where's Steve Pierce?" I asked. Normally I wouldn't cut straight to the chase, but clearly we had him. With his stash in the back, Calico had no choice. Either cooperate with us or his tattooed butt would be on its way to the slammer.

"He's doing his thing," Calico gasped.

"What thing?" Buddy asked, then suddenly turned Calico loose. The little guy sprawled to the floor and lay there, looking like an illustrated broom.

"Jeez, Buddy, lighten up." I reached down, offered Calico my hand, and pulled him to his feet. He couldn't have weighed one hundred pounds, but it was clear he hadn't always been so thin. On one thigh, Humphrey Bogart in a trench coat had shrunk from virile Sam Spade into an ancient, emaciated Bogieman.

"Where's Pierce doing his thing?" I asked.

Calico's smile leaked around gaping teeth. "Point Dume. Big redwood house overhanging the cliff. One little earthquake out there and that sucker's kindling on rocks. Couldn't get me to set foot in that place, I'll tell you."

"Relax. You aren't invited." Buddy pushed Calico out of the way and headed for the door, griped at leaving a doper holding, even though the unspoken agreement is *the guy snitches, you leave him alone.*

I waved at Calico. "Have a nice day." Then I followed Buddy out of the shop.

I stepped out in the sunshine, knowing my goodbye to Calico was definitely weird. But I was raised by a psychiatrist and, for me, closure is second nature.

No matter the circumstances, I *hello* at the beginning and *goodbye* at the end. Mother insisted, telling me that hello and goodbye are directional signposts she teaches her patients immediately. That way, they know where they've started and know where they end. It's the middle that's dangerous—the forks in the road, the detours, the highways to hope or oblivion. That's where the psychiatrists come in, selling the patient the road map.

Of course, when I look at Mother, her gigolo husband, and patients all with identical noses, I wonder why, if her maps for me and for others are so damn terrific, her own has brought her to a dead end.


By the time we reached Point Dume, the sun had set in a blaze of orange-and-gold glory, as specified in the real-estate contracts held by the residents of Malibu Colony.

We parked the car at the foot of an incline leading up to the house, which was surrounded by bushes, trees, and shrubs. Because Buddy had called back to the station, we knew that the house in question, designed by architect Olaf Blusdorf, was fourteen thousand square feet of opulence and belonged to Japanese industrial billionaire Yuko Omi, owner and CEO of the multinational conglomerate that produced almost everything made of plastic that had become a necessity since World War II. Mr. Omi, reputed to be a man of vision, had commissioned this residence for his use on business trips to Los Angeles, where he kept an eagle eye on investments and attended Dodger games.

"Stay behind me," Buddy ordered.

I laughed. "You gonna save me from a ninety-year-old baseball fan?"

Buddy's nasty retort was cut short by the special surprise appearance of two black-clad figures who dropped out of the trees over us onto the path just ahead.

"LAPD," Buddy said quickly, reaching for his badge.

Before his hand reached his back pocket, the two were on top of us.

"Shit," I grunted as the guy who'd picked me spun me around and wrapped his forearm around my throat. I dropped to my knees, a move he didn't expect. Still choking me, he dropped with me. I used the leverage to flip him. As he went over my head I braced myself, then sprang as he thudded to the ground. "Shit," I repeated, and clipped him in the throat. He made a weird gurgling noise, then went out like a light, just as my karate teacher had promised. I was pleasantly surprised. "Who knew it would work?"

I turned my attention to Buddy, who was kneeling on top of his assailant, slugging away.

I scooted over to Buddy and grabbed his arm. "Buddy, he's out. Cease and, for Christ's sake, desist."

"The son of a bitch scared the shit out of me," Buddy mumbled. But he got up. He reached into his back pocket and took out his handcuffs. "Let's see why Mr. Omi employs thugs who think LAPD means terminate with extreme prejudice."

We waited for the thugs to come around, then Buddy handcuffed them together and pushed them ahead of us on the path.

"Want to take off their hoods?" I asked. "They're twisted around backward."

"No." I could hear Buddy smiling in the dark. "They look like extras in an old Bruce Lee movie. Let them eat fuzz."

The doorway to the house was black lacquer. There weren't any doorknobs, just a small silver security plate set in the door.

"Punch in the code," Buddy whispered to assailant number one. The man stiffened. Buddy pressed his revolver into the man's neck. "Punch."

The man punched. A second later the huge double doors swung open soundlessly. Buddy pushed the two men in ahead of us.

• • •

Inside, the house was a cross between museum and palace. Walls rose eighteen feet to a ceiling with skylights. Pin-spotted sculptures seemed to float in the dark of subdued lighting. A floor-to-ceiling fish tank divided the entry hall from the next room, a massive gallery. We walked through the gallery to another set of double doors with yet another inset, silver panel.

"This must be the place," Buddy whispered.

"What place?" I whispered back.

Buddy's Doberman nose twitched. "Omi's in there." He placed his revolver at the base of number two's skull. "Do the right thing."

Number Two punched the buttons. The doors swung open and we stepped into an enormous round room, covered with an enormous round stained-glass skylight.

Beneath it, a dozen Japanese sat in a circle of club chairs listening raptly to Steve Pierce, who stood in the center of the circle, dressed in a long white robe, a blond wig that made him look like a bleached Jesus, and an earring made of feathers dangling from his left ear.

Steve spoke with his eyes shut in a high-pitched singsong. "From the galaxy Arcturus I come, traveling the astral plane to deliver a message from the mists of all-time. I am Morpho, instructing you to beware of European currency. The United States of Europe will never materialize."

Buddy looked at me. "Bunco."

Twelve Japanese heads turned. One of the men, the oldest, raised his hand. "Forgive us, Morpho," he said.

Steve opened his eyes, saw Buddy and me, and his knees buckled. He sat straight down, hard, on the floor.

The old Japanese rose and came toward us. "I am Yuko Omi. I see that you have met my gardeners."

"Is that what you call these assholes?" Buddy said pleasantly, then showed his badge. "LAPD."

"Welcome to my home." Mr. Omi bowed. "May I offer you refreshment?"

"You may offer us a reason why these two assholes tried to kill us outside." Buddy was pissed.

"These two men are employed to protect my gardens," Mr. Omi explained. "They are extremely contentious and sometimes excessive in their devotion."

"You want us to believe that you hired ninja gardeners to keep strangers from picking the posies?" Buddy asked. "Would you like to run this story by some of my buddies downtown?"

"No, I would not," Mr. Omi responded. "Nor would you like to explain to them later why you and they are patrolling the far edge of the Mojave."

I tugged Buddy's sleeve. "Don't mess with him, Buddy. He's tight with guys you don't want to know. Let's just do what we came to do."

"Which is?" Mr. Omi wanted to know.

Buddy stepped around Mr. Omi and headed for Steve while I explained, "We're here to arrest Steve Pierce."

"And the charge?" Mr. Omi's voice was soft as watered silk and smooth as a samurai blade.

"Murder," I answered.

Mr. Omi's expression didn't change. "Mr. Pierce is the vehicle for the entity Morpho. Though Morpho is eternal and omniscient, obviously his vehicle is unworthy. You understand you have no jurisdiction over Morpho?"

I nodded. "Morpho's free to go back to wherever he came from. And bon voyage."

Mr. Omi bowed. "I will not interfere with your arrest of the vehicle. We will await Morpho's return through another channel."

"Try public access," Buddy advised, pushing the handcuffed *vehicle* through the crowd of Japanese. "It's wall-to-wall wackos."

"Shit," Steve mumbled. "This was the best idea I ever had. A goddamned gold mine until you two fucked it up."

Buddy laughed. "That's showbiz."


The long ride back to town was made longer by a piss-and-moan contest between Steve and Buddy.

"You've got the wrong guy," Steve protested over and over. "I didn't kill Amy Westin."

"Shut up, Pierce," Buddy commanded. "You've been Miranda'd and cuffed. Save it for your lawyer."

"I didn't kill her. I was at the Devil's Punchbowl in the Mojave with some buddies of mine."

"We'll get your statement at the station. Quit bending my ear."

"Or what? You gonna shoot me?"

"Don't tempt me. Shut up."

But Steve wasn't through. "Where does it say in the Constitution that a guy who's arrested has to shut up? I'm innocent until you prove me guilty, Hart, and I'm not gonna shut up."

"I think you are," Buddy said through clenched teeth. "I'd put money on it."

"Yeah? What are you gonna do, open the car door and throw me out? Shoot me in the back and say I was trying to escape? Beat me into a bloody pulp and say I was resisting arrest? Your fascist LAPD buddies will cover for you, but Dutch here is a civilian. She won't let you get away with your bullshit cop tactics."

"That's enough, Pierce," Buddy said softly.

I looked at Buddy. By the light of the oncoming head-lights I could see his white-knuckled hands gripping the steering wheel. He had rounded angry and was sliding into ballistic. I crossed my fingers. In the past, situations less volatile than this had ended in violence.

Now Steve's voice was even softer than Buddy's. "That got you, didn't it, Hart? You can't do shit to me with *her* here. She's not one of you LAPD cowboys. She'd have your badge and your job and your goddamned pension. She's too straight for you, Hart, and besides, she's always had the hots for me."

In a second I was kneeling on the seat facing Steve and my gun was an inch from his face. *"Shut up!"*

"Whoa! Dutch! Hey!" Buddy reached frantically for me. "Put that away!"

The car swerved and I lurched to the side, banging my head on the roof. I felt gravel beneath us, then asphalt, then the car screeched to a stop.

Buddy jumped out of the car, ran around, jerked my door open, pulled my gun from my hand, then yanked me from the car. He slammed the car door behind me, then threw me against it.

"What the hell's the matter with you? You can't wave a gun in a guy's face!"

"*You* can't!" I screamed at him. "You're a cop. He can spit in your ear and you've got to take it. But the son of a bitch isn't going to spit on me!" I took a deep breath. "I left the safety on, Buddy. I wasn't going to shoot him."

"I didn't think you were," Buddy said automatically, then shook his head. "Hell, that's not true. I thought you might. It's not like you're squeamish. Or hair-trigger either. Damn it, Dutch, I didn't know what you were going to do. I never know. What the hell kind of woman are you, anyway?"

I looked at him levelly. Now, that was a question Mother would charge me seven hundred thousand dollars and eight years of my life to answer. "Tall," I said coolly. "Shall we go?"

Buddy looked at me warily. "In a minute. Let's get a cup of coffee in there." Buddy nodded toward a restaurant fifty yards away.

"What about Steve?"

"His hands are cuffed. I'll cuff his feet, then cuff him to the front seat."

"What if his buddy, Morpho, wings in from Arcturus to break him out?"

"I'll ask to see his green card, then bust him for being an illegal."

"Make mine cappuccino."

Buddy handcuffed Steve to everything in the car, then locked him in.

As we entered the restaurant Buddy remarked, "You know, Pierce said what he did to get to me. I was supposed to lose my cool and pop him. You'd be the witness, I'd be the goat, the department would have a lawsuit, and he'd be rich and walking around free."

"I knew that," I told him. "So I lost my cool first."

Buddy stopped dead. "You didn't. You're making that up. You just lost your temper. He rattled your cage and you reacted, just like everyone else."

I smiled at him. "Have it your way, Buddy."

Then I opened the door and went in. Buddy would follow, looking confused. And I'd never cop to the truth, whatever it was.


The restaurant was dark, woodsy with ferns, and full of couples wearing patched jean jackets and Rolexes. Our waiter's name was Dave and he recommended the swordfish with sorrel butter. Buddy ordered a hamburger, rare.

Dave looked pained. "You sure that's what you want?"

Buddy nodded slowly. "Go shoot the cow."

Dave seemed relieved when I said I wasn't hungry and ordered only cappuccino *without* sprinkles. His smile patted me on the head, then he drifted away.

Buddy shook his head. "Whole country's going to hell. Hungry homeless everywhere, and flakes like him worry about eating red meat."

Three cappuccinos later Buddy asked me to dance.

"Why not?" I accepted graciously. Between the cappuccinos and the Smarten-Up, something hot-wired and buzzy was going on in my head.

Buddy dropped quarters in the jukebox and the music came up. "Body and Soul."

"Hey, Buddy, you have taste."

"Surprise." He grinned, then swept me onto the dance floor.

For a few minutes we swayed, feeling each other out, then we got serious. Buddy's hand was firm on the small of my back and felt like a rudder, turning me effortlessly. The turn of his body guided my feet, which followed his, as though there were magnets attached. We moved to the music like Siamese twins joined at the hips and I wondered if I looked as amazed as I felt. Buddy could dance. I couldn't. Never could. Even with Michael I was all stumbles and trips. But I could dance with Buddy. Dance like a demon, like Rogers and Astaire, like Rhett and Scarlett at the Confederate fund-raising ball, her in widow's black and him laughing at her. I could dance with Buddy. Why? How could this be? I wasn't even sure I *liked* Buddy. But my body did. It liked him a lot. And the buzzing in my head was spreading all over, arms and legs and south of the border. If we didn't stop now, I'd jump him right here. And live to regret it. Buddy would see to that. . . .

The music came to an end. Buddy whirled me, then held me close. "You're delicious. I'm nuts about you. Another dance?"

"Negative," I mumbled, glad to have my wits back. I went back to the table, tossed a twenty on top of the bill, and went.

The car was locked and Buddy had the key, so I had to wait. A blurred reflection of the waning moon lay flat on the black asphalt. I stuck my toe in it, wondering how I could respond so hotly to Buddy when my heart and soul so clearly and firmly belonged to Michael.

How?

Maybe I was as confused as Morris, my mother-designated pinch-shrink, had claimed. Maybe my masculine and feminine sides *were* locked in some primeval conflict. Maybe Ethic and Eros were waging war for my soul. Maybe my moon was in the seventh house and I was about to explode into a great supernova.

Or maybe Buddy was just as sexy as hell and I was only human.

And maybe Buddy was heat and Michael was passion and I'd just learned the difference between the two.

Being booked and fingerprinted seemed to have a salubrious effect on Steve Pierce. He spoke only when spoken to and then quite amiably.

"What's this with the Japanese?" I asked him.

"Everybody thinks they're unscrewable or whatever that word is," Steve replied. "But those little guys are nervous breakdowns just waiting to happen. Especially about business and politics."

"I'm not sure about that, but say you're right. Nervous or

not, these are really smart people. Why would they be listening to a guy named Morpho from outer space?"

Steve's eyes narrowed and he grinned, looking like a weasel. "You gotta know history. These guys worship their ancestors, right?"

"Right."

"They think that dead relatives are out there somewhere either helping them out if they burn enough incense or cursing them out if they don't. Right?"

"Mmmm. I guess."

"It just makes sense that they think if they push the right button, someone smarter and more powerful than Uncle Fuji will float in from the ether and help them out. Psychics and channelers are the buttons."

"You're kidding."

"No. I was raking in five big ones a week until you and Hart did your Starsky and Hutch."

"Things are tough all over, Steve. See you around." I left the *button* wiping ink off his fingers.

"Why were you talking to Pierce?" Buddy wanted to know as we left the station. "This is the asshole who tried to kill you."

"I'm not so sure, Buddy."

"C'mon, he's our killer."

I got in the car. "Seems to me that if Steve had wanted to kill me, he would have made a direct attempt, say outside my building or in my parking lot or any number of places where he could have found me alone. He's not dumb. The last place he would have chosen was the place he worked. He'd know that you cops would be all over the studio lot and he'd be one of the first suspects. And that pipe bomb that blew up poor Frances was crude, Buddy, strictly amateur night. I'm not saying that Steve has any finesse, but he knows better than to sign, seal, and deliver himself as a killer."

"That's your opinion. You're wrong." Buddy pulled up in front of my apartment, killed the engine, then grabbed me. "Come here."

"Buddy!" The buzz was gone from my head and now all I wanted was ten hours of sleep, alone, under my patchwork quilt. "Stop." I wiggled away from him.

Buddy raised both his hands in surrender. "Okay, okay. You're driving me nuts."

"Short trip." I remembered the bon mot from third grade.

Buddy leaned closer but didn't touch me. "You listen to me, Dutch. I love you. I want you. And I'm going to have you. Whatever it takes."

"A threat if I ever heard one." I opened the car door.

"Sleep well, honey," Buddy called cheerfully. "I'm the best thing that ever happened to you. You just don't know it yet."

I ran up my apartment-house steps, my masculine side leading, my feminine side following.

What was it about Buddy that always made me smile? Even when I wanted to strangle him?

I took my cup of tea and my father's picture to the armchair near the window where the light was strongest. Settling in, I studied the picture.

At first glance his face seemed open, his expression easy. But on closer inspection, closer and closer, there was something less than straightforward, almost guarded, in his eyes. He had a secret. There was pain in the secret. Pain and guilt. Had he cheated someone? Or murdered someone? Or left someone to die by the side of the road? Did the secret have to do with his wife, my mother? Or with me, his child?

For a long time I sat with the photo in my hand, squinting and speculating. When my eyes began to water from staring, I stopped. Then shook myself.

What was I doing? Had the detective in me overwhelmed my good sense? Was I inventing scenarios remote from the truth? Just because this man had always been a mystery to me didn't mean that he was involved in a mystery. In another minute I'd have made him a criminal then solved the crime, just because my mind worked that way.

Still, his eyes—

I turned my attention to the house behind him. White, small, Thirties craftman's style, not one of the classics but a nice representation. I looked closer. On the porch was an old-fashioned wire milk-bottle container and, in it, four empty milk bottles. A lot of milk for one man. Could be that when this picture was taken he hadn't been living alone. Could it be that *I'd* once lived in this house with this man and my mother? Mommy and Daddy and little Demeter, all wearing milk mustaches?

A little simple arithmetic and that notion vanished. I'd be mid-fifties if I'd lived in this house, and the tiny mole in Mother's chin would have been lifted to her cheekbone by now.

One front window was open. An errant breeze had pulled the tail of lace curtain over the windowsill, making the house look like it was waving a lace hankie goodbye. Or maybe hello. I smiled at that oddly comforting notion.

Then I noticed something. On the right side of the top front step were four metal numbers, one hanging slightly askew and all far too small to make out. My father's address.

I upset my teacup leaping out of the chair.

In the next five minutes I pulled everything out of messy

kitchen drawers hunting for my magnifying glass. I found it. And looked. And was disappointed. The numbers were still too much in the background and too small.

But . . . I could have the picture blown up. Then look again. And maybe—

I ran for the shower, impatient to get to a photographer, to order extra copies and the enlargement, to call Michael and tell him what I knew. Somehow reality always became sharper and more real after I talked it over with Michael.

Odd. Wasn't love supposed to do just the opposite—make everything fuzzy? Why was Michael's first and consistent gift to me clarity?

I reached for the shampoo, thinking that I'd never really asked for much. Just the answers. To everything. Always. And that everything always make sense.

## Chapter 9

*I* called Michael, told him I was coming, and felt my heart leap at the happiness in his voice.

At least I assumed it was my heart, which hasn't often wobbled, not even on that Candlemas midnight when Willie Baylor, the embezzling accountant, had caught me rifling the files in his office and expressed his displeasure by sticking a gun in my neck. Fortunately, Willie was a thief, not a killer. His eyes were uncertain and his gun hand had trembled. I shouted "Boo" in his face, ducked, kicked him in the groin, then watched him double and fall. My heart never wavered.

But Willie wasn't Michael and the threat of imminent death isn't half as shocking or nearly as scary as being in love.

I rang Michael's bell and waited, photograph in hand, my mind racing ahead on the trail to my father. Until Michael opened the door.

Then, desire so mad and overwhelming it buckled my knees took me. I flung myself at Michael, who grabbed me, caught up in his own desire. My father forgotten, we kissed each other breathless in the doorway.

Eventually, a truck driver delivering a load of discount linens to a nearby Stroud's warehouse slowed to appreciate the spectacle we were making of ourselves, which he liked so much he honked encouragement. Michael pulled away, his face deeply flushed. "My God, what are we doing? Come inside."

I followed Michael in, amused at his embarrassment. I'd enjoyed the driver's enthusiasm. But that was me. Feckless. Where Michael had depth, Michael had soul, Michael had angst and conflict and torment, all I had was a job normal people thought of as sleazy—and a burning desire to make love to Michael as often as possible, anytime, anyplace. And my gun.

Michael moved closer, slipped an arm around me, and kissed me. "I can't get close enough to you," he whispered.

For the rest of the morning we tried to burrow inside of each other, and if ever lovers have, we did.

Later, after I showed him the photo, he smiled. "Go find your father, Dutch. When you do, you'll find it's only a part of your history you're missing, not part of your soul."

What a nice thought. It left life lacking, not me. Emboldened by the idea that I might be perfect, I threw my leg over his hips, pinning him, and asked a pertinent question. "Why do you love me?"

He kissed me. "I just do."

"Oh, no. That's too easy. I know why I love you. My reasons are complicated with more layers than baklava, but I know what they are." I kissed him, softly and quickly, starting with a gentle kiss on his forehead and ending with an ardent smooch on his lips. "Let's face it, Michael. I'm not the kind of woman a guy like you falls madly in love with. I'm too . . . something . . . and not enough . . . something else. So, what is it with you? Why me?"

I waited, expecting a "who knows?"—in which case I'd know his love for me was visceral, not rational. Or a laundry list of my better qualities, in which case I'd know he didn't know.

Instead, he laughed. "Blame it on *Gone With the Wind*."

"Excuse me?" Now there was a curveball.

"I was a kid the first time I saw it," he explained. "Adolescent. Very impressionable. With a very keen interest in history. Of course I loved it. Everyone does. I seemed to recognize that family immediately—the aunts, the cousins, the women in their petticoats getting ready for a party. Like my family. All those good women bustling around preserving the traditional life. Like my mother. My aunts. My cousins. I was born into a family of good women. Every one of them admirable. Several saintly. A family of Melanie Wilkeses. So, when I saw *Gone With the Wind*, of course I loved Melanie. I was conditioned to love her. But . . ." Michael hesitated, not for effect, but to give himself time to roll over on top of me. "I was unprepared for Scarlett," he whispered. "Scarlett set me on fire."

I pressed my lips to the curve of his neck, listening. In a second I wouldn't care why he loved me. Only that he did. In a second.

"Melanie was affection. Scarlett was desire. I thought I had to choose between one and the other." He kissed me. "Until I met you."

"I understand," I whispered back, moving against him. The second was over. I knew why he loved me.

Two weeks later, as I entered the office, Margo bounced toward me, her face flushed the color of her red curls with excitement. "Cassie's been calling you every ten minutes. Richard's sent a fax."

"From where?" Despite Buddy's insistence that Steve Pierce was the murderer, I was certain Richard Raymond was still in the running.

"Cassie would kill me if I told you." Margo pointed toward Cassie's office. "She's in there."

The moment I walked into Cassie's office, she looked up impatiently from her computer. "You're going to Brazil. Margo will make the arrangement."

Cassie's panic was plain in her eyes. She looked trapped, frantic, a small black bird beating its wings against its cage. She was in what Mother would call a *state*, the kind of state the killer must have been in when she/he severed Amy Westin's blonde head. Though Cassie's alibi had checked out—she did attend the screening—she'd gone alone and no one Buddy had interviewed could remember if she'd slipped out. All we knew was that she was there when the lights went down and when they came up. All cut-and-dried. Except that several people had remarked that Cassie Sayres seldom attended screenings and at this one she'd seemed to make a point of greeting industry people she knew both before and after the movie. Buddy considered Cassie a dead end, not because of her alibi but because of the nature of the crime. According to police profiles, women don't hack and slash and dismember. Women shoot, usually with their eyes closed and screaming louder than their victims, or sometimes in numbed silence, always expecting to be caught and punished. Women kill husbands and lovers. Crazy women kill their children. Women kill for love, rejection, revenge, abuse, when whatever it is they can't stand anymore has gone that one inch over the top, but never for sport like psychopaths do and certainly not for business. Buddy calls it the Y-chromosome factor; men have it, women don't. Y marks the violence. The profile agrees with Buddy.

I don't. I think the profile was made up by men to comfort themselves about women. Thinking about women and rage in one context makes men want to hide under the bed.

For me, Cassie Sayres was still the prime suspect. And right now she was looking at me like I was hers.

I approached her slowly, speaking softly to calm her. "Before I run home and pack, tell me what's happened."

"Richard's lost his mind. You have to find him." Cassie's hands were shaking.

"Okay." I spoke even more slowly. "Richard's sent a fax from somewhere in Brazil. You read the fax and believe he's gone crazy. What did he send?"

"A feature script!" Cassie exploded. "A goddamned feature script nobody's paid him to write and isn't for *Stone, Private Eye!*"

If writing a feature script was a symptom of insanity, then Margo, my dry cleaner, my pharmacist, and the cashier at my car wash were about to be fitted for straitjackets. "Why is that crazy?"

"You don't understand," Cassie wailed. "Richard writes television series. He's good, he's fast, and he's blatantly commercial, everything a TV writer aspires to be. He isn't interested in art. He doesn't have flights of fancy. He rolls the paper into the typewriter, and when it comes out, the camera starts rolling and Buck starts emoting. But this script he's sent isn't television. It's about revolution in South America and like nothing he's ever written before. He's in terrible trouble. I know it." She bent over and started rooting through piles of scripts on the floor around her chair. "I have it right here. I think. Well, it's somewhere." She straightened. "Why does my office always look like a Dumpster?"

That wasn't the kind of question you answer. "This script came from Brazil?"

"From a hospital somewhere near the rain forest."

"Give me the number." I took the fax number into Richard's office, tracked down the phone number, and called the hospital. The conversation was brief. Richard Raymond wasn't there. No one had ever heard of him.

I went back into Cassie's office. "Mr. Raymond doesn't want to be found."

"I don't care!" Cassie leaped out of her chair, ran around

her desk, and grabbed my arm. "Richard's my partner. If he thinks he's going to quit the television business *and* me to write funky screenplays I don't understand and no one with any sense will want to produce, he's got another think coming. By midnight tonight you'll be on a plane to Brazil. And don't come back without him!"

She looked so distraught, I tried to think of a kind way to reject her gently, then thought, What the hell? She's a grown woman. Her black is Chanel. The hoops in her ears are real diamonds, not Home Shopping Club CZs. She'd heard bad news before, even turned it into scripts, tempering her pain with a thirty share. She'll hear bad news again from people in her life far more important and connected than me, and live through that, too. I was small potatoes in the bad-news department, so the best thing to do was just spit it out.

"I'm not going to Brazil."

She lurched across her desk and grabbed my arm. "*What!*"

"Much as I'd love to hop down to the rain forest to find a man who doesn't want to be found, I'm not into wild-goose chases. He'll be gone by the time I get there." I pulled my arm free.

Cassie slumped in her chair. "You don't understand. If Richard quits television, I'm finished."

"Finished? You? Not as long as you have your computer. Or a typewriter. Or a pencil. You can write."

She seemed puzzled, as though this thought had never occurred to her. "Well . . . maybe. But Richard's the partner who talks to people."

"What people?"

"The people you have to talk to when you produce a TV series."

"What does Richard say to these people?"

Her brow furrowed. She stared into the space where her memory was located. "Usually he says, 'I'll get back to you.'"

"You can say that."

She grinned and reached for her cigarettes. "I can, can't I?" Her cheer lasted a second. She looked at me mournfully. A tear formed in one eye. "You still don't understand. Richard's my friend, my dear friend, maybe my only friend. We talk the same language. We understand each other. We finish each other's sentences. We go to the same bank. We have the same agent. We like the same movies. We hate the same people. We eat the same lunch. I wear his old shirts."

"You wear his old shirts?" I'd never heard that one before.

She shrugged. "He gives them to me. I like them a lot. They're all dark murky colors and they smell like him."

"You're in love with Richard," I deduced. Not a toughie.

Her smile froze. "No," she said slowly. "It's not love like *Casablanca* or *The Thorn Birds* or even *Mad About You.* It's like . . ." She trailed off, then snapped back. "It's like *The Waltons.* Richard's the brother I never had. And I'm the sister he always wanted."

Sure, I thought. And incest lives in the closet. But I didn't say it. Better to leave her with her sibling fantasy and the feelings she didn't want to understand.

"I miss him," Cassie continued. "So if you'll just ask Margo to call the travel agent . . ."

"Darling!" The door burst open, and a young man swooped in, made a beeline for Cassie, and swept her into his arms. She raised her face for his kiss. He started with her lips, moved to her ear, and was working his way down her neck when I decided our meeting was probably over and headed for the door.

"Dutch!" Cassie barked. "We're not finished."

I glanced at the lovebirds, still tangled up in each other.
"This can wait."

"No," Cassie was adamant. She glanced at the young
man. "Besides, it's not every day you can meet Joshua Ian.
You probably recognize the name." Beside her, Joshua smiled
modestly, preparing to be recognized.

I thought for a moment. "Sorry, I don't."

Joshua looked annoyed. He glared at Cassie, who immediately supplied me with his credits.

"Joshua is, quite simply, the literary sensation of New
York. His first novel, *They Always Eat Their Young*, speaks
for an entire generation. His second spent seventeen weeks on
*The New York Times* best-seller list and his third is about to
be published."

"Of course." I suddenly remembered. "Wasn't *They Always Eat Their Young* about a lot of rich, spoiled kids blowing cocaine and each other?"

Joshua bristled. "It's an artist's responsibility to hold a
mirror up to life. The ugly, the sordid, the degenerate are all
probes into the vast, decaying womb of society."

"As opposed to its impotent dangling penis?"

Cassie stepped between us. She looked shocked. "Dutch,
I've never seen you so hostile."

Behind her, Joshua smiled slyly. "It's an artist's responsibility to provoke strong emotions in the masses. Obviously,
I've succeeded. She's read it. She's furious. I fucked her right in
the gut."

He had me. He did. I hated him, not about something
real and important but about a book I couldn't abide.

"You're partly right," I admitted. "I started your book.
Couldn't finish it. Your rich spoiled kids weren't degenerate,
just boring."

He laughed. "Just the effect I was after. As an artist, I've sunk my teeth into the neck of the ennui and drained the last drop of blood."

"Sure."

Cassie's phone rang. She dove on it. "Margo, is it Richard?"

She listened, looked disappointed, and hung up. "Excuse me a moment. Buck is on Richard's private line, calling from the set. Margo says he's screaming."

After Cassie left, Joshua stared at me with what he obviously considered flattering intensity. "You're a television actress, aren't you?"

"How did you know?"

He grinned, pleased at his perception. "You have a television actress's body."

"Which is?"

"Part plastic, no offense. Part workout."

"You got me." I nodded agreeably, taking his notion that my breasts were plastic as some half-assed New York compliment.

He moved closer. "Maybe I can do something for you in the near future."

"Like what?"

His eyes gleamed and his voice was low. "I'm working on Cassie to get me an overall television deal at Paramount. A two-series commitment. Maybe three."

I tried not to laugh. "What about literature?"

"I've done that," he said. "Besides, the book business is in the toilet. I'm a best-selling writer, for Christ's sake. Every fucking literary journal in the country kisses my ass for an interview. Book reviewers go on for pages about my inalienable right to write whatever I want even when it makes them throw up. I have Truman Capote's old table at the Russian Tea Room. And what has it got me?"

He paused, waiting for an answer. I let him wait. I'm only the masses. What the hell do I know?

Finally, he went on. "I've got an overpriced apartment at a good address I bought at the top of the market, a Jag I can't drive in the city, and eleven maxed credit cards."

"Not much."

"Fucking A." His hand went to the back of his neck and rubbed hard. He looked very distracted. "The bucks are in television. Sure, I could do a feature script. That Eszterhas guy makes, what, two, three mil a pop? That's okay, but I want the brass ring. These TV guys throw an idea together, shove it on the air, and a few months later they're up to their asses in serious money. One hundred. Two hundred mil. I need that kind of money." He glanced at me speculatively. "You've known Cassie Sayres long?"

"A few months."

"New York's full of women like her. Career hags. Lonely. Doesn't admit it. When she starts to feel something, she buys a pair of shoes. Probably takes Dexedrine. Doesn't get laid. Nobody really wants to fuck her." He grinned. "Well, Cassie baby, your life's just improved."

"You want to fuck her?"

"In spades." He laughed. "Isn't that what it's all about? I get what I want. She gets what she wants?" He moved closer. "You want to star in my series?"

"What do I have to do?"

He giggled. "See? It's all so delicious, isn't it?"

The office door banged open and Cassie appeared, looking frazzled. "Some crisis!"

Joshua quickly moved to her side and draped his arm around her. "Darling, what is it?"

"Buck stopped production in the middle of a scene, left the cast and crew cooling their heels on location deep in the heart of Arleta, ordered a teamster to drive him home in his

Winnebago, then called me from his kitchen to scream at me that there's no peanut butter on the set."

"Peanut butter, darling?"

"He said he's always had peanut butter on the set since the days of *The Buck Stevens Good Time Roll Along Variety Show*. He said that having huge open jars of peanut butter on the snack table is his oldest, finest tradition—and fan magazines have written articles about it. He said that the absence of peanut butter for himself and his crew is an intentional insult and personal betrayal. He said that if Richard Raymond doesn't return by Tuesday, there will be hell to pay." Exhausted, Cassie sank into her chair.

Joshua whistled. "What did you say?"

Cassie glanced at me. "I told him I'd get back to him."

I gave her a thumbs-up. Joshua stared. "That's it?"

"Of course not," Cassie snapped at him. "I also sent a production assistant down to Safeway to get two dozen jars of plain and crunchy. The son of a bitch can take a bath in it." She lit a cigarette with a shaking hand. "Where the hell is Richard?"

Joshua leaned over her. "Poor baby."

Cassie looked up at him as though surprised to see him. "Look, can we table this for now? I'm up to my ass."

"Anything you say." Joshua was offended.

"Good." Cassie didn't seem to notice. "I'll meet you at seven-thirty at the bar at Mortons. If I'm late, start impressing people without me."

"Mortons." He cheered up. "Okay, see you later." He headed for the door, then looked back at me. "I saw your last show. Intense."

Then he was gone. Cassie squinted at me. "Your last film?"

"Everyone mistakes me for Sharon Stone."

"Writers," she said mysteriously, making it sound like a curse. "Look, Dutch—"

I interrupted. "I'm not going to Brazil." I sat on the edge of her desk. "Get this straight. If I was just doing my consult, reading your scripts, and telling you how much of *Stone, Private Eye* is thick-sliced baloney, I might go find Richard Raymond. I'd take a big fee and a first-class ticket and go spend a fat per diem wandering around Rio at the top of the season. I wouldn't find him. He's smart, has money. He can disappear. If I lucked out and found him, I couldn't make him come back, but eventually I'd come home with a tan and a story to tell and you'd turn it into a script. Wouldn't be the worst job I ever had. But I'm not just doing my consult. I'm tracking whoever turned Amy Westin into dog chow and blew up Frances, and trying to keep my own head out of a hatbox."

"But Steve Pierce has been arrested. You're safe."

"Not until I'm convinced he's the killer. Which I'm not. So, I'm here. Not Brazil. Case closed." I slid off her desk. "Now, there's something you should know about Joshua Ian."

Cassie held up her hand. "Don't bother. He's a zero. I know it."

Now I was surprised. "You do?"

"I'm not as crazy as you think." Cassie stubbed out her cigarette and immediately lit another. "I'll level with you. Before it's too late, I want a baby. I'm too busy to get married, and besides, I've never met a man I was so crazy about that I wanted to spend my life picking up his dry cleaning. Joshua, though an asshole, has a certified IQ of one sixty-eight. His body is sound, despite the abuses of his cocaine days, which, by the way, were largely self-invented. He snorted a little once in a while to get the feel, then dropped it when he noticed that real coke addicts look ravaged, not romantic. His family has longevity on both sides and there's no history of insanity, just arrogance. Once I get pregnant, I'll dump him."

"You're only after his DNA."

"You got it."

Okay. So I couldn't relate to Cassie's agenda, but I was thrilled for her that she had one. An agenda, no matter how bizarre, is the difference between eccentric and mad as a hatter. "Do you have any scripts you want me to read?"

Cassie delved into one of her piles. "Four." She handed them to me. "Slice the baloney."

I took them. "You wrote these?"

She turned back to her computer. "Baloney is what I do best."

A week later I arrived home to find three messages on my machine: Mother, Buddy, and the photo enlarger. I called the photo enlarger.

A whiny voice told me, "We lost your photo."

I gritted my teeth, resisting my first impulse to scream at the ninny. Ninnies like to be screamed at. Since they're basically passive-aggressive, being screamed at gives them a chance to feel wounded and withdraw. Then you never get your photo or dry cleaning or airline tickets or whatever it is they've screwed up. So I faked nonconcern. "Keep looking. I'm sure it's there somewhere."

"I'm closing in two minutes and I'll be closed for three days," he whined. "I'm going to a Star Trek convention."

"See you in three days," I said agreeably, ready to kill him. "Live long and prosper."

Mother's message puzzled me. Her voice, usually brisk and businesslike, was disturbingly hesitant. "I, uh . . . we, uh . . . since the quake did considerable damage, we need to remodel the house. If you have time . . . when you have time . . . well, if you want . . . come over and tell me what you want done with your room."

My room? I didn't have a room. I hadn't lived with my mother for years. I would rather eat nails and sleep on an off-ramp than live with my mother again. Especially with Dunn hovering around buttering up the bread Mother puts in his mouth and angling for a glimpse of my cleavage. But I would visit Mother. Something besides the foundation had cracked in her castle and I wanted to know what it was.

Buddy's message was . . . Buddy. "Hey, honey, baby, sweetie, Ms. O'Brien, the love of my life. Now that the bad guy is locked in the slammer, let's boogie. Anywhere you want to go. Tonight's the night!"

Sure. In his dreams. One thing I knew. I wasn't going to boogie with Buddy. Ever. Well . . . not unless Michael fell off the earth. Then maybe. Just maybe. On a cold night. After some hot dancing. Maybe. Probably not.

But . . . his message made me laugh. Buddy made me laugh. To me, that made Buddy sexy. Mother would tell me I'm demented. She would say I should be responding to men who are nurturing and loving and, above all, sensitive. I've known a few sensitive guys who've told me about their childhood and how Daddy ignored them and Mommy never cared. Their eyes tear up and run over. They jam the word *feelings* into every third sentence. They *relate*, they *identify*, they *empathize*. And it takes about ten minutes to realize that their empathy begins and ends in their own skin and their tears are all for themselves.

Better Buddy—the focused, the feckless, the guy out there mixing it up in the world—than Mother's sensitive ideal, the sensitive sitting in some corner of his own dented psyche endlessly inspecting his own boring navel.

I decided to call Buddy. Tomorrow.

Tonight I'd tackle Cassie's scripts with more than my usual attention. Compared with sixteen cramped hours on Brasilia Airlines listening to a seat mate who was probably

CIA pretending to be an Exotic Fruit, Ltd., exec, an evening of reading about murders set in colorful locations with an innocent accused and three suspects (two male, one female) was a no-brainer. Even with Buck's endless folkisms, which always made *Stone, Private Eye* sound like an old backwoods detective gone soft-brained and garrulous, moseying around out back of his house scolding birds off his scarecrow and philosophizing to his hogs.

In the first script, the woman murders her rival in love.

In the second script, a man murders a business rival.

In the third script, Buck runs out of tuna fish in the first act, ignores the murder altogether, and spends the entire hour scoring tuna from various down-home fishermen so he'll never run out again. I was impressed. How eerily similar this story was to Buck's recent real-life peanut-butter panic. Whoever had decided that art imitates life must have known Buck Stevens and his television persona.

I scribbled a few notes for Cassie, who was making fewer mistakes in the "detective stuff." Made sense. She'd been writing *Stone* from the beginning, and if anyone knew how, she did.

I gathered the scripts in a pile then saw there was a fifth—Richard Raymond's script, *Hot Pursuit*, which I'd picked up by mistake.

Curious about a Richard's-eye view of revolution in South America, I made a pot of tea, then sat down to read it.

Five pages in, it became apparent that this script wasn't about revolution, but about passion, and the hero was nothing like Richard. While Richard, aside from his words and his luck, was all cool logic, all well-modulated steady-stream conversation, all programmed communication with emotions on mute and conflicts fast-forwarded, his hero, Victor, by contrast, was all juice and heat, a man driven by passion to unrelenting pursuit of a woman. That the woman was nameless and as elusive as joy didn't daunt Victor. He pressed on, pursuing his love literally to the ends of the earth, continent to continent, first world to third.

I read casually, then faster, drawn in.

When, five pages from the end, Victor finds his love, I stopped and applauded. Way to go, Vic!

They meet, they make love, waves crash on the shore, fireworks go off, the earth rocks, and the heavens roll. My kind of lovers!

I turned the last page and found Victor dead. Shit!

I flung the script across the room.

What the hell happened?

I picked up the script and reread the last page. No one had shot him or stabbed him or pushed him out of a plane. He was just sprawled on the floor of a Rio hotel room with rigor mortis creeping up him like ivy.

And the woman? Who knew?

Maybe Richard had run out of ideas. Or energy. Or paper.

Maybe Richard had spun his story on hash, thinking his joke had a punch line and his plot had a point. Whatever, I could see why Cassie was worried. Richard was out of sight and out of touch, and if he didn't snap to and come in from the cold, Richard and Cassie could be out of business.


I'd just turned off the shower and was preparing to drip-dry, when I heard a sound I didn't like coming from my living room. I stepped out, slipped into my robe, and took my gun from its bathroom hiding place, the laundry hamper. I turned off the bathroom light, opened the door a crack, and peered out. No one in the bedroom.

I stepped into the bedroom.

According to the rules, I was supposed to call out, announce my presence, and declare myself to be armed. Otherwise, the asshole I shot in the act of trying to rape, rob, and kill me might recover to slap me with a civil suit for injury. Or his next of kin, should I shoot to kill, might file a similar suit for wrongful death. Or the cops might inquire as to why I'd fired at all when a warning might have scared off the perp. They wouldn't be happy about asking—they're required. When it comes to breaking and entering these days, the bad guys walk with the angels and the victims wind up pleading guilty.

I'm not a good victim. Being threatened annoys me. Being hurt is out of the question.

I don't care if the bad guy's father beat him. That doesn't give him the right to beat me. I don't care if he's poor. I have friends who are poor—and upright and honest and decent. I don't care if he's out of control on drugs and belongs in some rehab program. He shot himself up, I didn't. I don't care if some worm is eating his brain and Satan's voice is telling him to waste me. I didn't make him crazy and I won't let him make me dead.

Any son of a bitch who comes at me is going to find a hole where his right eye used to be. Period.

Gripping my gun, I moved slowly across the bedroom to the living room. Halfway there, I stopped and sniffed. Food. Chicken. Barbecue sauce. What the hell?

Then I heard whistling. "Thunder Road," for Christ's sake, with a squeak for the top note and a honk for the bottom.

I stepped into the living room. "How the fuck did you get in here, Buddy?"

He looked up from the food he was unwrapping and grinned like a cherub. "Hi, Dutch."

"Answer the question," I demanded. Thanks to Buddy's break and enter, my adrenaline was pumping with nowhere to go. "How did you get in?"

Now Buddy's grin was sheepish. "One time when I was here and you were in the bathroom, I took a wax impression of your keyhole and had a key made."

"I'm not sure I understand." I said it softly, like a first lady or lobotomy patient. "Would you care to repeat that?"

My quiet question did not deceive Buddy. Either my eyes had started glowing red or he simply knew me too well. He took a step backward. "I brought dinner, Dutch. I know you didn't call me, but I thought, what the hell. There's never any food in the kid's apartment, she's gotta eat, I gotta see her, we gotta talk. . . ." He took another step backward. " 'Fish gotta swim, birds gotta fly' . . . don't look at me like that." He gestured at the food. "I got chicken and ribs and gravy and mashed potatoes and coleslaw and biscuits and *what* are you *doing?*"

I was reaching for his hand. "Honey." I smiled at him. "How thoughtful. The Colonel is dead but his chicken lives on."

Hesitantly, he reached for my hand. Tenderly, I brushed his fingers with mine. Then grabbed him. And flipped him. He went down with a thud. I sat on him. "You fuck, you shit, you son of a bitch." I could feel my adrenaline leaking away. What a relief. I wouldn't have to maim him.

"Dutch," he squealed. "Get offa me."

I laughed. "But isn't this your favorite fantasy? You and me rolling around on the floor? Or maybe you don't like me on top."

I reached for the carton of mashed potatoes and, still sitting on Buddy, rubbed them in his hair.

"Shit! Knock it off!" Now Buddy was bucking, madder than hell.

So I cooled him off with the carton of gravy. It dripped over his hair and ran into his eyes. He shook his head like a spaniel, splashing gravy onto my wing chair. I could see myself tomorrow, scrubbing gravy out of velvet with a toothbrush.

"Goddamn it!" Buddy bucked under me. I held on to his ears and twisted a little. He bellowed. "Get *off*!"

"Maybe. If you promise not to retaliate," I offered, trying to sound generous. Truth was, Buddy was strong and I was getting tired. In another minute his adrenaline would blow and I'd find myself pinned under him. Not a place I longed to be. Not with potatoes and gravy dripping into my face. "Promise and I'll let you up."

For a moment there was just heavy breathing, his and mine.

Finally, he whispered, "Okay."

I twisted his left ear, just a half turn. "Swear."

"Swear," he mumbled.

I got off him.

He uncoiled, then sat on the floor with gravy running down his neck, looking more grieved than angry. "This is what I get for being a good guy." He reached for the packet of complimentary napkins and began dabbing. "I make a key so that if anything happens I can run over here and try to protect you. Not that you'll admit you need protecting and not that I ever thought you'd thank me. You're so goddamned independent you'll never admit you need anybody for anything, not even when the killer who's after you cuts off your head and mails it to me." Buddy stood up and began bagging the food. "I send you flowers, I bring you food, I worry about you and lust after you and can't sleep at night thinking about you. Me. The guy who spent his honeymoon at a police convention because women are boring, and after you've fucked 'em, what the hell else is there to do?" He threw the biscuits in last then mashed the bag down, making a garbage pancake.

"Well, for your information, O'Brien, my ex is still nuts about me. And every time I walk into a bar, bimbos unbutton their blouses just to get my attention. I can have any woman in this block twice before breakfast, so why the fuck do I need you?" He picked up the bag and slammed it against the wall. It split down the middle and a tornado of Kentucky Fried garbage flew everywhere, raining down on my sofa and spattering the drapes. Buddy looked at the mess, astonished. He cleared his throat. "Well, we're even."

His adrenaline was spent. Now I could talk.

"You said, 'the killer who's after me.' I thought Steve Pierce is the killer and he's in jail."

"Steve's alibi checked out. He isn't the killer. And he isn't in jail." Buddy opened the door. "Have a nice evening."

"Buddy . . ." I called after him. He hesitated. "Next time you come over, call first."

Buddy went, slamming the door behind him.

## Chapter 10

If Buddy's idea of a nice evening was scrubbing barbecue sauce off my wall, then I had a great time. I went to bed hungry and smelling of Lysol, a pissed-off Cinderella who then dreamed of a dark prince kissing her before chopping off her head.

The sky was still dark when I woke, startled out of fitful sleep by my nightmare. I sat straight up in bed and looked around wildly, afraid someone might be in the room. I snapped on the light. No one. Even the shadows had scuttled back to their corners. I was alone. My dark prince was fear.

I took a deep breath. My heart slowed to normal.

I got up, shrugged into my robe, staggered into the bathroom, and turned on the shower.

Twenty minutes later, my hair still wet, I was on my way to Steve Pierce's apartment.

In Steve's apartment house, the peeling paint on the walls had surrendered to attacking mildew.

I knocked on his door, then stepped back. At five-thirty A.M. he wouldn't be happy to see me. He answered the door, wearing an Iron Man T-shirt, and looking like a sleepwalker.

His eyes focused. He saw me, then tried to slam the door in my face. I stuck my foot in the door.

"I'm not going to hurt you," I promised. "I just want to talk."

Steve backed into his apartment. I followed. "I'll leave the door open if you like."

"Are you armed?" Steve wanted to know. "Where's the cop you hang out with?"

"Detective Hart is on assignment," I said, trying to sound reassuring. "I am armed, but don't worry. I just want to ask a few questions."

"You scared the living bejesus out of me," Steve complained. "You and that cop. Where the hell do you get off, pulling your gun on me? And him chaining me up like a dog. I'm in the back of his car twisted up like a pretzel, freezing my ass off, and I didn't kill anybody."

"Yeah. I know and I'm sorry. We all make mistakes, Steve. And you have to admit, you're a pretty fast hand with the square needle. You irritate people, you know that?"

He scowled. "If you can't stand the heat, honey—"

"Just a couple of questions," I interrupted him fast, wanting to get some answers before he slid into his standard, how-about-you-and-me-in-a-tub-of-Hershey's-syrup-baby? rap. "Who checked out your alibi?"

"LAPD homicide. I told them to find Alfie and Morgan and they'd tell them I was at the Devil's Punchbowl with them."

"The Devil's Punchbowl's a crater surrounded by rock in the Mojave. At night, it's got to be darker than the inside of a glove. What were you guys doing there?"

Steve shrugged. "Drinking beer. Beating on drums. Chanting."

"Why? Homoerotic or ritual slaying?"

Steve looked embarrassed. "You gotta understand. Alfie

and Morgan believe in this stuff. Alfie's a personal trainer and channeler. Morgan's a CPA who sides as a spiritual healer. They've been into this shit for years, both of them making a decent living with seminars and tapes and private clients. I met them one night at a place called Raves."

"I've been there. Lemonade guaranteed to make you a genius."

"All it made me was nauseous. I only went there to impress a weird New Age babe who talked nonstop but was double-jointed. Anyway, I met Alfie and Morgan. They told me what they did. I thought they were nuts. But Alfie was doing his channeling routine that night and the babe was hot to go, so we went." Steve chuckled. "I'd never seen so much bullshit shoveled by one guy in an hour. Alfie's standing up there on a platform at the Encino Women's Club, talking in a high squeaky voice, claiming to be some guy named Harlan, a superintelligent being from a galaxy twenty million light-years away. He's going on about peace and harmony and how we're all specks of light in the great mind of God and how there's no disease in his galaxy and how their brains have evolved into advanced computers that see the past, present, and future at once and . . . well, you get the picture. After a half hour of this, Alfie, or Harlan, asks for questions from the audience. And all these people—the place was jammed and they weren't weirdos either—they start asking this superbrain questions like 'Will my daughter get married?' and 'Where did I lose my aunt Tilly's garnet brooch?' Well, I start laughing and the babe gets mad. I wanted to go. She wouldn't budge. Later, when I saw the donations baskets and heard people offering Alfie two hundred a pop for a private session, I was glad I stayed. There were big bucks in that room and I wanted in."

"So you invented Morpho and started channeling."

"As fast as I could. Of course, I let Alfie and Morgan think I was both a true believer—and had the calling. That way, they'd give me client referrals. I was doing great, building the business. Even got an offer to work the next New Age convention in Sedona. I was about ready to quit my cameraman gig. Then you guys busted me." He shook his head. "But Alfie and Morgan, they believe in this shit."

"So, on the night Amy Westin was killed you and your friends were at the Devil's Punchbowl performing some New Age ritual?"

Steve nodded. "We were trying to attract a passing UFO. See, if you drum at the right frequency, they can hear—" He stopped. "You don't want to hear about this."

"Thanks. Why did it take several days for the LAPD to find Alfie and Morgan?"

"Right after the night at the Devil's Punchbowl, Alfie's entity Harlan told him that there would be a tidal wave out of Japan before the new moon. So Alfie and Morgan hopped a plane for Hawaii. And that's where the cops found them, sitting on surfboards on the northern shore of Oahu, waiting for the *big* one. They confirmed my alibi and the cops sprung me. Anything else?"

"Mind if I look around?"

Steve switched on a lamp. Beneath his Iron Man T-shirt, he was wearing boxer shorts splashed with Fred Flintstone, Barney Rubble, and the legend YABBA, DABBA, DOO, an ensemble enhanced only by his knobby knees and goose-bumped flanks. His apartment looked like a run-down New Age warehouse with crystals lying everywhere, occult magazines piled up, and posters of ethereal beings with electricity for hair.

"Help yourself."

I headed for the kitchen and looked around. No freezer. No freezer in the bathroom, no freezer in the bedroom, no freezer in the closets. Plenty of dust. Traces of cockroach, hint of spider. No freezer.

My circle took me back to the living room. "Thanks, that's it."

Steve saw me to the door. "Maybe some night we can—"

"No, we can't."

"Didn't think so."

Steve closed the door after me.

No freezer. No way to store Amy Westin. Though Steve could have used a friend's freezer or rented freezer space in a commercial facility, it seemed unlikely. Anyone storing his murder victim's remains would most likely want to keep them under his or her own roof. Besides, the recent earthquake had caused power failures. Power failures cause unplanned defrosting. And anyone other than the killer who opened a freezer containing Amy Westin would take one whiff and call the police.

Clearly, Steve Pierce wasn't the murderer.

I checked out my car before I got in. He was still out there somewhere, slithering through the high grass toward me. I only hoped he'd rattle before he struck.

The front of Mother's house looked like the aftermath of a terrorist attack. The entry was a gaping hole decorated with scaffolding. An army of Mexicans swarmed over the roof, tearing off shingles. Trees were uprooted, shrubs had disappeared, and the lawn was a memory. I parked my car, noticing that the right wing of the house had vanished. In its place was framework for an area twice the original size. The framework curved outward. A bay window?

I found Mother in the breakfast room, examining her face in an Art Nouveau mirror embellished with the gilt heads of temptresses trailing gold-leaf hair.

"I'm adding a veranda," she said, looking oppressed, as

though she'd been ordered by the Veranda Police to build the addition against her will. "It'll cost a fortune and won't be finished until doomsday."

"Then why do it?" Mother had lost weight. Either too much stress or too many aerobic videos.

"Because I'm in the phase of my life where I tinker. With myself. With my house. With my work. With my relationships. With my life."

I sat down at the table. "You're having a midlife crisis."

"Right on time. And draconian. How perceptive of you. Coffee?"

"Decaf?"

"Of course. And the grilled chicken is skinless, the fruit organic, and the sorbet nondairy. I'm going to live for fucking ever, the rich and thin vampire queen of Beverly Hills."

"Mother, what's wrong?"

Her eyes were infinitely sad and exquisitely made up in twelve shades of taupe for the natural look. She took my hand in hers. Her skin had the texture and look of vanilla pudding. "I woke up yesterday morning with one of those revelations that happens when the unconscious has been unraveling a problem your conscious never knew you had. The kind of nasty revelation you don't really want and people who aren't therapists or patients can ignore or attribute to gas." She turned my hand over and became absorbed in it, tracing the lines on my palm with a pale rose fingernail.

"If I pay for this session, will you tell me?" I prodded her.

She glanced up and smiled. "Patience, Demeter. Someday, God willing, you may discover for yourself that confiding your foolishness to your child isn't easy."

"What foolishness?" I asked hesitantly, hoping she wasn't about to divulge something sexual. If she told me she'd murdered Dunn, I'd help her dismember him and stuff him in the trash masher, but I didn't want to hear any stories that involved orgasms. "It's okay. You can tell me."

"Demeter, look at my face."

I looked. It was flawless. I peered closer, knowing she expected serious scrutiny. "You're perfect."

"I know." Her perfectly almond-shaped eyes filled with tears. "I can stay this way forever. I can be lifted over and over. They can take fat from my derriere, what little fat there is, make my lips pouty, and erase incipient nasolabial lines. I can look like Barbie and her best friend, Midge, until I'm ninety-nine and the smell of my decay wafts through the house like sweet, poison oleander." Her voice fell to a whisper. "The outside of me is immortal."

"But, Mother, isn't that what you want?"

"Is it?" She glanced into the mirror and shuddered. "The revelation I woke up with yesterday is that in ten years, maybe less, I'll look younger than you."

"Oh, no." I got up from the table. "I'm not having cosmetic surgery to look fifteen so you can be thirty-five forever. Forget it. Go tinker with somebody else, take lithium or estrogen or a straight-up martini. I don't care. Just leave me alone."

Mother grabbed my wrist in a surprisingly strong grip. "Sit down, Demeter. I wouldn't suggest something so preposterous."

Really. Wasn't this the woman who'd once suggested I pretend I didn't have a father, that, like Minerva, I'd sprung full-blown from the head of Zeus, herself being Zeus? Who'd admitted me to her clinic *suggesting* that my desire for Michael was, in fact, only rebellion against her? Who'd assigned me to Morris the shrink, who did double crostics while I'd poured out my grief? Why would I think she'd suggest anything preposterous? But I sat. I wanted to hear what she thought wasn't preposterous. "Okay. Shoot."

Mother released my hand, then patted it to let me know she approved. "Looking younger than your child is abnormal. It's perverse, inevitably depressing, and ultimately foolish."

"Then stop having yourself lifted."

"Furthermore, counseling patients who want cosmetic surgery is ridiculous. Whatever guilt they feel doesn't outlast the bruises, no matter how many protest marches they attended in the Sixties. Truth is, you couldn't keep them from surgery with armed guards."

I was beginning to see.

"And don't get me started on Dunn," she went on.

"I won't," I interjected quickly. "I mean, it's none of my business."

"You're right. Bad enough that it's mine." She sighed. "After all these years, all this working and striving and accomplishing, my career is foolish, my life is foolish, I am foolish."

"What are you going to do?"

"I don't know," she said sadly. "Maybe just go on the way I am. Then someday you'll sit at my deathbed. You'll be an old woman wearing wrinkles and character. I'll be ancient and thin and rich and beautiful. You'll ask me if I have any last thoughts. I'll reply, 'I wish I'd eaten more ice cream.' "

I shuddered. It could happen. I made a mental note to be out of town at the time. "You can eat more ice cream now," I suggested softly.

Mother glared at me. "All that fat and those calories! Are you crazy?" She sighed again. "You wouldn't want to move into this house with me, would you?"

"No, I wouldn't."

"I'll build your room to suit you. Anything you want. Private entrance. Gun rack." She leaned forward conspiratorially. "How about a master suite, sitting room, bath with Jacuzzi, kitchenette, laundry? Bigger than the apartment you're in and you'll never have to see Dunn."

"Why do you want me to do this, Mother?"

"Because I can. Currently I find myself with more money than common sense. I'd like to share it with you." She looked away. "And I'd like to see our relationship become closer. Before it's too late."

There it was. Mortality had arrived, wearing a party hat on his skull, prepared to hunker down in the guest room until he made off with his hostess. She hoped I'd move in and stand between them. Even better, throw him out.

Did she know this? I wondered. Probably not.

I did, but only because death is my job's bread and butter and I've looked into the faces of people who've seen him up close and personal. I knew how desperately they'd tried to fight him off.

"That's a very generous offer, Mother, but I'm an adult. An adult's self-esteem suffers when she lives with her mother."

"I told you that, didn't I?"

"When I was eleven. You didn't want your mother living with us."

"My mother was a bitch. Beyond therapy. Beyond miracles." Mother's look was rueful. "Do you remember everything I ever said to you?"

"Most of it."

"God help us both." Mother rose from the table. "Well, I tried. I'm glad it didn't work. I was right twenty years ago." She kissed me on the cheek. "Your self-esteem is safe. If you can, come to dinner more often. My foolishness hasn't affected the quality of the food I serve. Try, Demeter."

"I will," I lied. Before I went, I wanted to say something from the heart to make her feel better. "Get an estrogen count, Mother. It might help."

"Not a bad idea." She smiled at me, willing to be comforted. "Thank you for listening. I do feel much better."

"Good. See you soon."

I was heading for the door when her voice loomed up behind me. "Demeter."

"Yes."

"In the aftermath of the earthquake I apparently lost a photograph I'd kept for a very long time. A picture of a man, an old friend of your grandmother's. Have you seen it?"

"No. Is it important?"

"Not really. I just wondered if you'd seen it. Drive carefully."

I waved and left.


A couple of days later I went to the police station looking for Buddy, and found him, tilted back in his chair tossing Nerf basketballs through his wastebasket hoop.

He ignored me as I walked in. I sat on the edge of his desk.

"Don't tell me, Buddy. Let me guess. All the bad guys have gone to Mafia camp and you have nothing to do."

He glanced at me briefly, then resumed tossing. "Don't start with me, Dutch."

"Or what? You'll shoot me? Ignore me? Stop working on my case, which is exactly what you seem to have done?" I leaned over his desk, into his face. "You going to shuffle a few papers around your desk all day, then head for a cop bar where you can grouse about women? Well, grouse to me, Buddy. Get it out of your system."

Buddy eyed me warily. "You drunk?"

"No." I leaned an inch closer. Buddy didn't flinch. He dug his butt into his chair. I went for it. "Maybe it's a female thing, Buddy. Maybe I'm PMSing or on the rag. Maybe I'm just a stupid, crazy bitch hell-bent on making you miserable.

We all know how stupid and crazy bitches are. And sluts. And douche bags. C'mon, Buddy. Spit it out. I'm just another bitch trying to break your balls."

Buddy's eyes narrowed. "I should arrest you for fraud. You come on like the Virgin Mary with a hands-off sign on your belt. You act like I'm some fucking creep out to rape Orphan Annie. You're no virgin or orphan."

"Okay, I'm not your average maiden looking for a shining knight to sweep me off my feet," I said softly. "But you're no knight, Buddy. You come after me like Robocop. I feel like your target, not a woman. All I can think of is head for the hills."

For a moment Buddy was silent. He seemed to be mulling it over. "I come on the way I come on, Dutch. Maybe it's not what you want, but it's what I am. I'm nuts about you. I say it the way I say it. I show it the way I can. Maybe I *am* Robocop. But that's not the problem."

"It isn't?" I was beginning to feel uneasy. "What is?"

"We've worked on this case together, eaten together, pounded the crap out of ninja gardeners together. We've even danced together."

"So you think you know me?"

Buddy grinned. "Damn right. Just like you know me. No bullshit, Dutch. Like it or not, we know each other better than people who get married. I know how you smell."

"Smell?" Here he was at his best, Robocop the sweet talker.

"You give off a lot of heat when your adrenaline's up. And it's up all the time. *That's* the problem." Buddy put one hand on my shoulder and pulled me toward him. I didn't pull away. "Look me straight in the eye, Dutch, and tell me you aren't fucking someone else."

I looked him straight in the eye. "I am. I'm fucking someone else."

Buddy pushed me away. "Who is he? Where is he?" He was ready to fight.

"That's none of your business." Let him take his best shot.

Instead, he shrugged. "Okay. I can stop driving myself crazy wondering. I was right. But one thing I know. It won't last. Know why? Because you're just like me. We both pretend to ourselves that we want to settle down, have a relationship with one other person. But when we get down to it—and we both love to get down to it—what we want is an occasional roll in the hay with a buddy who wants the same. Because when the phone rings and the voice at the other end tells us that some stiff's just been found in some alley, we're gone."

My heart literally sank, dropping from my chest to some-where south of my pancreas. Maybe Buddy wasn't entirely right, but he wasn't wrong either. What if Michael decided to stop feeling guilty? What if he pardoned himself for crimes he never committed? What if he decided that the past was the past and that I was the future he wanted? What if we moved in together? And then the phone rang? What would Michael do when I slipped my gun in the holster, kissed him goodbye, and left, sometimes for weeks at a time? Would he decide I was as crazy as his wife? Would he . . . still love me?

At the moment I didn't have any of the answers, just a burning desire to pop Buddy for raising the questions.

I finally answered him. "Okay. So you think I'll dump my boyfriend for a stiff in an alley. Or he'll dump me because I hang around alleys with stiffs. All I can say is, we'll see. Now that we've turned over this rock and let everything crawl out, can we get back to what we were doing? I saw Steve Pierce."

Buddy looked surprised. "When?"

"Early this morning. He gave me the background on his release. The department's checked everything out?"

"Twice. And I released Pierce myself." Buddy laughed.

"He asked me to call the Japanese and tell them that we were mistaken, that he is a worthy vehicle for Morpho. I offered to introduce him to Bunko." Buddy tossed one final Nerf ball, then pulled a file from his drawer. "We're back where we started. Any ideas?"

"I still think Cassie Sayres is our killer." I tossed my pet theory in his lap.

Buddy shook his head. "No hunches, Dutch. I want to hear evidence."

"I don't have anything new."

"That's because she didn't do it." Buddy smirked. "Her alibi checked out. She has no history of violence. No priors." He looked speculatively at me. "You hang out around her. Has she said anything to make you suspicious?"

"Only that she wants to have a baby." I expected him to laugh in my face.

Buddy's laugh sailed past my left ear. "Now I know she didn't do it. A woman who's thinking about babies isn't thinking about murder."

"Are you sure, Buddy? Are you certain that Cassie isn't one of those people who can separate issues in her head? It's called compartmentalizing, like when a man tells his mistress he adores her, but he loves his wife, too. Are you absolutely positive that Cassie Sayres isn't capable of compartmentalizing a desire to give birth and a desire to kill?"

Buddy thought about that for a moment, then opened the file. "Men do that. Women can't."

"Really?" I took the file out of his hand, forcing him to look at me. "I can."

For a moment I thought he would argue with me. He wanted to and would have if he was certain. But he wasn't, so he backed down. "Okay." Buddy took the file from me and flipped it open. "When you come to a dead end, go back and start all over again. Let's start at the top."

For the next couple of hours Buddy and I went through
the file, rehashing every bit of evidence, every interview, every
thought or stray idea or coffee-buzzed fantasy we'd ever come
up with. Finally Buddy closed the file. "Shit!"

"Exactly."

"I hate cases like this. A killer kills. Threatens to kill
again, a specific target. The connection between the first victim and the threatened victim is so shaky it almost doesn't exist. The killer kills again, only this victim is a mistake. Or was
she? Or did the killer change his mind and kill his second victim in such a way that it looks like a mistake? Then the killer
backs off, lies low. We don't know why. Maybe the killer left
town, or had a heart attack or got carjacked or popped in a
drive-by. Maybe he got religion. Maybe it's over. Or maybe
he's just waiting for the next full moon."

"We just had one. I'm still alive."

"Okay. Cross off full moons. We're nowhere with
nothing."

"Okay. Now what?"

"Lunch. Lamb at Philippe's French Dip. Chili fries.
Lemonade."

"On you." I headed for the door.

Buddy followed. "Oh no. I'm out of the Robocop business, honey. No more Meals on Wheels and free home deliv-
ery. This tab's on Ms. O'Brien."

I laughed. Buddy thought he was being original, but I
knew better. The first thing guys do when they get pissed is
hand the woman the check. Your basic play-or-pay transac-
tion. With Buddy it was okay. Like he'd said. He could only
come on like himself.

Heading downtown, we tossed a few more lame ideas at
each other, then, knowing we'd hit a brick wall, switched to a
discussion of the local news. Everybody who'd ever had his or
her name in the papers seemed to be running for mayor. The

election battle would be long and tedious and fought in a field of mud.

There was one idea I didn't bounce off Buddy.

The killer was definitely involved with the show. If he was still after me, and instinct told me he was, the best way to lure him back into action was to stay very close to *Stone, Private Eye*.

It was a plan I didn't want to tell Buddy. I didn't want to hear the word *bait*.

For the next couple of weeks I hung out on the set, waving myself around like a red flag. Nobody charged. I kept waving.

And yawning. Sets are boring. Everyone does what they're hired to do, then waits for everyone else. While they wait they read. Mostly the trades, *Variety* and *The Hollywood Reporter*. I quickly became addicted to the gossip columns and was surprised to see Cassie's name pop up with increasing regularity. It seemed Cassie and Joshua were hitting all the restaurants, where, at some point after the drinks but before the main course, Cassie was dragging her boyfriend under the table for a quickie. So far they'd been thrown out of Spago, Citrus, Patina, and the assorted Bob's Big Boys they visited because Joshua seriously worshiped Quentin Tarantino and hoped to find him eating lunch there one day. I laughed at the columns but rooted for Cassie, whose single-minded assault on Joshua's gene pool was taking on Desert Storm proportions.

One day I walked into Cassie's office to find her staring at twenty-five EPT tests lined up on her desk, each one of them a glowing robin's-egg blue.

"You're pregnant," I told her.

"You think these things work?" she asked. "I mean, they've probably sat in some storeroom for months. Maybe they've fermented or gone stale."

"One or two maybe," I allowed. "But you've bought out the fertility section at Thrifty. You are most definitely with child."

Cassie leaped up and hugged me. "This is great! Now I can dump Joshua."

"You mean you haven't bonded with him?"

"Bonded?" Cassie lit a cigarette. "Joshua's only bond is with his reflection. His idea of foreplay is to read his book reviews out loud to me in bed. He pontificates about art and literature constantly, but his big turn-on is power and money." She thought for a moment. "I'm sure I got pregnant the night I introduced him to Mike Ovitz."

"Have you told Joshua you're pregnant?"

"No. And I won't." She mashed out her cigarette. "I've got to quit smoking. For the baby." She stared into space, her eyes a complete blank.

"Cassie, are you okay?"

"I can't think without smoking. I'll cut down." She lit a cigarette. Her eyes relit. "I'll pick a fight with Joshua tonight. Nothing to it. I'll tell him I read his last article, the one in *Vanity Fair* where he goes on for six pages discussing his last book as though Moses had brought the manuscript down from Mount Sinai. I'll say that I found the article even more boring than the book and the book put my teeth to sleep." She laughed. "He'll be gone in ten minutes, don't you think?"

"Six" was my opinion.

Cassie was delighted. "Isn't it the best, the very best, when you can dump someone and make him think he dumped you?"

"A natural high," I said, thinking that her relationships must be even more complicated than mine. "So, you're pregnant. Joshua's gone. What next?"

Cassie looked puzzled. "Well, I'll do what I'm doing. Write, eat, sleep, write. Only now I'll also be gestating. Think of it, Dutch. I can create *Stone, Private Eye* and a whole new human being, without ever leaving my office."

"You're a full-service facility." I approved. "Do you have a doctor?"

"I did. He died. Or retired to Acapulco. I forget which." She scribbled a note on her legal pad. *Obstetrician. Pronto.* "Do you know an obstetrician?"

"One. Ralph Tobias. He practices in Sherman Oaks. You don't want him. He's paranoid. Had me following his wife around for six months trying to prove she had a lover. All the poor woman ever did was attend mass and bake Bundt cakes for church bake sales."

"I'll find someone else," Cassie decided. "I must know women who've had babies." She thought for a moment. "Guess not."

"Pick some names from the phone book and I'll check them out," I offered.

For a moment I thought she was going to hug me again. "You would? That's terrific."

"Baby present." I watched her eyes drift back to her computer. In a moment I'd lose her. "Anything new happening?"

"No. Buck's rewriting more. Likes to throw in phrases like 'happier than a tick on an overfed dog.' He says I don't write *country* enough. If I write any more country, I'll be printing these scripts out on grits. But that's Buck. He thinks all America wants to return to his roots."

"Is he doing anything else peculiar?"

Cassie giggled. "Peculiar? Buck? What does he do that isn't peculiar?"

"Good point."

I left Cassie pounding furiously at her computer, her EPT tests, pregnancy, and Joshua forgotten.

First chance I got, I'd call Mother for an OB referral. She'd give me three. I'd check them out. Not that I felt responsible for Cassie, you understand, but I'd never met anyone who hovered so precariously between determined and helpless. Until the moment I proved her a killer, I was free to like Cassie Sayres and help her if I could.

It occurred to me that Cassie's pregnancy posed an interesting ethical question. She'd stolen Joshua's chromosomes, DNA, and a baby to carry them in. Was this legal? Moral? Did I really care? She'd gotten what she went after and I liked that. I liked it even better that Joshua didn't.

I was beginning to agree with Buddy. Our killer had relocated to a smog-free environment or had been whacked by high-spirited youth out for their nightly drive-by massacre.

In any event, I was getting tired of standing around the set, watching Buck mug into the camera. I was starting to hear his twang in my sleep and dream of ticks chewing on overfed dogs.

What I needed was advice. So I tracked down my mentor, Gus Whitlow.

I finally found him, recovering from a heart attack at the Motion Picture Country Home.

"You weren't easy to find," I told him.

"Good." His shrewd blue eyes glinted. "I didn't want you to find me. Bad enough I'm sitting here like some decrepit old man wrapped up in this ridiculous plaid robe."

"Come off it, Gus. You look very natty. And hardly decrepit." It was true. Gus looked, as always, like a big, oddly dignified bear. He moved slowly but with purpose. His eyes were bright. His gray pelt was shiny. How sick could he be?

"How sick are you?" I asked.

His familiar chuckle stayed deep in his throat. "Good. Just what I taught you. Make your questions quick and direct. Catches people off guard."

"Except you. How sick are you?"

"And be persistent. Never let them squirm away without answering."

*"Gus!"* I grabbed his knee and shook it. "Knock it off. Tell me."

"A mild heart attack."

"Mild? Are you telling the truth?"

"No bullshit. The doc here says mild. I gotta believe him. We play poker a lot. He doesn't cheat."

"You do, so you're winning. When did this heart attack happen?"

"Fifteen days ago at Santa Anita. I bet on a long shot, twenty to one, and the son of a bitch came in. Next thing I knew I was gasping for air with pain shooting down my left arm." He shook his head. "I'm too old and too accustomed to losing to score one that big."

"Congratulations, Gus. Maybe now you'll give up gambling."

"Why? Everybody gambles. When we open our eyes in the morning, first thing we all do is figure our odds for the day." He closed his eyes for a minute, then opened them. "Shit, I get pooped. What's up with you?"

I told him. About the case. About my current MO. He listened without comment. So I asked, "Any ideas?"

He shook his head. "I've waved myself in front of killers once or twice in my time and lived to tell the tale. Unless you get lucky or this asshole gets religion, breaks down, and confesses, you're on the right track."

"I thought so. Wanted to hear it from the pro."

"I don't like this," Gus complained. "I don't like sitting here feeling like a leaky balloon. I don't like being out of the game. And I particularly, most profoundly and sincerely, don't like the idea of someone trying to kill you."

I got up and kissed his cheek. "Thank you. He won't. After all, I was trained by the best."

Gus smiled his closemouthed smile. He only bared his teeth when angry. "If he kills you, I won't come to your funeral."

"Then I'll be damned if I'll die." I was ready to go when a thought struck me. "Why aren't you in a hospital? Why the Motion Picture Country Home?"

He grinned. "Chuck Heston owed me a favor."

"Half of Hollywood owes you favors. You never say why."

"It's all for the memoirs, to be published posthumously." He waved me away. "Go on, now. Come back when you've caught the miserable bastard. I'll have Dom Perignon on ice."

I went, hoping the memoirs wouldn't be published for at least thirty years.


The next morning, Mother was handing me a paper with the names of OBs.

"Any one of these is good. Hoffman tells sexist jokes without knowing they're sexist. He learned them in medical school."

"Cassie won't notice. She'll probably take her computer into the examining room and pound out a scene with her feet in the stirrups."

Mother looked interested. "Really? Sounds like she has a psychological problem."

I wished I'd kept my mouth shut. "Not one you're going to unravel, Mother. Cassie is who she is."

"You don't think therapy can help her?"

"I think it can only confuse her," I said slowly, thinking it through. "Suppose she comes to you because she's unmarried and pregnant. You ask her questions about her life. You make your shrinky discoveries. She's a workaholic. She seems to live in her office. She talks about nothing but business. She took time out for a month to get pregnant by a man she selected for that purpose and planned to dump immediately after. And has."

"The Black Widow syndrome." Mother was fascinated. "I must meet this woman."

"And then what? You reach your shrinky conclusions. You tell her she has problems. You tell her she's dysfunctional. You tell her that her dysfunctional problems go back to her dysfunctional childhood, to the original dysfunctional triangle, her mommy and her daddy and her. You drag Oedipus and Electra out of her closet and set them on each other, and pretty soon she's spending all her time mucking around in her childhood, trying to remember if Daddy fucked her or if she wanted to fuck him and kill her mother and that's why she has no friends except a guy wandering around in Brazil writing stories with endings that don't make sense."

"Who's wandering around in Brazil?" Mother was rapt.

"Never mind. The point is, Mother, that everyone's childhood was dysfunctional. And everyone's life goes on."

Mother got up from her desk and sat in the chair next to me. "You feel that your childhood was dysfunctional?"

"No. Not for a minute. Just because I don't know who my father was. Because my mother told me it isn't important. Why would you ask a question like that?"

"How long have you been seeing Michael?"

I was shocked. "How did you know?"

She shrugged. "You look happy. You're not exactly serene, but then you never were."

"I'm seeing Michael," I admitted.

"You know, darling," Mother said, using the phrase and dispassionate tone she enlisted in her role as shrink-mother. "I've been thinking over your case. I'm sure you must know that your inordinate passion for Michael, who I'm sure is a fine man, is merely an acting out of the feelings you have for your fantasy father."

I got up. "You're wrong and I don't want to hear it. If I have to choose between Michael and you, I'll do it right now and you won't like it."

"You aren't going to send your friend Cassie to chat with me?" Mother changed subjects in a hurry.

"Her job is demanding and she's pregnant. Her present is enough of a challenge. Adding the past would be overload."

I'd reached the door before Mother's obligatory *last word* floated from her chair. "About your father, Demeter. It was a judgment call. My assessment of the situation and your feelings about it are two different things. I felt I acted in your best interests."

"I never doubted that. I only said you were wrong. Maybe when you've finished with your midlife hoedown, you'll see that."

I waited but she didn't respond. I'd had the last word. Her midlife crisis was worse than I thought.


A few days later, on a hunch, I dropped by Buck Stevens's house at a time I knew he'd be on the set. Without Buck at home to intimidate her, maybe Mary Lou would tell me something.

A large, tough-looking woman dressed in a nurse's uniform opened the door. "What do you want?"

"I'm Dutch O'Brien. I work on *Stone, Private Eye* and I'm a friend of Mary Lou's. I'd like to see her."

"You can't. She's resting." The woman started to close the door. I got my shoe in there first.

"Is Mary Lou sick?"

The woman's cold gray eyes told me she didn't want to

answer, but knew I wouldn't go away until she did. "She was. She's getting better."

"What's wrong with her?"

"You'll have to ask her husband, miss. I'm just the nurse."

"And a splendid one I'm sure you are, too." This woman could stonewall forever. I removed my foot. "Please tell Mr. Stevens I was here. Thank you for your time."

She slammed the door in my face.

I walked away from the house feeling more than uneasy. At the end of the path I looked back at the house, thinking I'd heard something.

I had. Tapping. Metal on glass. I looked up.

From a bedroom window, Mary Lou Stevens was looking down at me, her face a welter of bruises. As I watched, horrified, a burly, white-clad arm grabbed her from behind and pulled her away from the window.

I ran back to the door and began pounding. "Open up. Open up."

I could have pounded till my arm dropped off. The door was locked and no one was coming.

I headed for my car.

# Chapter 11

*I*n less than an hour, I returned with Buddy.

And this time Buck himself opened the door. "Well, isn't this a treat." His trademark ingratiating grin spread wide across his face. "Detective Hart, if I remember correctly. Come on in."

Buddy stepped in. I followed.

Buck gave me his usual once-over, the short version: slide over the face, hit the tits, slide over the waist, and hit the jackpot. "How you doing, Dutch? Every time I turn around on the set, there you are, just starin' at me. Keep checking to see if my fly is open." He turned to Buddy. "What can I do for you, Detective?"

Buddy stepped forward. "We're here to investigate possible domestic violence."

Buck cocked his head to one side like an Airedale, another trademark mannerism he usually reserved for close-ups. "In my house, Detective?" He sounded wounded. "You thinkin' maybe somebody livin' under this roof is pounding on somebody else? You think maybe Buck's temper runs away with itself? That what you're saying, Detective?"

"We want to see Mary Lou," I added.

Buck looked sad, like a tick on a starving dog. "Seeing

my poor sweet Mary Lou ain't no Sunday picnic these days. But I'll get her." He started up the steps, then paused. "You folks want something to drink? Maybe a glass of white wine or some cold lemonade?"

"We want to see Mary Lou," I repeated.

"Coming right up." Buck flashed a smile before continuing up the stairs.

I watched him go, wondering if he'd always suffered from spasms of charm or if he'd acquired the skill in the business. I looked around. "Wonder where the nurse is?"

"I'll check out Mary Lou, then talk to the nurse." Buddy pulled out his notebook. "Did you catch her name?"

I was shaking my head no when we heard them coming, first Buck's low voice urging, "Hold on to me, honey."

Then we saw them. On one side Buck, on the other Nurse Muscle, and in the middle Mary Lou, unsteady on her feet and terribly bruised. I started up the stairs. "Mary Lou. What happened?"

"Hold on, hold on." Buck waved me away. "Let's just get her downstairs." They descended slowly with Buck holding Mary Lou upright, whispering encouragement. "Just a little farther, sweetheart. Just a few more steps."

Buddy's eyes were wide and guilty. "Mr. Stevens, sir. We can interview Mrs. Stevens in her bedroom."

Buck stopped. Keeping a firm grip on Mary Lou, he fixed Buddy with a grieving stare. "Now, I wish you'd said that five minutes ago. You could have saved this poor little girl a world of pain if only you'd been thinking about her. Now she's halfway down and half fainting, and dragging her back's only going to rile up her pain. What would you like me to do now, Detective?"

"Bring her down," Buddy said. "I'll get a chair."

"No, she'll lie flat on the sofa," the nurse ordered. "She's having trouble bending in the middle."

It took several minutes, but finally Mary Lou was stretched out on the sofa looking like the victim of a hit-and-run forklift. I sat on the sofa next to her. "What happened, Mary Lou? How did you get hurt?"

Her eyes fluttered and finally focused on me. "Dutch, how nice to see you. Would you like some cold lemonade?"

"No thanks. I'd just like to know what happened to you."

She tried to smile but couldn't. Her lip was split and some doctor had slipped in a couple of stitches. "Oh, honey, I'm just never gonna learn."

"Learn what?" Buddy asked, glancing at Buck, who hovered over Mary Lou, catching every word as it fell from her torn mouth.

Mary Lou grimaced. "I'm always wandering around the house at night, tripping over stuff I leave on the floor. I mean to turn on the light, honest I do. But I forget. The moonlight shining through the rose window up there at the top of the stairs is just too pretty." She closed her eyes.

"What happened, Mary Lou?" Buddy's voice was sharp and insistent. He wanted to keep her awake.

Mary Lou opened her eyes. "I was up there thinking about coming down for some lemonade. I didn't turn on the light. I tripped over a cleaning caddy—you know, one of those boxes like shoeshine kits, full of cleaning supplies. I fell, ass over teakettle, all the way down. Buck said I screamed, but I don't remember. Next thing I know the doctor was here and Buck was bawling his eyes out." She turned a loving eye, the one that wasn't swollen shut, to Buck.

"You fell?" I repeated.

"I fell," Mary Lou answered.

Buddy leaned over her. "If you'd gotten hurt any other way, would you tell us?"

"Sure." Mary Lou looked into my eyes. "I'd tell Dutch. She's my friend."

I wanted to squeeze her hand, but didn't. Later Buck's lawyer might take this as undue influence. "You're right, Mary Lou. I am your friend. And I hope you know that if anyone hurt you, you can say it right now out loud and I'll see to it personally no one will ever hurt you again. I promise."

Mary Lou's eyes filled. "You're such a sweet lady."

"Tell me again. What happened?"

"Dutch, honey, I fell down the steps. I tripped on a cleaning caddy and fell down the steps." She closed her eyes. "I'm so very tired."

Buck softly patted Mary Lou's shoulder. "You sleep now, honey." He turned to Buddy. "You got what you come for, Detective?"

"I'd like to see the cleaning caddy," Buddy told him. His jaw muscles were twitching. He was hoping Buck would give him cause to arrest him. Anything, even a missing cleaning caddy.

But he didn't. Buck fetched it himself and presented it to Buddy. "Black box. Dark night. I woulda tripped over it myself."

"But you never trip over anything, do you, Buck?" I couldn't help the edge in my voice. "Mary Lou does all the tripping and falling in this house, doesn't she, Buck?"

Buck shrugged. "I turn on the lights."

Buddy approached the nurse. "When did Mr. Stevens call you?"

"Right after the accident. The doctor said Mrs. Stevens should go to the hospital, but she could stay home with proper care."

"Why didn't you want Mary Lou in the hospital, Buck?" I asked him.

"You been in a hospital lately?" Buck asked. "Drab and dreary and full of people with God knows what. If I can afford to do better by Mary Lou at home—and thank God I can—then, by God, I'm gonna do it. The doctor comes every day. You can ask him."

"We will." Buddy closed his notebook. "Thank you for your time, Mr. Stevens."

"No problem. I'll walk you out." Buck turned to the nurse. "We'll let her sleep here for as long as she likes."

Once outside, Buck's charm slipped from his face like makeup. "You listen to me, Detective Hart, and listen real good. First thing tomorrow morning three lawyers in Armani suits, which I bought and paid for, will show up at your office. They're sharks, Detective, lean, mean, and hungry, and they're going to rip your LAPD ass with a lawsuit. Understand?"

"You have no basis for a suit," Buddy told him.

"You pushed your way into my home without a warrant and for no reason."

"You invited us in," Buddy pointed out.

"Don't remember that." Buck shook his head.

"I'll testify to it," I added.

"You?" Buck gave me the once-over, the long version. "You started all this by coming here uninvited. Now you're going to testify that your boyfriend here didn't break any laws. We'll see if any court in this land takes the word of a badass cop and the slut he's fucking against the word of America's down-home hero, Buck Stevens. Now get off my property. I gotta call the cops to report a civil rights abuse."

"Mr. Stevens"—Buddy was polite, evidently intent on reasoning with him—"we can talk about this."

Buck turned away. "Just take that girl home and fuck her, Detective. She's hotter than a pistol. I oughta know."

Buddy stepped toward Buck. I grabbed Buddy's sleeve. "Don't. He wants you to hit him."

Buddy backed off. "Good night, Mr. Stevens."

Buck smiled. "At first, I was going to call my good friend the police chief and just carry on a little—nothing serious, just enough so he'd bust you down to a street cop. But you had to go and call my wife by her first name and, Detective Hart, I can't forgive that."

Buck went into the house. The door closed. I looked at Buddy. "I'm sorry."

"Don't be. That son of a bitch beat his wife half-dead. She won't make a complaint and we have no proof, but we'll get him, Dutch. For that and for killing Amy Westin."

"I believe you," I said. In the last half hour Buck Stevens had promoted himself from suspect to prime suspect to probable killer.

The following morning I was in Cassie's office reading about Joshua's departure, a story *Variety* headlined as LITERARY SENSATION ANKLES BIG ORANGE FOR BIG APPLE. I showed it to Cassie.

"At least he ankled in style" was her comment. "I paid for the ticket, first-class on MGM Grand." She switched on her computer then waited impatiently for the program to boot up. "He told me that I'm a television whore. That's after he spent a month here running around town shaking his cute little booty in the face of every agent and producer he could find. Nobody hit on him. Right now Joshua is somewhere over Chicago wondering why a guy with his talent couldn't turn the money trick in L.A. I'm sure we'll read the whole story in *Vanity Fair* with himself as the artist-hero who wouldn't sell out."

"You writers have all the fun. If life doesn't give you the ending you want, you just make up another one." I tossed *Variety* into the wastebasket. "How are you feeling?"

"Great. Nauseous. Exhausted. The very warp and woof of gestation. I think next I'm supposed to get some sort of rash."

"Rash? I never heard that one."

"I read that on an insert that came with my vitamins." Cassie blinked at her screen. "Or maybe that was my cat's thyroid medication. Damn! Where is that file?"

I was beginning to worry. "You are going to the doctor, aren't you, Cassie?"

"This afternoon. Ah, there it is." Cassie started typing, then hesitated. "I plan to take notes on my pregnancy. If there are enough complications, I could turn it into a movie of the week. If everything goes perfectly, it can still be an episode of *Stone, Private Eye.* Buck can deliver a woman's baby in the back of his pickup. I'll write folksy insights about the miracle of birth and we'll end the show with Buck playing his banjo to the baby."

"You'll redefine birth trauma." I laughed, thinking that Cassie's pregnancy was going to have more uses than the peanut. "What are you working on now?"

"She's working on nothing." The voice came from behind me.

I twisted around in my chair and saw Buck, dressed in his at-home overalls, leaning against the doorjamb, his evil-twin smile cracking his face. "She's fired." Buck stepped into the office, shambled across the room, and loomed over Cassie. "I warned you, but either you ignored me or you're a stone-stupid bitch."

Cassie hit save, then smiled pleasantly at Buck. "Is there something I can do for you?"

"Get out!" Buck bellowed. "Take your skinny, smoky ass on out of here and don't ever let me see you again!"

Cassie continued to smile, but her eyes seemed to glaze over. "Buck, I have a contract."

"I just bought it out, fifty cents on the dollar." Buck

fished in his pocket, pulled out a check, and tossed it on her desk. "Take it or leave it, either way you're gone."

Cassie looked at the check, but didn't touch it. "Why are you doing this?"

"I told you I wanted my show down where the rubber meets the road. But you refused to make it more country. You despise the plain folks I come from. You despise me."

"That's not true," Cassie protested. "I've been using a lexicon of colorful Southern aphorisms and I even like them. Look here, Buck—act two, scene three of next week's script. I have Stone telling his sidekick Wheezer that he's happier than a pig eating shit. Of course I can't say *shit* in the final draft, but won't *garbage* do? Or maybe *sludge?*"

Buck kicked Cassie's desk. The desk jumped. So did Cassie. I got up and moved closer to Cassie, still a spectator but preparing to play. Buck's face went white. His voice was a whisper. "Now listen to me, you weird little cunt. My people have talked to the network people and the result of all this high-priced yammering is that I'm taking over the show. It's done. It's over. You're out."

"Are you saying you're going to write the show?"

"Damn straight. And direct. And produce." Buck's whisper turned to a rasp with a catch in it. "I'm a disappointed man, Cassie Sayres. When I started this show with you and Richard, I thought I'd died and gone to hog heaven with a creative team I could trust. Now half of the team isn't here no more and the other half can't cut the mustard. I've been betrayed in my time by experts, but never nothing like this." He took a deep breath, then glanced sideways, seeming surprised that a camera wasn't there.

I couldn't blame him. This performance had been one of his best. Now with no director to call *cut*, Buck had to end his scene with an improvised exit, which he accomplished slowly. With limping.

"There is a God," I told Cassie. "He broke his toe kicking your desk. What are you going to do?"

"Call my agent." Cassie dialed quickly, spoke briefly to her agent, then hung up. "Buck wasn't lying. His hit men told the network powers that Buck's either running the show or he's quitting. I'm out of a job."

"I'm sorry. Can I do anything for you?"

"No." Cassie looked shell-shocked. "I'm going to cash my check, then see my doctor, then . . . go home?" She got up slowly and moved stiffly, like a sleepwalker. "There is something you can do for me, Dutch. Help me get my computer into the car. It belongs to the company, but to hell with 'em. To hell with Buck. To hell with everyone."

"Good for you."

While Cassie said goodbye to a tearful Margo, I unplugged the computer and rolled all the cords. Twenty minutes later everything was stacked in Cassie's car trunk and she was slamming the lid. "If Richard had been here, this wouldn't have happened."

"Call me if you need anything or just to talk. Promise?"

"Promise." She stared into space for a moment. "You know, Dutch, I've never been personally fucked over by a real-life bad guy before. I am consumed by desire for revenge." She started her engine. "I think I can turn this into a miniseries, maybe even a feature."

Then she was gone. As I watched her car disappear through the studio's main gate, I knew that if Buddy and I had anything to do with it, Cassie would have her revenge.

Two weeks later, Buck's first solo effort was ready. I read the script and called Buddy.

"You won't believe this, Buddy. Buck's first script, besides being incoherent, has Sam Stone stalking a killer who murders and dismembers women."

"You're kidding!" Buddy all but leaped through the phone. "Don't move. I'll be right over."

He was. In ten minutes. I answered the door and must have looked disappointed. Buddy scowled. "What's wrong?"

"You didn't bring food."

"I'm damned if I do and damned if I don't. C'mon. We'll go for pizza."

We did. And argued. "You're out of your mind, Buddy. Nobody who likes pizza orders thin crust."

"I do."

Neither of us would budge, so we ordered two pizzas, thin with mushroom and sausage for him, thick with everything on it for me. Then Buddy read the script. "Christ, Dutch, Buck Stevens is some piece of work. First he kills Amy Westin, then he writes about it. How can he do this?"

"He's a writer. Or he thinks he is. But the question is: Can we consider this a confession?"

"Are you nuts?" Buddy took a swig at his beer. "You expect me to go down to the station with a television script in my hand and try to convince the captain it's a confession? I've got enough grief as it is."

"You mean the lawsuit?"

"You got it. Buck's lawyers are all over the place. I've got Internal Affairs breathing down my neck and the captain telling me to lay low." He finished his beer. "It'll be okay. I can't prove he invited us in even with you as a witness. You're too involved in the case. But he can't prove we forced our way in either, even with Nurse Rocco as witness. So the investigation will eventually end and this will all go away."

"Until then, we can't touch Buck?"

"Not with a script, honey. Crummy, isn't it?"

We finished the pizza, went back to my place, and watched TV for a while. I would have kissed Buddy good night when he left, just to be friendly, but he didn't make a move. So I didn't.

I went to bed sad. Poor Robocop was beginning to rust.

With Buddy on temporary hold, I devoted my time to tracking Buck alone. I arrived on the set minutes before he did and hung around all day, hoping I'd hear or see something, anything at all to nail him.

Buck ran the show like he ran everything else, amuck but with enthusiasm. He placed the camera, supervised the lighting, rewrote scenes as they shot them, browbeat the other actors, and screamed at everyone. Eventually he'd yell "Cut," tell the boom man how lucky he was to watch Buck Stevens make television history, then roll off to his trailer for a Jack Daniel's break.

Everyone on the show was bewildered. The editor, a quiet, bespectacled man named Fred, dropped by, his eyes glassy from an overdose of migraine pills. "It's hopeless," he moaned. "I'll never cut this show together. Everything's either out of frame or out of focus. People come and go from all directions and there aren't any close-ups except of Buck."

"Maybe you should talk to the writer and director and producer," I suggested. "He's in his trailer, getting drunk."

"Not until I line up another job." Fred popped another pill and left.

One night at home, it suddenly occurred to me that I'd been doing it wrong—spending my days on the set looking at what everyone could see instead of scoping out what was hidden.

The following morning, when Buck walked onto the set, I slipped out the back and went to his trailer.

The lock jimmied easily. I climbed inside. Piles of script pages littered every surface, along with empty Cheez-It boxes and empty Snapple bottles, all diet peach. An open bottle of Jack Daniel's sat on the counter and another in the middle of the table. I started looking, for what I didn't know, just the elusive something that might nail Buck.

I found it tucked under a blanket inside the bedroom window seat: a long thick roll of black felt that unwrapped to reveal a set of surgical saws.

I buttoned the roll under my jacket, left the trailer, and called Buddy, who picked me up ten minutes later.

Buddy looked at the saws and whistled. "You could dismember a herd of cows with these."

"Get a warrant," I pleaded.

"Can't. Having them is bizarre, but it isn't illegal. We have to prove he used them on Amy Westin." He thought for a minute. "I'll take them downtown and run them through forensics. Think Buck will notice they're gone?"

"I don't know. Maybe he hid them and never looks at them. Or maybe he likes to take them out and play with them—you know, relive the scene. No way of telling."

Buddy rerolled the saws. "I'll have them back as soon as I can. In the meantime don't take any chances. And remember, you were never in his trailer and these saws don't exist."

"Right. I'll be waiting. You can call me on the set."

Buddy went. I returned to the set feeling like a cat backing a mouse into a blind corner. I was going to get him. Finally. And I hoped they'd invite me to the hanging.

I fidgeted through the day, waiting to hear from Buddy. Finally a production assistant approached me with a cellular phone. I grabbed it. "Buddy, what's up?"

"Sorry, Dutch, the saws are clean. No blood, no bone, no gristle."

"Damn."

"Yeah, but here's the kicker. Forensics says they're not just trophies. They've been used, cleaned, and sterilized."

"Then they're evidence!"

"Insufficient. Sorry." Buddy hesitated. "Okay, so this is a roadblock not a dead end. We'll get him some other way. I'm bringing them back, Dutch. Think you can get them back where you found them without any trouble?"

"Sure. I'll meet you at the gate." I pressed the off button then stood there while anticipation and excitement drained out of me. I'd been so sure. So damn sure this was our breakthrough. Now I was beginning to feel it would never happen, that we'd never pin anything on Buck, not wife beating, not murder. Nothing. He'd go on being America's enduring folk hero until Forest Lawn claimed him, and even then, he'd live on in his reruns—the dead undead and his goddamned banjo.

At the gate I took the saws from Buddy, said thank you, and kissed him quickly, which seemed to shock him. He was still rooted to the spot and staring at me when I rounded the corner and made for Buck's trailer.

Inside, the only thing that had changed in the course of the day was the level of liquor in the bottles. In the bedroom I returned the saws to the window seat and was making my way to the door, when it suddenly banged open and Buck appeared. "Well," he said slowly, "what have we here?"

"Just little old me, Buck." I smiled quickly. "I thought of more of that detective stuff you like to hear about, so I dropped by."

"Don't need more detective stuff. I'm taking my show in a whole new direction. Stone's not going to solve crimes anymore. He's going to go from place to place helping folks, like Jesus."

"Sounds great. Well, I'll be going." I moved toward the door Buck was blocking.

"What's the hurry?" Buck didn't move. "You know you

and I got a bone to pick, some might even say a score to settle. That little party you arranged at my house? Well, I stuck it to your cop friend real good, so now you've moved to the top of my list."

I gritted my teeth. My immediate desire to deck him was playing hell with my goal: to catch him. I tried to make my voice soft. "I'm sorry if the incident upset you, Buck, but you can't fault me or the detective either for being concerned about Mary Lou."

Buck thought about that. As he thought he moved deeper into the trailer, still blocking the door but closer to me. "Okay. You made your point. I know you came to my house to make mischief, but you came back for Mary Lou. That's not a bad thing."

"Then I'll be going." I tried to brush past him.

Buck grabbed my wrist, then my neck, and held me. "That's not a good thing, either. Good news is, I'm gonna let you make it up to me." His grip tightened. I didn't struggle. Mentally, I gauged the position of his groin relative to my knee, then shifted my balance onto my left foot. "And don't give me any shit about female trouble. Your boyfriend don't look sick."

His kiss was a lip masher and his tongue a lizard trying to crawl down my throat. His breath was Cheez-Its and alcohol and decaying incisors. I gagged, but that didn't stop him. He was fumbling under my sweater and I was inching back toward the wall, knowing that having my back against a hard surface would give me more leverage. When my knee shot up, his balls would go through the roof of his mouth.

There was a knock at the door, first a polite tap that became louder and more insistent until even Buck heard it through his slurping. His lizard slithered back into his throat. He turned to the door. "Who's there? What you want?"

"You're wanted on the set, sir." The AD's voice floated faintly through the door.

"Tell them to wait." Buck turned back to me. I braced myself.

"But, sir," the second AD persisted, "network people are here."

"Network!" Buck dropped me like a hot rock. "Why the hell didn't you say so, you pissant? Tell 'em I'm coming."

As Buck hopped from the trailer he smiled at me. "We'll finish this later."

"I certainly hope so." When Buck was gone I threw up in his sink, not a reaction to Buck so much as to the adrenaline trapped in a pool above my kidneys. My body had to do something to release it, so, as usual, it did the first thing it thought of, and, as always, the result was quick, cheap, and dirty.


Late that night, Cassie called me. "You said I could call you."

"Of course. How are you?"

"Fine. But I need paper for my computer printer. Will you bring me some?"

"Sure."

"Now?"

"Now?" On television Ted Koppel was interviewing a recently indicted member of Congress. "Tonight?"

"I'll give you the address."

"You're not at home?"

"Not really."

After I scribbled down the address, Cassie told me to go to the office and take the paper from the supply cabinet. "See you soon." She hung up.

I said good night to Ted Koppel and his elected crook, who was saying that the American people understand human weakness and will probably elect him again.

The address Cassie had given me was on a gently shabby street in Los Feliz. I checked twice to make sure, then opened the gate and entered the grounds of St. Anne's Home for Unwed Mothers.

Cassie herself opened the door. "I've been looking out the window for you. Come in."

I stepped in. The home, like the street, was frayed genteel but obviously lovingly kept and very homey. Cassie took me by the hand. "We'll talk in my room."

I scanned her room. "How long have you been here?"

"Only a week. Why?"

"It looks like your office." It did. She'd pushed the bed into the corner to make way for her computer, which dominated the room. An easy chair had been shoved in the closet and a card-table desk set up in its place. "I'm curious, Cassie. I thought these homes were only for teenagers."

"They are. Impoverished teenagers." Cassie sat in the straight-backed chair, hugging her computer paper to her bosom. "I know what you're thinking. I'm hardly impoverished and thirty-eight, so why am I here?"

"That's exactly what I'm thinking. If you want to tell me."

"Sure. But don't tell anybody. Swear?"

"Swear."

"Fine. You see, lately I've become aware that I'm engaged in a personal conflict that can only be resolved in a spiritual and serene setting. So I came here to the sisters and persuaded them to let me stay. They didn't want to at first, of course. I'm too old and too rich and not in need of vocational training.

But I told them I'd stay out of their way, and after the baby's delivered, I'll make a nice donation to the home."

I felt my PI hackles rising. "What kind of conflict?"

"I can't tell you." Cassie was gripping the paper so hard her knuckles showed white. "My conflict is so unsettling, so fraught with guilt, I can't confide it in anyone. Until I deliver the baby, I need to be here where I'm protected from the world and the world's protected from me."

Bingo! Maybe.

"If this is where you feel safe, I'm glad you're here." I squatted down so we were eye level. "If there's anything you'd like to get off your chest, I'll be happy to listen."

She shook her head. "Not yet. Thank you for coming. And for the paper."

I stood. "What are you writing?"

"*Stone, Private Eye.*"

"But you were fired."

"The network called me. They've seen Buck's first effort. They told me two in a row like this show and they'll lose their whole Thursday night. I'm back writing the show."

"Buck'll go nuts."

"No. The network told Buck that even a man with his talent can't do everything himself. So they offered him help, a real Southern writer who'll fax in scripts from Atlanta. That's me. I'll be writing the show under an assumed name."

"Buck's going along with this?"

"The alternative they presented to him was moving the show to Saturday morning."

"Buck'll go along with this," I agreed. "Well, you have fun here in Atlanta. And call me anytime at all, for any reason."

"I will."

She was still hugging her paper when I left her.

• • •

"I woke you," I told Buddy when he opened his door.

"No. I always open my door with my eyes closed." He stepped back. "Come in."

His apartment was surprisingly neat. I headed for the kitchen. "I'll make coffee. We have to talk."

Buddy was instantly alert. "You've gotten a break on the case?"

"Maybe. Maybe not." In the kitchen, I looked for the coffeepot.

"I'll do it." Buddy pulled the pot from a cupboard and turned on the water. "What's up?"

I told Buddy about Cassie—her present location and newly discovered personal conflict. He frowned. "Okay, she's a nut. So what?"

"So, she might be a homicidal nut, Buddy. Look at it this way. A woman who has Cassie's difficulty in distinguishing reality from fiction may well have blurred the lines between the murders she's writing and the murders she's committing. Add that to her connection to the show, her self-stated personal conflict, and her generally repressed anger and you have a murder suspect."

"I don't know, Dutch. Maybe."

"We have to check her out, Buddy."

"I know." He didn't look happy. "Our suspects are all on some flying trapeze. One's up, one's down, one's in midair. Then they change places."

I understood. "You hate having to consider anyone else besides Buck."

"He's a creep. I want him to be the killer."

"So do I. But we have to check out Cassie Sayres."

"I'll get on it first thing in the morning. Coffee's ready."

"Gotta go." I kissed him on the top of the head and headed for the door.

He followed me into the living rom. "But you wanted coffee."

"No. I just wanted you awake. Call me tomorrow, Buddy."

"Fat chance." He slammed the door behind me.

He'd call. I knew it. He knew it. This was business. He'd call.

*Chapter 12*

Mother's clinic had changed in ways that surprised me.

Interspersed among the upscale neurotics giving each other manicures in the parlor and the guilt-ridden cosmetic-surgery patients hiding out in their rooms waiting for their noses to gel, there was a scattering of patients with actual wrinkles who seemed to be genuinely depressed.

"You've picked up a new clientele." I greeted Mother as I walked into her office.

"Yes. Would you believe it? Actual sick people." Her eyes smiled. "I'm trying to direct my midlife crisis outward. Not that I'm ignoring my inner work."

"God forbid." But I smiled back. Something about her had changed. She seemed not happy, but somewhere in the vicinity of happy, maybe the waiting room. "You might be right about Cassie Sayres. She could be a lunatic."

"Really? Tell me."

I did. The whole story and as quickly as possible. In Mother's office I always heard the meter running. Mother listened attentively. "What do you think?"

Mother pondered. "Have you ever seen her overtly violent?"

"No."

"To the best of your knowledge has she had a relationship that's lasted more than a few weeks, other than this genital assault on Joshua, which, of course, wasn't a relationship?"

"No."

"Maybe she's incapable of a relationship," Mother speculated. "But then, who is? Especially in the Nineties? Especially in L.A.?"

"I know people who have relationships," I said, thinking of Michael.

"And I know people, young women people, who mistake an obsessive sexual affair for the intimacy they can't handle."

"And I know mothers who are also psychiatrists who make snap judgments about situations they know nothing about just because they don't fit some arcane, arbitrary, misperceived model. And furthermore—"

"Demeter!" Mother interrupted sharply. "We were talking about Cassie Sayres. If you want my opinion, shut up and listen."

How interesting. Mother was actually testy. How real, how lifelike of her. "Okay, shoot."

"She may be a borderline personality or she may have underlying psychopathology. Isn't there anyone who knows her more than casually?"

My turn to ponder. Then I remembered. "Richard Raymond. Cassie's been in a close working relationship with her partner and coproducer, Richard Raymond, for over six years."

Mother beamed. "Wonderful. Talk to Mr. Raymond. He'll tell you everything you need to know."

"A lot of people, including Cassie Sayres, would like to talk to Richard Raymond if they could only find him. He's the man I mentioned, the one wandering around in Brazil."

"Doing what?"

I shrugged and told her the story. The hospitals, the continents, the faxes, Christian Dior. "None of it makes sense, does it?"

"Sure it does." Mother nodded wisely. "Think CIA."

"You mean the Central Intelligence Agency CIA?"

"That very one." Mother leaned forward. "Review the facts, Demeter. He's been incommunicado, traveling from country to country. No one can reach him. But he can reach them. Calls made to his current location are stonewalled by the person on the other end. The man is a CIA operative."

"But he faxed in a screenplay."

"So? Is there a law that says spies don't have free time? Don't they spend most of their time in foreign hotels waiting for contacts to show up?"

"I suppose so." Though Mother's idea didn't make much sense, Richard's behavior was definitely *Three Days of the Condor*. Who knows? At this point I'd check any theory. "Thank you. I'll check it out."

"Glad I could help you." Mother walked me to the door, her arm around my waist. "We're not so different, are we? Both investigators. I sense that transference is finally taking place in our relationship. We're going to be great friends."

I nodded, just to be agreeable, then walked to my car wondering how we could possibly be great friends until she answered The Question. Would my relationship with my mother ever actually improve or would it remain what it was, brief and rare flashes of connection scattered among Maalox Moments?

Just as I thought, my photo developer's memory had beamed back up at the Star Trek convention. He found my photo. I ordered copies, an insane number of copies.

At home, my living room looked like it had been papered

with enlarged photos of my father. But stare as I would, and did for hours, I couldn't see anything new.

Something was there. I knew it. Something plain and in the open, something so obvious I couldn't see it. Something that would tell me where he'd been when this picture was taken so I'd know where to start looking. Something.

I called Buddy, who listened to Mother's CIA hypothesis and surprised me by not laughing. "Anything's possible. I'll check it out."

"Something's wrong?" I was worried. Buddy sounded so glum.

"What could be wrong? Internal Affairs is ready to throw my hide at Buck's sharks, I'm investigating a pregnant-woman murder suspect, and the woman I'm crazy about is going to spend tonight in some other guy's bed." He paused. "Am I wrong?"

This wasn't Buddy's business. I didn't have to answer. But I didn't have to lie to him either. Why make my life a secret, even to spare his feelings? "Right on all counts, Buddy."

"Give me the number where I can reach you."

"What for?"

"In case something breaks."

"Nothing's going to break, Buddy. You just want his number."

"I get nervous when I don't know where you are."

"Then get nervous." I hung up, hating Buddy for making me hurt his feelings. Especially now when his life was turning to oatmeal.

I pulled off my sweater and headed for the shower. Michael was waiting, and, as usual, I was late.


While Michael made dinner he described a project he was designing, a movie-studio complex in four levels with six office buildings, a park, and recreational facility, to be financed in part by foreign investors. He'd been working on the project for more than six months and expected the financial negotiations to take six more.

"Especially negotiating through translators," I remarked.

"Not a problem. I'm fluent in French, conversant in German, and working on Spanish." Michael handed me a glass of wine, smiling at the expression on my face. "Don't look so impressed. The seminary trained me in language. I was supposed to hit the fast track to international church diplomacy."

That surprised me. "I've never thought of the church in terms of career." Then it made sense. "Why, of course. Catholic is the religion, church is the business. But you didn't become a church diplomat. You were a teacher."

"My choice. I wanted to contribute on a level I thought was more relevant." Michael sprinkled salt and pepper on the salmon he was preparing. "So here I am—secular, up to my neck in business, and enjoying it. My seminary counselor, Monsignor Monihan, knew me better than I knew myself."

So Michael had an in-house shrink, too, a man who'd believed he could tap into Michael's soul and describe the landscape to Michael. The only difference was that Michael's shrink had been right, whereas mine, Dr. Karen O'Brien, shrink to the stars and one daughter-detective, had looked into my psyche and only described the landscape she wanted to see.

I sat quietly listening to Michael, impressed by the methodical way that his mind worked. He had plans that he implemented step-by-step to his goals. Not for Michael were the sudden intuitions and the impulse to act on them immediately that seemed to be my professional MO. That is, if I had one. Not for him the reliance on timing and luck, on a clue popping up at just the right moment, on the bad guy making one fatal mistake. When Michael opened his eyes every morning,

he knew where he was going and exactly how to get there. I
woke every morning to a piñata ready to crack and rain God
knows what on my head.

How had we gotten together? I wondered. Since I'd
known him, our affair had been the only unscheduled event in
Michael's life, but in mine it was the only goal I'd ever pursued with persistence. In our relationship, I was Michael and
he was me and I'd be damned if I knew what that meant.
Something deep and profound or maybe just coincidental.

Michael was laying the salmon carefully in an oddly
shaped pan. "What's that?" I asked.

"A fish poacher. You've never seen one?"

"Never." I thought about it. "Maybe I have, but I don't
remember." I got up and wandered around the kitchen, examining the contents of cupboards and drawers. "I've never seen
half the stuff you have here. What's this?"

"Garlic press. Standard item in most kitchens."

"Not mine. I have a microwave for frozen dinners and a
big pan for boiling meals in a bag. And a frying pan I keep my
mail in."

Michael laughed. "You don't have to cook, Dutch."

"I know," I agreed cheerfully. "My mother didn't and I
don't. It's the only family tradition we have."

The salmon was terrific and so was the wine and later the
lovemaking that was fast becoming an art form. Eventually, I
pulled the blanket up over Michael's long body and kissed him.

"You're tucking me in," he observed.

"I am?" What an odd thing for me to do. "Do you
mind?"

"No. Tenderness counts." He rolled up on one elbow and
faced me. "Are you happy with me?"

"Yes. I am."

"I didn't ask if you love me. I know that you do. I asked
if you're happy."

"Then yes again."

"You don't want more than this? Don't you want marriage?"

I touched his face, wishing he didn't look so troubled. "On my list of things I can't live without, marriage comes somewhere between learning French and whitewater rafting."

"Why?"

"Because."

"Why because?"

"You're going to make me think about this, aren't you?"

"Yes. I am."

"Okay." I sat up in bed. "Because I've never connected the word *marriage* to love. I don't know why. Nor do I care. I do have other words, though. Words I connect to love."

"Such as."

"Commitment. Passion. Telepathy."

At that he laughed out loud. "Telepathy?"

"Yes. You and I knew each other the moment we met. Do you deny that?"

"No. You'd barely walked through the door of my office and I knew that I'd love you. And instantly wanted you."

"Why?"

"I don't know. It just happened. Like lightning."

"Me, too." I leaned over and kissed Michael's nose. "That part's a mystery. But this part isn't. I love you, Michael. No matter what happens, I'll love you for the rest of my life. Marriage won't make that truer or deeper."

For a long time Michael was silent. "You're right," he said finally.

It was my turn. "Now I have a question, Michael. What if we're together and the phone rings. And I have to be gone on a case for days, maybe weeks. What will you do?"

"I'll keep a light in the window until you get home. Is that all that's bothering you?"

"It's no small deal, Michael. Most men want their women to be . . . there."

"You just told me that no matter what happens, you'll love me forever. Don't you think I feel the same way? You can be here in my bed or off doing your job. My feelings won't change. Or my desire for you. Or my commitment." He kissed me. "I'm surprised you don't know that. Has our telepathy blown a fuse?"

"No. Just a temporary disconnect caused by an unreasonable doubt."

I fell asleep vowing that never again would I allow a barb thrown by Buddy or Mother through to my heart. My life was my case to solve, not theirs. With reasonable luck and timing and an occasional clue, I'd follow its mystery right to the end. And then die as they would, enlightened and confused.

Early the next morning the phone rang. Michael answered, then handed it to me. "For you. Buddy Hart."

I took the phone. "How did you get this number, Buddy?" I demanded.

"I'm a cop," he reminded me. "Meet me for breakfast. I have background on Cassie Sayres." He hung up.

"Buddy Hart's a cop I'm working with on the Westin case," I told Michael.

"He sounded like a cop. You want breakfast?"

"Thanks. No time." I headed for the shower. Fifteen minutes later I was kissing Michael goodbye. "See you later?"

"I'll be here." Michael opened the door. "This is going to be easier than you think, Dutch. Contrary to popular belief, true love can run smoothly."

I nodded but didn't say anything. We'd said all the important stuff last night.

I drove away thinking about the evening we'd shared,

how cozy and domestic it had felt. I'd loved every minute—
the cooking, the talking, and Michael. I couldn't wait to do it
again. It occurred to me that my life with Michael could be an
unbroken stream of those evenings, the day-to-day comfort of
coming home to a man who loved me. If I wanted.

Did I want? A good question.

By the time I turned the corner on Michael's street, I had
the answer. Not yet.

At Dupar's in the farmers' market, I slipped into the booth opposite Buddy.

"You followed me last night. I'm going to kill you."

"Kill me later. I have some leads."

"Cut the crap, Buddy. You have no right to spy on me."

"Your boyfriend's got money." Buddy poured half the
container of sugar in his coffee. "A ton."

"None of your business."

"He recently divorced or legally separated?"

Now I was curious. "What makes you think either?"

"That house isn't more than three or four years old. It's
not a house a man buys for himself. Where's his wife?"

"None of your *damn* business. I'm leaving."

I started to slide out of the booth; Buddy stopped me
cold. "Cassie Sayres has been married three times. I have the
husbands' names and addresses."

"Then what are we waiting for? Finish your coffee."

He did. I paid. We went.

We found the first husband, a Valley architect named Joe
Farina, in his office in Encino. We asked him about Cassie.

"She left me," he said. "We were married three months.
I thought we were happy. One day I came home and found
her packing. Said she'd made a mistake. Then she left. The
next time I heard from her was when her lawyer sent the di-

vorce papers. She didn't want anything except my name on the paper."

"Did she say what went wrong?" Buddy asked.

Joe shrugged. "She just said she couldn't write with me in the house. Said I used up all the space, there was no room for ideas. Tell you the truth, looking back, I think I was lucky. She didn't cook. She didn't screw. She just smoked and pounded on her goddamned typewriter. She wasn't a wife, if you know what I mean."

"Gotcha." Buddy shook hands with Joe, who nodded and smiled at me. "Nice to meet you."

I nodded back. We were halfway to the door when Farina asked, "She's not in any trouble, is she?"

"No," I assured him. "She couldn't be better."

"Glad to hear that," he said, meaning: *Thanks for not telling me.* The last news this man wanted was that the wife who'd abandoned him might need some help.

Our tour of Cassie's husbands took us to the Palisades, where we found Albert Cochran at a table in his very pleasant, very upscale garden restaurant. He jumped when Buddy mentioned Cassie. "Is she dead?"

"No," I answered quickly. "Why do you ask?"

"I haven't heard from her since the divorce and all of a sudden a policeman comes in." He shrugged. "What would you think?"

"Your former wife is alive and well," Buddy told him. "How long were you married?"

Cochran seemed to be calculating. "Twelve days."

"You're kidding," Buddy blurted. "What happened?"

"Beats me." Cochran shrugged. "We were on our honeymoon at the Mauna Kea on Hawaii, one of the finest hotels in the world. Built by Davis Rockefeller and a group of his friends. Everything top quality. Service impeccable. And the food—"

"What about Cassie?" Buddy interrupted. "What happened at the Mauna Kea?"

"I came back from a swim. The suite was empty. It was a suite, not a room, beautifully appointed. She was gone. Her clothes were gone. Her suitcase was gone. All she left was a note."

"Saying what?" I pressed him.

"Saying she'd made a mistake and she was sorry. That was it."

"That must have been hard to take," Buddy remarked.

"Between you and me, I wasn't with her long enough to get really attached. I've had dates longer than my marriage."

"What did you do?" I asked.

"I stayed another four days and had a fling with a cocktail waitress from another hotel. What was I supposed to do, sit around and wait for Miss Wacko?"

"Guess not." I tried to sound sympathetic. "You and Cassie divorced?"

"She sent papers. I sent them to my lawyer. He took care of everything. If I wasn't divorced, the man would have told me. That's what I pay him for. Anything else?"

"That about does it." Buddy closed his notebook.

"You should stay for lunch," Cochran advised. "We're featuring snapper."

"Some other time." Buddy and Cochran shook hands. Cochran smiled at me. "Nice to meet you."

So far, the only connection between Cassie's husbands was that neither of them shook hands with women.

We found Cassie's third husband, Larry Brand, a Century City attorney, eating lunch at Harry's Bar and Grill. He went dead white when Buddy mentioned Cassie's name. "Whatever she's done, I don't want to hear about it. I don't want to talk about her. I don't want to think about her. I just want to pretend I never knew her."

"This'll just take a minute." Buddy tried to soothe him. "How long were you married?"

"How long? You want to know how long?"

"If you don't mind, sir." Buddy was pushing cool cop to the limit.

"I'll tell you a story, then you tell me how long." Brand quickly sipped some water and went on. "Our wedding reception was at the Bel Air Hotel. A beautiful day. She was beautiful. I was beautiful. The ceremony was beautiful. We were cutting our beautiful wedding cake when Cassie threw down the knife, knocked over the cake, took off her wedding ring, threw it in my face, and ran out of the hotel and across the bridge, throwing her veil and her shoes at the swans as she went. Killed a swan with her pump. Cost me three hundred dollars. So, you tell me. How long was I married?"

"Ten minutes," I guessed.

"Ten minutes too long." Brand straightened his tie. "Go away. I've had one coronary and I have two plugged valves that haven't responded to angioplasty. I'll be damned if I'm going to upset myself talking about Cassie and die at this table."

"Thank you for your time, sir." We left quickly.

In the car, I asked Buddy, "What do you think?"

"Cassie Sayres is a deeply disturbed individual."

"Agreed. But is she a killer?"

"Who the hell knows?" Buddy stretched, arching his back like a cat, working out kinks. Then he grinned. "Well, at least I know someone who's worse at marriage than I am, and that's saying something. What say we go back to the Palisades and score some snapper?"

A Buddy cheered up was a Buddy hungry. The snapper was excellent.

Driving back, Buddy asked, "Where should I drop you?"

"At Dupar's, Buddy. That's where I left my car."

"Right." He'd forgotten. "Then where are you go-ing?"

I looked at my watch. "Work."

"Not the boyfriend's?"

"No."

"You'll go over there later, after work?"

"Possibly. Probably." I looked out the window. Orange-jacketed Cal Trans workers picking trash out of ground cover looked like pumpkins dotting the grass. "Why are you doing this to me, Buddy?"

"Doing what?" He lifted his eyebrows at me.

I wasn't impressed. "Save that innocent schoolboy act for the women you date. You're grinding me about Michael."

"Who's grinding? We're partners. Partners talk about their personal lives all the time. We are partners, aren't we, Dutch?"

I didn't answer. I tried to remember the moment when we'd become partners and couldn't. But we had. Like it or not, and I didn't, we were in this together until the end. "There's Dupar's."

Buddy walked me to my car. "I'll run a check on Richard Raymond, but it can't be through channels. Last thing I need is the CIA wondering why a cop in L.A. is poking his nose into their business. Those spooks like nothing better than cut-ting off noses. But I do have a couple of contacts."

"Contacts who owe you a favor?"

"Only kind to have. Where can I call you later?"

"I'll call you." I started the car. Buddy leaned in the win-dow. "When your ass needs saving, the boyfriend won't do it. I will, Dutch. I'm the guy who'll be there."

"And maybe it's your ass that I'll be saving. That's what partners are for."

• • •

At the office I found Margo yawning and listlessly typing a script. "Buck's been calling. He wants you on the set."

"Did he say why?"

"Does he ever?" She flexed her wrists, looking pained. "He's screaming for me to finish typing this script, but he keeps making changes. He's giving me carpal tunnel."

"You need some help," I told her, quickly adding: "Too bad I don't type."

Margo's eyes brimmed with sudden tears. "I used to love this job. I loved Frances and Cassie and Richard. Sure, Richard and Cassie were weird, but they were weird like relatives you eventually get used to, and they never forgot my birthday. And Frances was my friend. I'd cover for her when she took a long lunch and she'd cover for me. Now she's dead and Richard and Cassie are gone and I'm here alone typing the worst script I've ever read and nobody cares if I starve to death."

"I do," I told her. "I'll cover the phones. You go to lunch."

She brightened immediately. "You will? You mean it?"

"Sure. And don't worry about finishing that script. I hear that the show's bringing on a new writer."

Margo jumped up, overjoyed. "I'll have somebody to talk to! When's he coming?"

I wished I'd kept my mouth shut. Now I had to throw cold water. "Uh . . . he's not actually coming. He's going to . . . fax."

"Not another one!" Margo sat down, disappointed. "I hate fax machines. I hate writers who fax. Why can't they just come to work like normal people. And they're never at home when I call to ask where a scene goes or what word they're trying to spell. They just send whatever comes into their heads, then go to lunch or the beach or to buy a new Mercedes. And I'm supposed to make sense of it." Her long, stiff fingers pulled at her fiery-red curls. She was thinking. "Well, whoever this writer is, he's got to be better than Buck. In this script I'm typing, Buck is playing himself, his evil twin brother, and their maniacal mother. I think he ripped it off from a movie."

"Sounds familiar," I agreed. "Go eat."

Before Margo left, she apologized. "I'm sorry I bent your ear, but I've had no one to talk to. I know I should look for another job, but Buck's been working me twelve hours a day. Why can't things be like they used to be?"

"Beats me."

Margo gave me the numbers of three restaurants to call in case of an emergency. In her excitement about finally going to lunch, she couldn't decide if she wanted Italian, Mexican, or Chinese. She'd make up her mind on the way.

The moment she left, the fax bell rang. I jumped up, feeling like Pavlov's dog. The cover letter grabbed my attention. The material about to pour out of the fax was a revision of Richard Raymond's *Hot Pursuit*, sent from the Saturnia Health and Beauty Spa in Florence.

I called Buddy. "Forget Brazil. He's in Italy."

Buddy was excited. "Give me the number of the spa."

While I waited for Buddy to call me back, I scanned the pages the machine spit out, disappointed to find that at the end the hero was still mysteriously dead. Only the woman he'd been chasing had changed. She was actually onstage, real rather than fantasy. She was tall, agile, had long blonde hair, and smoked Tiparillos. She never spoke but appeared now and then, always moving away from the hero. In one scene he looks in the mirror and sees her reflected behind him. When he turns around, she's gone.

This revision was no better than the first script, if anything more aggravating, like a joke without a punch line. Why write a mystery woman and a mystery death if everything was still a mystery at the end? If Buddy found Richard, that was the first question I'd ask him.

Buddy called back. "The spa disavows any knowledge of Richard Raymond. According to them, he isn't there, never was, and never will be. Sounds like this spa is a CIA cover. I'll keep checking."

"I'll call if he faxes anything else."

Two hours later Margo returned, bringing egg rolls, lasagna, chips, guacamole, and two wrist splints. "The man at the medical supply house told me these are the cure for carpal tunnel." She slipped them on. "How do they look?"

"Like the Velcro version of Wonder Woman's bracelets. Didn't you eat?"

"I couldn't decide, so I went to all three and brought it all back. Want some?"

We had gone through the chips and were hitting the lasagna when Buddy called back. "Dead end, Dutch. Richard Raymond is definitely *not* CIA."

"You sure?"

"I got it from the source, honey. This guy's played poker with Deep Throat and knows which politicians are in Heidi Fleiss's notebook. Richard Raymond's just swung from *up* to *midair*."

I hung up feeling frustrated.

An hour later the fax bell rang. Neither of us jumped. We were too full. Eventually, I ambled to the machine, plucked out the paper, and read. It was a message from Richard to Cassie. *I'm coming home soon. I have much to share with you. I think of you every day. Take care, Richard.*

I called Buddy. "Dinner at my place. I've got something."

*Chapter 13*

**M**y fake Tiffany lamp cast green-gold shadows on Buddy as he scanned the fax.

"Call Interpol," I urged him.

He scanned the fax. "Can't, Dutch. He's not wanted for anything. Besides, this fax says he's coming home."

"He says *soon*. For Richard *soon* could be a week or a month or never." Then I had an idea. "Buddy, listen, what if Richard Raymond never left L.A.? What if he hired people all over the world to send faxes with his name on them? Even his script. Cassie Sayres knows him best and she told me he's never written anything like it. What if he's been here all along, hiding somewhere? What if he put the bomb in my car? What if he's close by right now, waiting to kill me?"

Buddy thought about it. "I hate this case, Dutch. Every time we think we're about to crack it, something else pops up and it all slides away."

"I know. All we can do is keep going." I tossed my TV remote control into Buddy's lap. "There's a football game on. I'll be back."

Buddy scowled. "I'm supposed to sit here watching the Rams roll over Denver while you're at the boyfriend's?"

"I'm going to see Cassie. This fax is for her. Maybe she can tell me how Richard defines *soon*."

"Good luck." Buddy snapped on the set and was cheering the Rams before I even closed the door.


I found Cassie in her room, hunched over her computer. When I handed her the fax, she read it, then squealed with delight. "He's coming back!" She threw her arms around me. "Richard's coming back. How can I thank you!"

And with that, she kissed me full on the mouth, an exuberant little girl's kiss that quickly matured to the woman variety, intent, intense, and exploding with passion. I was so surprised I just stood there, my arms at my sides, while Cassie tried to suck my lips from my face.

Suddenly she jumped back and covered her face with her hands. "Oh, my God, I'm sorry. I didn't mean to jump at you like that, but you are an attractive woman and I forgot myself and . . . oh, my." Cassie slumped against the wall, her face gone dead white.

"Don't faint." I put my arm around her and helped her toward the bed. "Do you want some water? Should I call a nun?"

"I'm sorry. I'm sorry," she moaned. She sank back on the bed.

"Look, it's all right." I sat down next to her. "Forget it."

"It's not all right, not for me!" Cassie wailed. "I've been fighting it and fighting it. I'm so tired." She closed her eyes and sighed. "I don't know how to say this, Dutch, but I don't think I like men."

No shit, Sherlock, I thought, but I didn't think this was the time to bring up her ex-husbands. "Okay, so you don't like men. You like women. So what?"

She looked at me gratefully, then sighed. "It isn't that

easy. I wasn't raised that way. My mother would kill me. My father would die. The nuns would be shocked out of their wimples. What will the baby say?"

"One thing at a time," I told her. "Have the baby and sort out the rest later."

"Later? I never thought of later." She sat up and smoothed her hair. "I don't have to think about this now, do I? I mean, just because I've suddenly realized how and what I am doesn't mean I have to run out and actually do anything about it, does it? Anyway, what would I do? I'm not a joiner, so organizations are out of the question, and I already own three pair of Birkenstock shoes. I don't have to do anything! What a relief!" She smiled, something she did rarely but well. "You like men, don't you?"

"A lot."

"I thought so. I've never seen you with anybody, but when I just kissed you . . ."

"Dud?"

"Yeah." She smiled. "Friends?"

"Sure. You're okay?"

"I think so." She got up and went to her computer. "The nice thing is I have plenty to do. There's the script and the baby and Richard's coming home!"

When I left she was typing and gestating and waiting for Richard, activity enough even for Cassie.

When I got home, Buddy looked up from the game. "The bums are losing."

I didn't ask which bums. "Take Cassie Sayres off the list of suspects. She's keeping a secret all right, but it's personal."

"Murder is personal. What's her secret?"

"She's just discovered she's gay."

Buddy gawked. "No shit? What do you mean discovered? Didn't she know?"

"Apparently not. I suppose my mother would say she always knew and her whole life has been denial, but according to the lady herself, her true sexual preference has come as a news bulletin."

Buddy squirmed. "You mean that can happen? You can wake up one morning and discover you're gay? You just open your closet and there you are? Jesus Christ, Dutch!"

"You worried it's going to happen to you?" I laughed.

"Me? Are you crazy?" Buddy hit the remote-control button. Denver and the Rams disappeared. He got up and stretched elaborately. "Okay. You got home in one piece. Cassie Sayres is off the list. Want to go down to Malley's for a beer?"

"Maybe some other time. I'm going to bed."

"Here?"

"Where else?"

"These days, who knows?"

"Buddy."

"Okay. I'll call you tomorrow. The way things are looking, Amy Westin committed suicide, then hacked herself into stew. We couldn't be colder."

After he went, I sat in the wing chair, still warm from Buddy, and hit the remote button. Denver and the Rams popped in, two yards from where Buddy had left them.

I thought about Buddy swaggering into Malley's, joining his cop buddies for a cop beer. Clearly, Cassie's revelation had rattled him. Not so much about being gay. Buddy's self-doubts, whatever they were, didn't include his masculinity. It was more the idea he could wake up one day and find himself to be someone he'd never met. If it had happened to Cassie, it could happen to anyone. A thought scary enough to rattle even Buddy. Enough to rattle anyone. Even me.

My newspaper comes at six A.M. By then, I've usually showered and nuked my instant coffee. I read the paper slowly, front to back—national news, local news, international news—enjoying the sensation that I'm sitting center stage with the world on view revolving around me.

This morning I couldn't concentrate. All the news I wanted to know was lying somewhere in the back of my head, hidden by cobwebs. I didn't have a clue and that's just what I needed. I knew there had to be one somewhere in the debris of this case, hiding in plain sight, laughing at me. I knew because a murder always has clues. Killers, except the pros, don't rehearse. They improvise and they make mistakes. They're sloppy and messy and they establish a pattern, and when they kill again, they repeat it. And I wasn't seeing it.

I put down the paper and stared at the wall, which meant I was staring at my photo blowups, the crooked mosaic of my father. And finally I saw something. I looked closer.

I looked past his crooked smile to the house behind him and focused on the porch, on the glass milk bottles in the wire holder. On the sides of the bottles were ridges of raised glass and, between the ridges, soft indentations. The name of the dairy was printed on the glass.

I untacked the blowup. I'd need one more enlargement with computer enhancement. If I could read the name of the dairy, I could track down the company. Maybe, just maybe, with luck and timing, they'd still have old records of their routes. If they did, I could match the house's address numbers to a street and a city and then . . .

I snatched up the phone. My call woke Buddy, who sounded hung over. "Christ, it's still dark!"

"Buddy, I need a favor. I want you to take this photo of my father into the police lab and ask them to enlarge the section I'll circle. Will you do that for me?"

"Your old man? This couldn't wait for another two hours?"

"Will you or won't you?"

"Okay. I'll even stop by and get it."

"I'll nuke you some instant."

My offer must not have appealed to Buddy. When I opened the door an hour later, there he was, balancing foil-wrapped plates piled with pancakes and sausage, a large thermos of very hot, real coffee, and a gardenia plant. He greeted me with a heartfelt announcement: "You're the worst pain in the ass I've ever had for a partner."

"And you're the best, Buddy. Come in."

I wasted a week running from the office to the set, looking for clues in all the wrong places. In the office, my company made Margo so happy she chattered nonstop, mostly about heavy-metal musicians and over-the-counter remedies for yeast infections. Both topics were strictly conjecture, as she'd never had either, but she wanted to be ready in case.

On the set, Buck projected high spirits. "So the network assholes are bringing in a writer. What the fuck do I care? I'm still producing and acting and directing. Hell, I'm a fucking auteur!" Everybody laughed as required, then Buck yelled "Action" and the tape rolled, capturing for all time Buck as he was, including the dangerous glint in his eye. For all Buck's bravado, he had lost this round.

Back in the office, Margo had acclimated to the novelty of company and was quietly working. I scanned *Variety*, skimming stories about movers and shakers I'd never met who were winging off to Gotham and jetting in from Rome. The skies over L.A. seemed to be full of these people transporting their ambitions first-class. If a collision occurred, we on the ground would be showered with a thousand pocket electronic Rolodexes and two thousand copies of *The Art of the Deal*.

A knock at the door interrupted my scanning. Margo and

I looked at each other. This was an office. No one ever knocked.

"Stay there, Margo. I'll get it."

I opened the door with one hand under my jacket close to my gun.

"Hi." It was Cassie, carrying a large box. "I couldn't open the door, so I knocked with my foot."

I took the box from her. "What are you doing here?"

She slipped past me into the office, where Margo jumped up and hugged her. "I'm so glad to see you. Does this mean things are normal?"

"When were they ever?" Cassie laughed. "But I've been thinking. When Richard comes back—"

Margo squealed. "Richard's coming back! When?"

"Soon," Cassie told her. "When he does, I want to be here. So I'm going to work here during the day, then at night go back to where I'm living." She glanced at me. "What do you think?"

"Sounds like a plan."

Cassie nodded. "It's the only one I could think of. I'm not good at plotting real life." She turned back to Margo. "I need your help. I'm going to be working in Richard's office. I don't want anyone, especially Buck, knowing I'm here."

"I won't say a word," Margo promised. "You keep the door shut. I'll bring you lunch. No one will know that you're back."

"Perfect." Cassie took a script from the box and handed it to Margo. "This is finished."

Margo took it. "I'll retype it." She laid the script on her desk, then took Cassie's box from me. Then Cassie and Margo went into Richard's office, chattering.

I stayed where I was, thinking that the concept of *normal* was as much conjecture in this office as musicians and yeast remedies. I glanced at the script, then picked it up, staring at the title page.

A second later I was in Richard's office holding the script under her nose and demanding, "Okay, explain this."

"Explain what?" Cassie seemed mystified.

"Explain why this page reads: 'The Case of the Mauled Mobster' written by D. O'Brien."

"Oh, that." Cassie took the script. "You know I can't use my own name, so I borrowed yours. Or part of it anyway. Don't worry. Buck won't recognize it. He'll be sure the initial stands for a man's name and there are a million O'Briens."

"Buck'll notice and go nuts," I predicted.

"Then let him." Cassie was adamant. "If I can't write under my own name, then I have to write under a name I know. I can't just make up a person."

"But you do, every day."

"The people I make up are characters. Writers are real." Cassie put her small hand on my arm. "I'm trying to learn the difference, Dutch. Will you help me?"

What could I do? "Okay. Borrow my name or whatever part of it works. But when Buck comes bellowing that I'm fucking up his show, what would you like me to say?"

"Tell him you have a third cousin named Dennis who takes his stories from real police files. Tell him Dennis lives in Amsterdam, Holland, and you've never met him. Tell him Dennis is married to a Norwegian woman who is the illegitimate daughter of a Mafia don and the female mayor of a small fishing village. Tell him Dennis has one blue eye and one brown and is being considered for a Nobel Prize."

"Think that will convince him?"

Cassie nodded solemnly. "You can convince anyone of anything if you use enough detail. That's the secret of politics."

"You just made up a writer named Dennis. Change his last name to Murphy and use that."

"But then I wouldn't feel any rapport for the name because it would only be a character. Next thing I know, I'll feel like a character, too." Cassie looked at me anxiously. "Is this really such a big deal?"

I hesitated. Yes. Your name is the only thing that's yours absolutely and forever unless of course some road-show prince comes along with a ring, in which case most women toss their names over their shoulder along with the rose-and-baby's-breath bouquet. But not me. I'll never do it. Not even for Michael. I'm O'Brien forever. And now Cassie wants to make off with my name.

Cassie was waiting, anxiously plucking at her hair. Her long, black eyelashes fluttered. "Dutch, I'm having a baby alone."

Whose fault is that? I wanted to ask her. Who raped the literatus with the stellar IQ? Who . . . ? I sighed. Who hasn't a clue as to what she's gotten herself into? Who's in way over her head? Who should have a husband? Or a lover? Or a friend? Or maybe a keeper, someone to stand by her when she wakes up to what she's done? "Use my name, Cassie. We'll worry about it later."

Cassie hugged me. "I love *later*," she enthused. "Later makes everything simple. Thank you, Dutch."

"You're welcome." I patted her shoulder, deciding I'd never tell Buddy. He'd snicker and murmur *sucker* not just once but three times a day until the millennium.

When I left the office, Cassie was typing, Margo was dusting, and normal was a promise that hung in the air.

I knew better than to stop at a deserted ATM machine at night. Even machines with people milling around don't come with a guarantee that one of the millers isn't a bad guy willing to shoot you dead for a handful of twenties. I knew better and did it anyway, approaching the machine without even looking around, like some hick tourist from Ashcan, Alabama.

I'd just punched in my code when he grabbed me from behind, his arm around my throat. Out of the corner of my eye, I saw a knife flash in his hand. I had a couple of seconds.

I lunged forward to throw him off balance, grabbing wildly at his fingers. I spun in a circle with him hanging on my back, wheezing into my ear. Then something that felt like a fingernail scratched my side at the same time my fingers found one of his and pulled it back sharply. It snapped like a string bean. The louse gave a muffled cry, dumped me, and ran off, a figure in black, wearing a ski mask.

Later, after I'd called myself every name I could think of, cleaned myself up, and disinfected the knife scratch, I called Buddy and told him what happened.

"Dummy," he said. "I'm coming right over."

While I waited for Buddy I pondered the assault. Something wasn't quite kosher.

"He didn't rob me," I greeted Buddy.

"Maybe he didn't have time."

"He didn't try. He didn't wait for the machine to spit out the money. He just tried to kill me."

Buddy grinned. "Maybe we're getting somewhere. You say you broke his finger?"

"Sounded like it."

"And your assailant was definitely male?"

"Absolutely."

"You're thinking that the guy who attacked you could be our killer?"

"Possibly."

"Great." Buddy closed his notebook. "Tomorrow morning first thing, we'll go see if Buck Stevens has any bent digits. Do you need anything, Dutch?"

"Just a brain."

"Tell me about it." Buddy's good-night kiss grazed my cheek. "Lock the door after me."

Buddy went. I locked the door, then went back to my wing chair, where I sat with the lights off, feeling fragile and stupid, a one-two combination that kept me on the canvas all night, replaying the fight in my head. It took me a couple of hours to get the replay right, but when I did, my assailant lay at my feet dead.

Not only were all of Buck's digits intact, they were all in the air, rosy and wiggling.

"Why is he waving his arms around like that?" Buddy whispered as we watched Buck from behind the scenery.

"He's acting," I explained. "That's the mannerism he uses when Stone has figured out the case. He started using it on *Sheriff Buck and His Banjo* and says that people wrote in, they liked it so much."

"People write in about crap like that?"

"Buck says so. Every time a director suggests that his little war dance might be a tad over the top, he says that his audience loves it and he's got the letters to prove it. Nobody's ever seen any letters. Now we know Buck's a ham, but he didn't attack me."

"Not last night, anyway," Buddy agreed.

A few days later Buck summoned Margo to his trailer. She returned an hour later, looking flushed and unhappy, carrying a pile of personal correspondence he wanted her to type.

The typing wasn't the problem.

"He started telling me how pretty I am," Margo reported indignantly. "He said I should be in front of the camera, not stuck in the office. He said he wants to make me a star. What does he think I am, some bimbo?"

"What did you say?" I asked quickly, knowing that this could be important.

"Nothing. I just gave him one of those smiles that doesn't mean anything, then got out of there as fast as I could."

"Good. If he asks you down there again, and it's a safe bet that he will, don't get within grabbing distance, don't get him angry, and don't smile. He'll take it as an invitation and move in. Just ask him what he wants and wait for him to tell you. He'll almost certainly make up something about work. Then you come back."

"And what if he . . . you know?" Margo went shy.

I showed her where to kick, how high, and how hard. She practiced on the door a few times, then turned to me for approval. I nodded. "You got it. Now don't be afraid to use it."

"I won't." She suddenly relaxed. "I feel so much better."

"Karate'll do that. It's not exactly a gun, but it's not Swiss cheese either."

That afternoon Margo handed me the phone. "For you. Somebody named Buddy."

Buddy came straight to the point. "I'm in the studio commissary, Dutch. One of Amy Westin's arms has been found in a cupboard, behind the frozen yogurt machine."

By the time I got down there, Buddy's boys were fine-combing the place for evidence and Buddy was interviewing the hysterical kitchen worker who'd opened the cupboard.

"The arm's still frozen," Buddy told me. "Whoever put it there had to have done it within the last couple of hours. It was wrapped in a Hefty bag."

Buddy and the boys cordoned off the studio, then

checked every car as it went through the gate. Late that night they still hadn't found anyone who couldn't explain why he or she was on the lot.

"Either the killer dumped the arm and took off or, more likely, the killer works here."

Late the next afternoon, Margo returned from Buck's trailer looking flushed but very happy. "It works!"

"You kicked him?"

"And how! He sent word to the set that filming's done for the day. He claims to have food poisoning." Margo laughed. "I can't believe I did it."

I could, and though I was glad she had, I was nervous for her. The only link between Amy Westin and me had been our mutual rejection of Buck. "Do you live alone, Margo?"

"No. I share a house with three roommates."

"Good. Go straight home after work and stay there. Tell your roommates you need their company. Tell them what happened with Buck."

Margo's lower lip trembled. "I'm in trouble, aren't I?"

"Not if you do as I say." I patted her shoulder. "I'm not trying to scare you, honey."

"But you are," she said. "You're scaring me silly."

In the end, I drove Margo home, handed her over to her roommates, and waited on the porch till I heard the dead bolt drop in the lock.

When I got home, Buddy was waiting for me in the hallway. "I have good news and bad news and good news. What do you want first?"

"What's that under your arm?" I pointed at the cardboard tube he was carrying.

"Your blowup." He handed it to me. "I take it I'm invited in."

Inside I unrolled the blowup and showed it to Buddy.
"Look, on the milk bottles, the name of the company. Morgan
Dairy."

"Don't get too excited," Buddy warned. "For all you
know, this is just a dead end."

"It won't be! I know it!" I threw my arms around Buddy.
"I'm going to find my father!"

Buddy hugged me tightly, going along with my optimism
so long as it involved hugging. Finally, I kissed his cheek and
stepped back. "Thank you, Buddy. You're a pal. What's the
news?"

He'd frowned at *pal*, but answered my question. "Good
news. We found your assailant. You know a guy named Donald Miller?"

"Miller? Miller?" I rolled the name around in my memory. It slipped into a groove and stuck. "He's the squatter I
threw out of Mrs. Ramirez's apartment!"

"That's him. Only the way he tells the story he was an
ideal tenant only a few days late with the rent when you broke
into his apartment, threatened him with a gun, and threw him
out bodily. Any truth to that story?"

"Absolutely not. He'd already been evicted. I just showed
him the door."

"With a gun in your hand?"

"Would you answer that question if you were me,
Buddy?"

"I never asked. Anyway, this Miller decided you're the
reason he's one of the homeless. He's been following you
around for weeks, waiting for a chance to pay you back."

I shuddered. I'd never even sensed him watching. Me,
who'd been trained to watch other people.

Buddy seemed to know what I was thinking. "If somebody really wants to get you, he will. You know that as well
as I do, Dutch."

I knew, but I didn't want to think about it. "What's the other good news and the bad news?"

"The good news is that forensics has found hair under Amy Westin's fingernails that has to belong to the killer. This is the break we've been looking for. The bad news is that the sample is seriously deteriorated with freezer burn, so testing will take some time."

"Buddy, this is great. The good news is terrific and the bad news isn't that bad. Once the lab processes the hair, we'll round up the suspects and clip them."

Buddy laughed. "It won't be as simple as that, but close, very close. Buy me a beer at Malley's?"

"Anything you want."

Malley's was crowded and hot and noisy. The beer was cold and went down easy. We sat at the bar with the other cops, bullshitting about nothing. Every time Buddy caught my eye, we grinned at each other. This was good, very good, as good as it gets with real partners.

The next morning I made a few calls to offices downtown and discovered that Morgan Dairy had been bought out by Vita Industries sometime in the Seventies.

I was there when Vita Industries opened for business. In the accounting department I found an earnest-looking young man who told me his name was Bill Yates. I introduced myself and told him why I was there. He didn't hold out much hope. "I suppose there could be old route records somewhere, but finding them—I don't know."

"I'll pay for your time," I offered. "With a bonus for doing it fast."

"I could use the money. I'm a medical student." He hesitated for a moment, then he decided. "I'll give it a shot."

I pulled out a hundred dollars. "Here's a down payment on a stethoscope. Call me when you've got something."


When I got to the office, Cassie was alone, hunting through Margo's desk for paper clips.

"Where's Margo?" I asked.

"She called from a friend's house. She said she'll be in later."

Instinct raised the hair on my neck. "Margo's all right?"

Cassie looked up. "Sure. Why wouldn't she be?"

"No reason." I helped Cassie find the clips, which she carried like treasure into Richard's office. After she closed the door behind her, I made a pot of coffee, Instant Vanilla Mocha Crème, dashed in some cinnamon and Dairy Mate, poured it into a cup, and sipped. It tasted like a McDonald's vanilla-and-Styrofoam shake only hot, but I hadn't had breakfast. I sat at Margo's desk, debating with myself about calling Buddy.

I was still debating when the door opened and a tall, striking blonde came in. As the door closed behind her she hesitated, looking expectantly in my direction. And I stared at her.

Her hair was platinum, cut in a short bob, longer in the front than the back and so shiny it looked like a neat, chic halo. She was wearing a black suit, elegantly tailored, with a black silk turtleneck blouse and espresso-brown stockings. Her long legs were well muscled. Her shoes were Italian. Her makeup was perfect, subtle yet defined—taupe shadow, coffee liner, three coats of mascara, peach blush, and nearly nude lip gloss. As she walked toward me I thought of Mother's collection of Thirties *Vogue* covers, with their elegant, stylized models, elongated women with incredible panache.

This woman was all of that and more. This woman was Richard Raymond.

"Hello, Dutch," he said, smiling shyly. His voice was higher, softer, somewhere between Brenda Vaccaro and Lauren Bacall. Husky, as in sexy. Not masculine if you think Clint Eastwood, but in the ballpark if you think Tom Cruise.

"Hello, Richard," I answered. "What's new?"

He/she chuckled deep in his/her throat. "My name is Roberta."

"Okay." Ever adaptable though thoroughly astonished, I prepared to let Richard Raymond be whoever he wanted. So long as I got to ask questions. "Are you . . . I mean . . . um . . ." Some questions are easier to ask than others.

"Do you mean am I real or just a cross-dresser?" Richard supplied the question then answered it. "I'm a woman. I always knew I was born to be female, but sometimes nature makes a mistake. With the help of several competent doctors, I rectified that mistake. Now I'm what I was always meant to be. And I'm happy."

"Good." He looked happy. And fashionable. And groomed to the max. Like a Hollywood wife, only with taste. And I still had a million questions. "Isn't a sex-change operation complicated?"

"Very."

"All those hospitals in all those places? And all the tests you've had since I started here. It was all about the sex change, wasn't it?"

"Of course. The hormone therapy alone began nearly a year ago." He shook his head, then looked surprised as his hair floated around his face. Still getting used to the female pelt. "I didn't exactly advertise what I was doing. Just in case I changed my mind. Though I knew I wouldn't. How could I not decide to be what I am?"

He'd been glancing surreptitiously at Cassie's office and now he did it again. This time he sighed. "I'm so disappointed Cassie's not here."

"But she is," I said quickly. "She's working in your office."

"Why?" His voice deepened. Suzanne Pleshette. "She never did that before."

I got up, noticing that Roberta was still a lot taller than me, even taller than Richard in her three-inch heels. "It's a long story. Maybe Cassie should tell you herself."

Roberta hurried toward his office, then stopped with his hand on his doorknob. He cleared his throat, stalling. "Uh . . . Dutch . . . would you go in with me?"

Would I? I'd buy tickets for this. To see this, Mother would give her next face peel. Who wouldn't want to go in with Richard? Except Buddy, who'd call it a freak show. "Glad to, Richard . . . uh . . . Roberta."

I opened the office door and stepped back, gesturing Richard in. He stepped past me, his eyes on Cassie, who was sitting at his desk typing furiously on her computer. She didn't look up. "Margo, I'm out of cigarettes," she said. "So don't buy me any. Not even if I beg."

Richard moved toward her slowly. "Hello, Cassie," he said.

Now she looked up, her eyes unfocused, her head swinging at the sound of his voice. "Richard! You're here!"

Cassie flew from behind the desk and straight to Richard. She flung herself into his arms and held him tightly, chanting "I've missed you. I've missed you. I've . . ." With her arms around him and looking down, she'd glimpsed his Italian pumps. She blinked, then looked again, seeing the stockings, then the skirt hem, a fashionably discreet two inches above his knee. She blinked rapidly, not trusting her vision, then stepped back and looked at him. Her face drained of color. She swayed. He caught her.

"I'm sorry." He held her tightly. "I've shocked you. But I couldn't tell anyone, not even you. And you're the only one I wanted to tell, the only opinion that mattered." He stepped away from her, bending to examine her face. He looked like he was about to cry. "You're repulsed."

"No! Just very surprised," she cried, then frowned thoughtfully. "But not shocked. Something inside me always knew. But I didn't know what I knew. I just knew I didn't know. My whole life's like that. Maybe I find out what I know when it's time." Her hands reached for his face. She held it tenderly, then kissed him full on the mouth. Richard/Roberta didn't resist. His eyes widened, then closed. He kissed her back. Finally Cassie released him, then with a laugh: "Richard, you're beautiful!"

"Not as beautiful as you," Richard told her. "I can't believe that you missed me. You look almost radiant. You've even gained weight."

"I'm pregnant," Cassie said triumphantly. "I'm having a baby. Isn't that wonderful?"

Now Roberta looked shocked. And unhappy. "I didn't know you were . . . with . . . anyone."

Cassie laughed. "I'm not." She glanced at me, a look that both pleaded and warned. "I had artificial insemination. Dutch went with me."

Richard glanced at me. I nodded. Well, why not? Cassie's conception by Joshua was as artificial as insemination ever gets. So why not bend the past for the sake of the future?

Richard grinned, not his usual ear-to-ear, but a softer, gentler Roberta grin, sweet and frosted with lip gloss. He folded Cassie in his arms. "I couldn't be happier."

Obviously, neither could she. And even more obviously, I was no longer needed by either Richard/Roberta or Cassie Sayres.

I left the office quietly, closing the door behind me.

Once outside, I resisted an urge to shout "Hallelujah!" only because I knew they'd hear me. But I was thrilled, shot through with an electric current of joy, exhilarated beyond all reason.

Despite the odds, despite the world, despite what they'd been taught was right and wrong, despite the rules made by dusty old men, despite what people would think . . . and say . . . and condemn . . . despite their pasts and in the face of their future, they'd decided to be what they were.

I applauded. With my whole heart. And softly, so as not to disturb them.

I was on my way out of the office when Margo came in, sobbing hysterically. She threw herself at me, screaming, "He's dead!"

I held her away from me, shaking her a little. "Who's dead?"

"My kitty, Alice Cooper," she cried. "I came out of the house and found him hanging from a tree. It was so awful I ran down the street to a friend's house. I tried to call you, but you weren't home."

"I'm sorry." I patted her back, trying to soothe her. "This is terrible and I'm sorry it happened. I can't let you go back home."

"Where will I go?" Margo had the look of a very small girl who's been badly hurt and is waiting for some grown-up to fix it.

"I know somewhere safe."

I took Margo's hand and, with a regretful glance at Cassie's closed door, took her out of the office, eased her into my car, and drove her to Mother's clinic.

## Chapter 14

"The girl's in shock. Of course I'll look after her." Mother leaned against the front of her desk, looking down at me. "This has something to do with that murder you're investigating, doesn't it?"

"Yes."

"And that's all you're going to tell me?"

"For the moment."

"Until it's over?"

"Yes."

Mother walked around her desk and sat in her chair. She was wearing glasses. Since I'd never seen her in glasses before, I stared at her face as I would at a stranger. She was as beautiful with glasses as without them, but different, less like a still life and more like a sculpture.

"I like your hair," I told her. I did.

"I'm letting the roots grow out."

"Oh?" I was surprised. "What color is it?"

"Who gives a shit?" She took off her glasses. "I'll give you one million in cash to go back to law school."

For the first time in my life Mother had truly shocked me. "You don't mean that."

"I do. I'll write out the check this minute."

"No! I don't want your money. And I don't understand. What happened to all your shrink stuff about establishing transference and not interfering and talking it out for a decade or two?"

"To hell with all that. You're about to do something dangerous. I can feel it and smell it. You're going to get yourself killed."

"That's ridiculous." I laughed just to underline *ridiculous*. "I never do anything dangerous."

"You do. You just don't tell me about it."

"No. Honest to God, Mother, I never—"

"Shut up!" she shouted at me. "I'm your mother, goddamn it. I know!"

I could only stare, wondering what alien had made off with my mother and left this pod-mother in her place. This woman, whoever she was, sounded like the mothers in books I'd read, mothers who reacted emotionally, mothers who'd never been analyzed. In a way she was interesting or would be, once I was ten miles away.

I decided to reason with her, which meant lie. "I'm working with a police officer named Buddy Hart, who takes care of all the dangerous stuff."

"He's good, this Buddy?" She grasped eagerly at Buddy, wanting to believe, instantly hopeful. Who was this woman?

"Buddy's the best. I couldn't be safer."

She sighed. "You wouldn't lie to me, would you?"

"Of course not." I eased out of the chair, went around the desk, and kissed the top of her head. "You're worried about nothing."

"I hope so." She looked up at me with eyes so warm and soft I couldn't help thinking of Bambi's mother. "You're my daughter, Demeter. I love you."

"Me, too," I told her, thinking that this part might be close to the truth. "I'll call you tomorrow."

I drove away from the clinic feeling that some torch might have been passed. But what kind of torch it was and who had passed it to whom, I hadn't a clue.

Back in the office, the day was ending and Cassie's door was still shut. I debated whether or not to knock, then decided against it. I'd wait as patiently as I could. If they didn't come out in another ten minutes, I could always yell "Fire."

But they did, five minutes later, their arms around each other's waists and their lovely faces glowing.

"Where's Margo?" Cassie asked me, not really caring.

"Not here. I'll give her a message."

"Tell her we'll be gone for a few days." Roberta delivered the message. "We have a lot to talk over. We'll call."

"I'll tell her. Have a nice time."

I don't think either of them heard me as they left, smiling into each other's eyes.

Alone, I ran my hands through my hair. What a day. Dead cats, happy endings, mothers from space going gray. I knew I wanted to tell Michael about it. I wanted to see the look on his face and ask him what he thought it all meant.

But most of all, I wanted to go home, take a hot shower, and get into bed. Alone. Where I could form my own opinion first.

It wasn't that easy.

At home, I stood in the shower a very long time, letting the hot water beat down on my head, pound over my shoulders, and rain down my back. Gradually my muscles uncoiled and tension rolled off, disappearing down the drain with my rose-scented soap.

Wrapped in a towel, I drip-dried while brushing my teeth. In the bedroom I sat on the edge of my bed, massaging rose-scented lotion into every inch of my skin, starting with my throat and ending with my soles. Finally I slipped into my robe, dried my hair, and went to sit in my wing chair, cleaned and polished within an inch of my life and much too awake. My ritual had failed me. I was wired.

I switched on the Tiffany. In the gold-green light that washed over me, I examined my fingers. Square and sturdy with short clipped nails, they bore no resemblance to Mother's long tapered fingers tipped with perfect pale ovals.

They were the fingers of the man in the photos tacked on the wall, my father's hands, the hands of a stranger who'd left me a grab bag of genetic surprises before disappearing. Some of them I could see, like my fingers, but the rest were a mystery. Where was my father in me, in the drive and emotion Mother would call personality? In the tilt of my head and the rhythm of my speech? Was he stubborn like me? Did he like spicy food? Like me, did he experience a physical response to music, a literal lifting of the heart? Was his music the background score of his time, the slow Fifties ballads, or did he like jazz? Warm or cool, hip or square, what was his music? Did he hum under his breath? Was he a loner like me? Had he ever tried to picture himself as an animal and come up with the image of a wolf, warily circling the edge of the campfire, wanting the warmth, the food, and the company but not at the price of leaving the wild? Did he laugh? What kind of jokes did he like? Did he see the humor in everything human, including himself?

Was he alive? If so, where was he and did his thoughts ever, even once in the mythical blue moon, turn to me?

Was he dead? If so, did he die alone or with someone there, holding his hand and saying goodbye? And how did he die? Was it violently or by accident or of some disease that had carried him off slowly or quickly and that he may have passed on in his grab bag to me?

Who was he and why should I care? There was only one reason. The clues to him were clues to me, and seeing a case through to the end is my calling, the motor that drives me in my unlikely profession, the reward and the curse of the private detective.

At three o'clock I gave up the notion of sleep, so I got up and nuked some coffee. Taking my grocery-list notepad, I hunkered down in the wing chair and started reviewing the case from the top, putting the events into chronological order. There had to be sense here, no matter how elusive. Later, when the pieces had fallen into place, I'd be amazed I hadn't seen it. Amazed and frustrated and complaining to Buddy, if I lived to complain to Buddy.

The sense in this case had to lie in the connection between Amy Westin, myself, and now Margo.

The connection among the three of us was obvious and made a perfect circle, coming back to Buck. The only thing lacking was proof, and if proof wouldn't come to me, I had to go get it.

Just after dawn, rose-scented and decked out in a bloodred dress and real makeup, I was knocking on the door of Buck's trailer.

When he saw me, his astonishment was so real and so immediate, I grinned. "Look at you!" he exclaimed. "A real-life girl!"

"I get like that sometimes. May I come in?"

Scrambling past him into the trailer, I suddenly remembered the Chinese woman shaman who'd cautioned me to be careful what I prayed for. It would come quivering at me, out of the air, like it or not, and I'd be stuck with it.

This early morning Buck bore no resemblance to an answered prayer. He looked like what he was, an old actor with Jack Daniel's in his coffee and his career winding down, while a younger version of himself still sparkled and popped, every day at four o'clock, in syndicated reruns. The Buck in reruns

still had a future—ambitions and plans and the energy to ful-
fill them. The Buck standing here in this trailer was over. And
if I had anything to do with it, he'd soon be over and out.

Buck slammed the trailer door behind him, then blocked
the way out with his body. His shrewd eyes narrowed. If I was
about to give him a bad time, he was ready. If I wasn't, he'd
cope with that, too. A fucking auteur thinks on his feet. So
does a killer.

He sipped his coffee and eyed me, appreciating the dress.
"Well, well, what have we here? The bitch all gussied up at
this hour of the morning, standing here heaving her bosom at
Buck?"

Now that Buck had selected the tune, I could start
dancing.

"I hope you don't mind me just showing up like this?" I
began, warming up.

"No, no. There's nothing more inspiring on a wretched
cold morning than a hot-looking woman." Buck smiled. "Better than coffee to get your heart going."

"Thank you, Buck. Coming from you, that's a compliment. If there's one thing you know, it's women."

"Shit!" he snorted. "You're out of your mind. No man
knows women, 'cept in pieces, and any man knows that the
best pieces start at the neck and end at the knees. It's what's
between their ears, not their legs, that gets them in trouble.
Why the good Lord went and gave them a brain without giving them any notion of how to use it is a mystery way beyond
Buck."

"You have a point there, Buck," I said quickly.

"You think so?" He leaned toward me, looking interested
but puzzled. "It's not a point I thought you would like. Something's happened to you, something female. What is it?"

This was it. Showtime. I took a deep breath. "Even the
stubbornest woman eventually comes to her senses. I'm tired

of fighting the attraction between us. If you want me, I'm yours."

"Holy shit!" Buck covered the three feet between us with one step. One hand gripped my waist while the other mauled at my red silk bosom. "You and me are going to rock this trailer!" He kissed me and I inhaled a mélange of old man and stale whiskey. I stood it as long as I could, then started what I hoped he would interpret as a coy, feminine struggle. "Buck . . . uh . . . Buck." My lips twisted away from his, but not harshly. "Buck . . . honey?"

*"What!"* He turned my lips loose and glared, the glint in his eye glowing dangerously. "You just come over here to fuck with me? 'Cause if you have, honey, you're the one getting fucked."

"No," I protested, then softened my voice. "I wouldn't do that to you; honest, Buck. It's just that it's taken me so long to make up my mind, I'd like it to be nicer than this."

"And what the fuck's the matter with this?" Buck was indignant. "There ain't a bigger Winnebago on the lot and I'm not due on the set for forty-five minutes."

"That's great, but it could be even nicer, you know, like . . . almost romantic."

That stopped him. "Romantic?"

"If you'd like to come over to my place tonight, I'll make the trip worth your while." I smiled, I hoped sweetly, submissively, pliantly. Melanie rather than Scarlett. It worked. Some Southern gentleman back there in his lineage rose from the grave and kicked him in the ass. He glanced at me almost shyly. "I've done more than my share of fucking without a shred of romance and that's good. Screwing should be like food when you're hungry, just grab it and run. But sometimes you like to sit down to a meal, take time to enjoy, linger a little. What time tonight do you want me?"

"Eight o'clock would be fine," I told him, hoping I didn't look as relieved as I felt.

"Eight it is." Buck opened the trailer door for me. "I'll bring a bottle of wine. Wear that dress."

I sprang out of the trailer and made for my car, shivering with fatigue and excitement. I had him! I had him!

At home I fell into the sleep that had eluded me the night before and slept dreamlessly until the ringing phone woke me. It was Mother.

"How are you?" she asked.

"Fine. How's Margo?"

"I've discontinued sedation and she's coming around. Poor kid. Finding her kitty dead that way has opened her Pandora's box of childhood trauma."

"Hmmm . . ." I said ambiguously. Sympathetic as I was to Margo—in Mother's world eating lunch can unleash childhood demons—so much as she wanted me to, I wasn't about to suggest that Mother keep Margo forever or until she completed analysis, whichever came first. "Margo's a healthy girl, Mother. I'll pick her up and take her home tomorrow."

"I'm her doctor. I'll decide when she's ready." Mother's voice was chilly. "Have you given my offer any more thought?"

"No."

There was silence. Obviously, Mother had expected a response longer and more palatable than the truth. Finally, I broke the silence. "Is there anything else, Mother?"

"Given your attitude, no."

"I'll call you tomorrow." I was pulling the receiver from my ear when Mother's voice called me back. "Demeter. Wait."

"What is it?"

"This man you work for, this actor?"

"Buck Stevens?"

"He has serious pathology."

I was intrigued. "How do you know?"

"Margo told me that not only did he attempt to rape her, but he attempted to rape her with his wife present."

"In the room?" I couldn't keep the shock out of my voice. This was a new one, even for Buck.

"No, no. They weren't in a room. They were in some sort of mobile home. And the wife, Margo believed, had been locked in the bathroom. When Margo ran away she saw her, looking out of the window." Mother sighed heavily. I could picture her, shaking her head. "He's a sick man in a sick situation. Stay away from him, Demeter. Promise!"

"I promise," I said quickly, then hung up and checked my watch. Buck would be here in a couple of hours and I still had one thing to do before redressing, repainting, and rescenting with roses.

For the next twenty minutes I sat in my wing chair and tape-recorded a message to Buddy, explaining my plan.

"I've invited Buck for a romantic evening," I said, trying to sound cheery and confident. "I know what you're thinking. I'm nuts. But we've waited long enough for him to make the first move. He's too foxy and shrewd to trip up. Since we both know that the key to Amy's murder and the attempt on me is romantic rejection of Buck, I'm luring him up here just to reject him. He won't take it well. In fact, I expect him to try to kill me." I let the tape run for a few seconds, to give Buddy room for swearing. Then I resumed. "Don't worry. I'll be ready. I'll get him and then I'll call you. And . . ." I hesitated, caught by an impulse I hadn't expected. "I want you to know that I think you're a really good guy and I've enjoyed working with you. I wouldn't mind doing it again. Only next time, Buddy, a little less food, and maybe even a little less arguing. Not that I don't enjoy it, but . . ." I hesitated again. I was rambling, holding to Buddy's lapels to feel safe. I went on. "Don't get crazy. This tape is only for backup in case . . ."

I switched off the recorder without finishing the thought: ". . . for backup in case I don't make it."

I hid the tape in my dresser, then called Buddy's answering machine, telling him that I had a tape he'd like and letting him know where to find it. Then I nuked a bowl of oatmeal in the new cinnamon-toast flavor and ate it deliberately, as befits sensible food. I washed and dried the bowl, then headed for the shower to prepare for my performance, my first starring role as Buck's leading lady.

I was in the bedroom, dry and dressed in my underwear, when I heard a small clicking noise from the living room. Someone was at my front door, clumsily picking my lock.

I snapped off the light, grabbed my gun, and waited, wondering what the hell was going on. It couldn't be Buddy. I'd forgotten to get back my key. And it wouldn't be Buck. He was invited. If some son-of-a-bitch random burglar had chosen this moment and my apartment to sharpen his skills, I'd tear him in half. After what I'd gone through in Buck's trailer, no two-bit punk with a habit was going to spoil my plan.

I went cold, then angry. The rules said I had to identify myself, to warn the punk I was armed. A ridiculous rule, not even a law really. A glitch in a citizen's right to self-defense. A flaw in the program intended only to prevent terrified citizens from popping a burglar who might turn out to be an unarmed fifteen-year-old boy.

Shit. Was there ever a rule that didn't get me in trouble?

Whoever he was, he was in. I heard him stumbling around in the living room. I stood for a moment, deciding, then put down my gun. He didn't know I was here. I could surprise him. Better unarmed surprise than armed announcement. Besides, my hands were a lethal weapon of sorts, or would be if I kept practicing.

Hoping my breathing wouldn't give me away, I slid toward the living room. At the door, I hesitated, listening, hearing nothing. He'd stopped moving. Had he heard me? I waited, it seemed forever, until I heard what I thought was a careful footstep close to my wing chair. Then I slipped into the room.

My goddamned ears had misplaced the sound. He hit me from behind with something blunt and heavy. I dropped like a rock, straight down on my knees, feeling like my brains were blowing out my nose. It hurt, God, it hurt, like a son of a bitch, but even so, one part of what was left of my brain remained detached, noting with surprise that what Gus had taught me was true: You get hit over the head, you see red. Bloodred.

Through the bloodred haze I saw the carpet and out of one eye the flash of a knife. I rolled away. The knife flashed down beside me. I swiped at the hand holding the knife and missed. My attacker had already regained his feet and was winding up for another plunge. I kicked at his feet. I had to get up to get leverage. I had to get up if I didn't want to die.

Kicking madly, I scooted backward until I was just out of knife reach, then scrambled to my feet.

As he rushed me I grabbed him. He was wiry, almost slight, but very strong, and his knife hand was flailing wildly in the direction of my face. I kicked out at his knee and caught the cap square. He grunted and almost buckled but didn't go down. I let go for a second, put my fists together, and swung from my shoulders. The roundhouse connected. He went down. And stayed.

I stood over him wheezing, gulping at air, my heart and my head both pounding. When I could breathe again, I switched on the light. My assailant lay on the floor, dressed in black sweats and wearing a hood.

I bent over, pulled off the hood, and stared into the sweet, swelling face of Mary Lou Stevens.

"Damn it," I said, feeling stupid. "Of course." With the last pieces in place, I saw the whole puzzle. As always, everything made sense.

I tied Mary Lou up with extension cords and had just gotten dressed when there was a knock at my door. Buddy, I thought.

But when I opened the door, it was Buck, holding a bottle of wine and a bouquet of flowers. "I'm sure looking forward to this."

"I doubt it," I told him. "Come in."

He did, saw Mary Lou on the floor, and flung himself at her. "Honey, honey . . . Mary Lou?"

I headed for the bedroom and came back with my gun. Buck looked up at me and growled, "What the hell have you done to her?" Then he saw the gun in my hand. "Oh, Jesus," he moaned, "you're going to kill us."

"No, I'm not. I just want you to stay put while I tell you what happened. If you make one move, I'll shoot you in the leg. Understand?"

"I'm not gonna move," Buck said angrily.

"Good." I sat down on the floor opposite Buck and held the gun loosely. "Mary Lou killed Amy Westin."

"My Mary Lou?" But the way Buck said it, it wasn't a question. It was a lament.

"I think that you knew it. All along I thought you'd murdered Amy because she rejected you. And tried to kill me for the same reason. But it wasn't rejection that triggered the murder. It was you chasing us. Mary Lou couldn't stand it. For whatever reason, she loves you, and the thought of you with other women just drove her crazy."

Buck shook his head. "No. My chasing didn't help, I admit it. But she was crazy when I found her, you know, up in the hills with her brothers and father. All beat up and used up and out of her head. I thought she'd get better. I tried. Took her to doctors. Even found some raggedy-ass minister to pray over her, and I don't hold with praying, but she does. Prays all the time when she isn't throwing herself down the stairs trying to commit suicide."

"I thought you beat her up." He'd surprised me.

"Me beat Mary Lou?" Buck looked genuinely wounded. "Hell, no. I love Mary Lou. But she's always beating herself. Put her on a footstool and she'll dive off headfirst. Never saw anything like it."

"That's why you hired the nurse."

"I hadda have somebody at home keeping an eye on her. The rest of the time I kept her with me in my trailer."

I could have told Buck then that what had gone on in his trailer had only pushed Mary Lou over the edge, but I didn't. Sooner or later he'd figure it out for himself. "What happened the night Amy Westin was murdered?"

"I don't know," Buck said slowly, sounding defeated. "I think she put something in my drink then left the house when I passed out. All I know is that I woke up the next morning with a terrible hangover and there she was, all beat up and sleeping like an angel next to me."

"I found surgical saws in your trailer."

Buck shrugged. "She brought them home one day and showed them to me. Said they reminded her of her daddy's slaughtering house, only these would be nicer for cutting up pigs. I told her I'd keep them for her and I did, until—"

"They disappeared one day, and when you next saw them, they were bloody. So you cleaned them and hid them."

Buck looked away. "She said she'd been cutting up chickens."

"You have a freezer?"

"Out in the shed behind the garage. Been empty for years."

"Not anymore."

By the time Buddy arrived, Mary Lou had come around and Buck was kneeling beside her, promising to buy her the best defense in the world. She wasn't exactly listening. Something fine and strung tight had snapped in her head and she thought she was back in her nightmare hills listening to hogs scream.

As for me, I was listening to Buddy do some screaming of his own. "Why didn't you tell me? Why didn't you tell me? How could you do this to me?"

"To you? I did something to *you*?"

"You could have been killed."

"My plan worked, Buddy. Maybe not the way I thought it would, but the killer is caught and the case is over and you're just pissed because you weren't here."

"I don't give a fuck about the case!" Buddy shouted. "Don't ever do this again!"

Buddy's face was so furious and his eyes so dark, and he looked so absurd standing there shouting with his hands in his pockets and his nose getting red, that suddenly I wanted to hug him. But mostly I wanted to faint. I swayed. Buddy caught me. "Jeez, you okay?"

I held on to his arm. "My head."

He felt it and whistled. "Some lump. I'm taking you down to the hospital."

On the way to his car I held on to him just a little more tightly than necessary. If Buddy needed to feel that he was my hero, it was all right with me. I'd aced him out of the good stuff, but I could give him his moment. That's what partners are for.

•  •  •

The hospital X-rayed my skull, pronounced me dented but not cracked, and sent me home with a handful of Tylenol.

I slept round the clock and more, finally waking in sunshine. I felt almost normal. Certainly hungry.

My answering machine resembled a Christmas tree. Buddy had called, my mother and Michael, and at the end of the tape, Bill Yates.

I called Bill Yates.

"I've got something," he announced. "Not the old route exactly. I'm still looking for that. But somebody remembered the name of an old Morgan Dairy milkman because he raised such a commotion at the stockholders meeting when Vita took over. He has to know something. I have his name and address."

I reached for my grocery-list notebook. "Shoot."

Two hours later I was showered and dressed and carrying an overnight bag to my car.

I'd called Mother and told her I was going to spend a few days in San Francisco investigating a nice genteel insurance-fraud case. She told me she hoped I'd take in the opera and think over her offer.

I told Buddy I was going to a spa in Ojai for a few days where I could work out the kinks incognito. I promised to call the minute I got back. He didn't buy it, but he didn't call me on it either. He just said he'd see me when he saw me and hung up.

My call to Michael had been interrupted by a knock at my door. When I opened it, there he was, looking worried.

"I had to come. Something happened. I know it."

I smiled. Stupid of me not to know that he'd know. "Come in."

I took his hand and led him into the bedroom. "Take off your shoes and lie down and I'll tell you about it."

We stretched out on the bed together and I told him, sliding over the rough stuff but not missing a beat. When I finished he said, "Promise me, promise me . . ." He trailed off.

"What?"

"I'm sorry. I can't tell you what to do. I don't have the right."

"You can tell me. I might not do what you ask, but I've given you the right."

"Promise me you'll stay out of danger."

"I can't."

"I know."

For a while we lay quietly, Michael's hand on mine, each of us trapped in the skin of our separate lives. Then I sensed him beginning that long, slow turn away from his separateness and I began mine. We turned to each other and twined. In time I received him, took his grief and his guilt and his vast cold loneliness, and warmed them inside me until all that remained was my love for him, and I poured that back into him like honey.

"I love you," he said, his lips against mine. And I knew that no matter what happened to either of us, apart or together, we were mated for life.


"Come home with me," Michael said later.

"I can't." I kissed him. "I'll see you day after tomorrow."

"Why?"

I told him where I was going and what I was going to do. "Will you keep a light in the window for me?"

He laughed. "Always. You know that, Dutch."

I knew. Whatever happened in the next forty-eight hours, or ever, Michael and I were together. I loved him, something of a miracle really. Growing up, I'd listened to girlfriends mooning over boys I wouldn't have wanted even as friends, and I'd wondered. What was this love they all fell into like lemmings heading over the cliff? Later, I went to their weddings and marveled that they could turn themselves over so willingly to absolute strangers. I marveled and left with cake on a plate, glad to be going home alone, thinking that love was all domestic adjustment, who picked the movies, and who did the dishes.

I hadn't known about love that explodes from the soul, that burns into the bone, that fuses one heart to another. Now I knew. I knew Michael.

I tossed my bag in the car, started the engine, slipped a tape in the deck, then pointed my car north toward the Mojave.

## About the Author

JOYCE BURDITT is the author of *The Cracker Factory* and *Triplets*. For the last eight years she has been a writer and producer of numerous successful mystery series for TV: *Perry Mason*, *Matlock*, and *The Father Dowling Mysteries*. She is also the creator and supervising producer of *Diagnosis: Murder*, starring Dick Van Dyke.